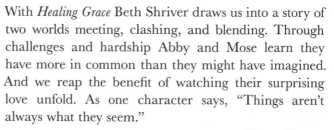
With *Healing Grace* Beth Shriver draws us into a story of two worlds meeting, clashing, and blending. Through challenges and hardship Abby and Mose learn they have more in common than they might have imagined. And we reap the benefit of watching their surprising love unfold. As one character says, "Things aren't always what they seem."

—TRISH PERRY
AUTHOR, *THE MIDWIFE'S LEGACY* AND
LOVE FINDS YOU ON CHRISTMAS MORNING

Healing Grace is a story fraught with tension. An accident and abuse force the protagonists together. But they both ultimately must face forgiveness and tough decisions. Beth Shriver does a great job of bring us into the lives of these characters. Fans of Amish fiction will want to read *Healing Grace*.

—LAURA V. HILTON
AUTHOR, *AWAKENED LOVE*

Beth Shriver has written a tender love story that is sure to please readers. It also had me wanting to run out and purchase a horse! Filled with vivid details and well-rounded characters.

—VANNETTA CHAPMAN
AUTHOR OF THE PEBBLE CREEK SERIES

HEALING Grace

Touch of Grace

BOOK THREE

Healing Grace

Touch of Grace

BOOK THREE

Beth Shriver

REALMS

Most CHARISMA HOUSE BOOK GROUP products are available at special quantity discounts for bulk purchase for sales promotions, premiums, fund-raising, and educational needs. For details, write Charisma House Book Group, 600 Rinehart Road, Lake Mary, Florida 32746, or telephone (407) 333-0600.

HEALING GRACE by Beth Shriver
Published by Realms
Charisma Media/Charisma House Book Group
600 Rinehart Road
Lake Mary, Florida 32746
www.charismahouse.com

Scripture quotations are from the King James Version of the Bible and from the Holy Bible, New International Version, copyright © 1973, 1978, 1984, International Bible Society. Used by permission.

Although this story is depicted from the real town of Beeville and the surrounding area, the characters created are fictitious. The traditions are similar to the Amish ways, but because all groups are different with dialogue, rules, and culture, they may vary from your conception.

Cover design by Bill Johnson

Visit the author's website at www.BethShriverWriter.com.

Library of Congress Cataloging-in-Publication Data:
Shriver, Beth.
  Healing Grace / Beth Shriver. -- First edition.
      pages cm. -- (Touch of Grace ; Book 3)
   ISBN 978-1-62136-297-5 (trade paper) -- ISBN 978-1-62136-298-2 (ebook)
   1. Amish--Fiction. 2. Texas--Fiction. 3. Christian fiction. I. Title.
   PS3619.H7746H43 2013
   813'.6--dc23
                                        2013022994

First edition

13 14 15 16 17 — 9 8 7 6 5 4 3 2 1
Printed in the United States of America

To Jan Halvorson

Some friends encourage, and some support, but
to find a friend who completely believes in
you, that person is a true friend. Many thanks
for helping me get this story started.

"If you admire our faith, strengthen yours. If you admire our sense of commitment, deepen yours. If you admire our community spirit, build yours. If you admire deep character and enduring values, live them yourself."

—*Amish writer quoted in* Small Farmer's Journal

Chapter One

THIS IS ALL I have." Abby flashed the money at the horse trader. It was more than she had planned to spend, but the filly was worth it. Did this man know the value of what he had, or did he just feel sorry for her? It hadn't been all that long since her mother passed away, but he and everyone else in town knew her dad was a swindler. He wouldn't be empathetic.

"That's what they all say." He grinned. "You know your horses." He leaned back against a wooden post by the stall.

She studied him for a moment, trying to decide if she trusted him. Abby did have a knack for picking horses. Focusing on conformation, temperament, and breed, she also had a good eye to go with her knowledge and experience. All of this told her that this equine had bloodlines for excellent breeding. Abby had learned the process from her father, Jim, who once was one of the best breeders around. But Abby's dream was to train them for shows, something Jim thought was ridiculous. With a horse like this, they could make it happen.

The last bit of sunlight disappeared, darkening the old barn. She didn't like this part of town, and she was still unsure about this dealer, but he had the horse she wanted. She flipped her long blonde ponytail behind her and studied the filly before locking eyes with the trader. "She hasn't been used on the track, has she?"

When he hesitated, Abby moved toward the horse.

"'Course not," he scoffed.

She lifted the filly's upper lip. No tattoo, the mark of a racer. She didn't want a three-year-old burned-out horse. "Just checking."

His dark eyebrows drew together, changing along with his demeanor. "I'm an honest horse seller, unlike your old man."

Abby froze and stared at the horse until the heat in her face cooled down. She tried to think of how to respond, but she knew he was right, so she decided to ignore the comment. "Can I see the papers?"

"Sure." He pulled some folded documents out of his back pocket and handed them to her. "Sign this one, and our business is done." He pointed to the line where she was to write her name.

Abby paused. This was all the money her mother had given her—money Jim didn't know about. How would she be able to explain this?

She looked over at the bay-colored mare. The brown tones contrasted beautifully with the white socks on all four of her legs, and her sleek body structure was the making of a fine competitor.

"Second thoughts?" His tone was flat, not friendly, but not flippant either.

"No...I—"

"You can wait and come back another time and see if she's still here." He almost sounded sincere.

She looked up at him to see a confident smirk appear. She knew the lines and had heard every spiel. Jim was the master of horse-selling tactics.

"You know better." There was something about him she didn't trust, so she stuck the money back in her pocket. "And so do I." He was getting a good deal, and Abby hoped she was too.

He grunted, amused, then conceded with a nod.

She signed the papers and kept her copy. "This way you'll know I'll be back," she said. Abby took one more look at the filly. "Yeah, this is the one," she whispered, and she walked out of the barn.

~~ Chapter Two ~~

THE SUN WAS hot as blazes. Sweat drenched Mose's shirt as he drove his buggy down the road. In the distance something moved on the heat-waved pavement. He blinked and then refocused. A vehicle—no, two vehicles—came into focus as they moved toward him, one gaining speed on the other from behind. Now close enough for him to make out, the faster vehicle, a car, recklessly careened around a slower truck that was pulling a horse trailer. As the car passed, the driver of the truck swerved, seeming to lose control. The trailer fishtailed, forcing the truck onto the shoulder and off the road.

Tires screeched as the driver yanked the truck to the left. The weight of the trailer pulled them down into the ditch.

Though it happened fast, Mose felt like he was moving through sludge as he jumped out of the buggy, wanting to get to the victims in time to help. The smell of burnt rubber wafted to his nostrils as cars whizzed by, creating hot gusts of wind. His hat blew off and sailed to heaven knew where. He barely noticed in his hurry to get to the accident scene.

He picked up speed when he saw the trailer tilting dangerously to one side and heard the horses screaming and kicking, trying to get out.

An older man and a young woman crawled out of the truck. Though they appeared stunned, they didn't seem injured, so Mose turned his attention to the trailer.

He got to the trailer's rear gate and grabbed the trailer handle as the driver and passenger moved toward him. The handle was jammed. He stepped back, got a better grip, and then put all his weight into it.

"Let me try." The young woman didn't look at him, just moved his hands and wiggled the lever until it clicked. Mose strained to pull the metal gate open. The angle of the trailer made it difficult, so she grabbed and pulled with him. The hinge squeaked as the door opened. The sound and movement caused the horses to thrash around wildly in the trailer.

Speaking softly, Mose calmed the larger of the two horses and then started to move toward the second horse. He felt a hand grip his forearm.

"I've got this." The young woman spoke in a calm tone to the two animals as she made her way to the front of the trailer. They pranced around nervously as she moved forward, landing a kick to her leg and nearly a blow to her back, but she moved quickly and didn't stop until she untied them.

Mose held out his hand. "Give me a lead." She took two seconds before giving him a rope and grasping the other, urging the bay out of the trailer. Mose gave them room and then clucked to the black gelding, noting the missing tufts of hair, swayback, and worn hooves. When the gelding kicked, he had little range of motion, but it wasn't because he was hurt. He was about the oldest horse Mose had seen. Mose dropped his voice to a whisper. Old Blackie moved, slow but sure, and made his way out. Mose checked for injuries and found none.

"Let me see if I can get this rig out of here." The driver walked to the truck and started it up.

Mose barely had time to shut the trailer door and step out of the way before the man hit the gas.

The tires sped until they caught the asphalt, which caused the filly to spook. She tried to run, but one of her legs couldn't take the weight.

"She's hurt," the young woman said while holding on to Blackie.

"I know. I hope it's not too bad."

She met his gaze before holding out her hand to shake his. "Thank you for taking care of Wart." Her expression seemed frozen with worry. Maybe it was from the shock of the event, or maybe she was troubled because her daed didn't seem to have any manners.

"Wart?" Mose preferred his name for the old black horse. The English didn't seem to think of good horse names.

When he clasped her hand, he felt a heaviness about her. Her gaze was focused on their hands. She quickly tried to pull away, but Mose held on a second longer. "I can help you load them back in, if you like."

She glanced at the truck and then back to him. "I can manage."

Mose put his hands in his pockets, not ready to leave just yet. "You gave me Wart because you didn't think I could handle the filly?"

"I just bought her. Spent a lot of money too." She looked down at the horse's damaged leg.

Mose had a passion for horses and hated to see one in pain that he couldn't get his hands on to doctor. "Do you want me to take a look at it?" he offered, but by the way she kept looking over her shoulder, he already knew the answer.

"No, I better not." She looked at him straight-on, but that only increased the tension. He could have continued the debate, but he wanted to ease her discomfort, and it seemed the only way to do that was to leave. "What's your name?"

She hesitated, taken off guard that he changed the conversation. "Abigail."

"That's a mouthful." He grinned, but she didn't. "Pretty, though." The Amish used nicknames, made it friendlier. He wanted to know if she went by one, then wondered why he cared. "Mose Fisher."

"Thanks, Mose." She turned away. The expression on her pretty face remained frozen during their entire conversation. Mose wondered what she'd look like if she smiled but didn't figure he'd find out.

"Abby!" The man came around the trailer.

She sucked in air as he came closer. And her hair fell over her face, covering her pinched forehead. She immediately moved away from Mose and began to coax the filly into the trailer. It took everything he had not to help her with the horse, but he knew his services were no longer wanted.

"Get those horses loaded." Her daed nodded to Mose and walked off.

Mose tethered Wart and turned to leave. He looked back once, to see her look away.

Abby.

He'd remember the name.

⌒⌐ Chapter Three ⌐⌒

JIM KEPT HIS eyes on the road. "Told you not to talk to strangers." He had one hand on the steering wheel and held a handkerchief with the other. His gray hair needed a trimming, hanging down across his forehead and into his dull hazel eyes.

"I was worried the horses might be hurt worse than they were." At twenty years of age, Abby felt like she was twelve, with the way he treated her.

"Well, they weren't. And even if they would have been, we didn't need help from a stranger." He coughed into the kerchief.

"He was Amish." She bit her tongue. Abby knew how Jim felt about the Amish. He said their "zealous" religious ways were too much. But Abby's mom had had a different view of them, so Abby decided not to form an opinion. There were enough other issues to deal with that affected her more directly than stirring that pot.

He grunted. "That don't make 'im perfect."

Abby looked out the window as they drove passed the sprawling fields where the Amish planted cotton and corn. She fingered the straw hat she'd found and stuck between the door and her seat. At first glance she wouldn't have figured the stranger was Amish. He didn't wear suspenders, and she didn't see the hat until she walked back to the truck. But the dark clothes and slight German accent gave him away.

She pictured Mose's eyes. It was as if she was staring at her own. The light blue intensity of them had caught her attention the minute he looked at her. But she'd had guys stare at her that way before, and it never turned out well. Even if it had, Jim would make it difficult, claiming he was protecting her, but Abby knew it was to hide their hardships. Jim wouldn't accept help from anyone, so that left just the two of them in their small world.

Her thoughts switched to the filly. She still questioned how much money she'd spent and not told Jim about. Abby worked at a local school, but it didn't pay much. She'd saved some, but it was hers to spend. Her mother would have understood. A part of her felt guilty spending the money, knowing months would come that Jim would have trouble making ends meet, but riding gave her a sense of peace and reminded her of her mother. When her mom had found out she was sick, she'd given Abby the money she'd stashed away, just in case she needed it. She shared Abby's passion to show horses, and she wanted her to continue riding after she was gone.

The filly's leg had to heal. That's all there was to it. If it didn't, everything Abby put into her dream would be lost.

"Make an early dinner. I got things to do later tonight," Jim informed her as they pulled up to the gate leading to their farm. They only grew what they and the horses they bred needed to live on.

Jim had made a few bad business deals and lost his reputation as an honest seller. Abby used to cringe when she heard him telling potential buyers what they were getting, knowing it was fudged enough that even a horse person couldn't tell the lie from the truth. That was about the time she quit calling him dad; they were on a first-name basis. It was too difficult to accept such a liar as her own flesh and blood.

Their once-green pastures were dirt. Pigs, goats, and chickens took over the barnyard, with no pens to keep them in their specified areas. Ducks, turtles, and frogs used to inhabit a good-sized fishpond. She'd spent many summers fishing there, catching sunfish. Now it was a marsh, infested with insects and whatever else grew in the muck and mire. It was as if when her mother died, the farm had too.

"What are you sittin' there for?" Abby snapped out of the memories and realized Jim was staring at her.

She shut the door and stepped down onto the gravel road that led to their two-bedroom house. The quicker she got inside, the better chance he wouldn't nag at her about something she'd done wrong or hadn't done. Abby never knew what to expect from him. He sometimes went into fits for no good reason, so she kept to herself and got her chores done to avoid the outbreaks.

She usually went straight to the kitchen to make supper, but she wanted to check on Ginger first. "I'll be right in," she told him, and went to the back of the trailer. He mumbled and walked to the house.

She let Wart out and set him out in the corral before going back to let out the filly. Her leg had stiffened, making it hard for her to bend it enough to walk. "It's all right, girl." Ginger protested, but Abby kept encouraging her until she was halfway down the ramp. She let her take a short break and then asked her to slowly move. "Back, girl."

When all four hooves hit the ground, Abby praised her and relaxed a little. Getting her out of the trailer was the hardest part. Now she had to make her comfortable until after dinner, when she could tend to the wound. The walk to the barn took some time, but once there, Abby decided she should take a look at the injury. Jim might be upset, but she'd dealt with that before, and this was worth the chastising. The leg was swollen just below the knee joint. As long as the swelling went down, there was a good chance it would heal on its own. That's what she hoped for, because they didn't have the money to pay a vet.

She felt rushed, knowing Jim didn't like to wait on his meals, so she let the leg breathe until she could get back to the horse after supper.

When she got to the old, one-story ranch-style house, she washed and got to work. She was careful not to trip over the bubbled linoleum floors at the corners of the kitchen and looked past the avocado green countertops with matching appliances. "Waste not, want not" was Jim's motto, so she did her best to keep the place clean and sanitary, but she never felt it was.

Jim was in the kitchen with a drink in hand, common since the loss of her mother, but a sure sign he would be difficult once the liquor sunk in. She could see his boots out of the corner of her eye, but she ignored him, busy preparing the food. They always had one of three dishes, none she ate much of—chicken, pork, or beef with potato, baked or mashed. The repetition kept her figure slim—more than was healthy—but it kept Jim satisfied, and that was what mattered.

He turned and leaned his back against the counter, crossed his arms, and stared at her. "You got something on your mind?" He was a frail man, but his brash personality made her forget that most of the time. His intimidation pulled on her self-consciousness.

"Just thinking about the filly." She pushed her food around in the pan, waiting for him to leave so she could finish preparing the meal.

He'd stared her down many times, but this was different. "And what else?" His fingers tightened against his ribs, turning them white at the tips.

"Nothing." She frowned. The fewer words, the better.

"Humph." He pushed off the counter and walked outside, and she heard him hack and spit. He chalked it up to allergies and didn't want to bother with doctors to get any relief, so Abby guiltily let it go.

She was ready to finish frying the rest of the chicken. Abby methodically prepared the meal and was setting the table when Jim walked down the hall. A sudden panic rushed over her, worrying that he would find the hat. It had been childish for her to hide it. She would get rid of it the first chance she had.

She held her breath when he started back to the kitchen. He sat in one of the three chairs. She filled his plate and sat next to him, leaving her mother's chair empty. They rarely talked at meals, so she was surprised to hear him speak.

"How's the horse?"

"I'm not sure yet. I'll check her again after dinner." She could tell he knew something was wrong, but she didn't want him to know. Animals paid the bills and put food in their stomachs. If they didn't, they were done away with.

"She walked to the barn, didn't she?" He stuffed a chunk of chicken in his mouth and chewed.

"Yeah, she did."

On three legs.

But he didn't need to know that. She'd fix her up before he had a chance to even wonder about it.

"Hope you didn't spend much on her." He lifted his head just enough to catch her attention. "I won't be paying to board a horse that isn't gonna produce."

Abby wasn't exactly sure what he meant by that, but when it came to money, he was a shrewd man. He reasoned with dollar signs, not emotions. A new sense of urgency grew in her chest, and she lost any appetite she had.

When Jim glanced up at her, she knew he was suspicious. He took an extra few moments to study her before he set down his fork and pushed his plate away.

"Do we understand one another?"

She didn't. Abby didn't want to know—not yet. Whatever he was suggesting was premature. Once she got her hands on that horse, she'd make things right. She just had to keep him out of it.

"I haven't had a chance to work on her yet."

He grunted. "One more mouth to feed." One side of his upper lip lifted as he stood and walked out of the room. His loud, long strides warned her not to explain. He wanted results, and that meant seeing to believe.

Abby hurried through her meal and left the dishes for later. The house needed to be picked up too, but driving to get Ginger had taken up her entire day, and the accident had made the drive longer. She slipped out before he decided it bothered him enough to make her clean up. The one good thing was that she didn't have to cook another meal.

He must be going into town to watch some sports game we can't get on our television...or maybe he didn't pay the bill again and it doesn't work at all.

She rarely watched any shows; there never seemed to be anything worth watching. She preferred the outdoors where she could be around the animals, smell the air, and feel the sun on her back. And Jim was always inside.

The locusts sang their lonely song as she walked to the barn. Ginger had the injured leg lifted just far enough off the ground to keep from touching. The swelling hadn't gone down, but it wasn't any worse. She calmed her with long strokes from her neck down to her thighs and then took her out by the hose. She turned the water on low and let it run over the wound to soothe the pain and decrease the swelling.

Flipping a pail over, she sat while she moved the hose around and then let her mind wander, fretting over what would happen if the filly's leg didn't heal. With no money for a vet and unable to ask anyone for help, she was on her own.

But then a realization made her suck in her breath.

I've been on my own since Mother died.

⟿ Chapter Four ⟿

MOSE WALKED THROUGH the furniture store glancing from left to right, looking for his lost hat among the rockers, tables, benches, and chairs that he'd made. He'd misplaced it somewhere. He hadn't had time to deal with it earlier.

He'd completed his day of work early and was determined to find that hat before he left. He nearly always finished the pieces he was working on before the English woodworkers and felt somewhat guilty taking off before they did. But the owner didn't go by a clock; instead, thankfully, he judged by the quality of a man's work.

Mose missed working the land on his family's farm, but this was a season to grow, not to harvest or plant. Besides, he liked the extra income.

He was halfway through the large building when he noticed another Amish from his community walk out of the manager's office. Mose could easily duck past him and hide behind the pieces of large furniture.

He groaned inside. It was Joe Lapp. He wondered if Joe was looking for work. Ever since Elsie Yoder had chosen Joe's brother, Gideon, over Mose, things had been awkward. And Mose hadn't found anyone to take her place in his heart.

Their community hadn't grown much since their move to Texas, and the new community on the other side of town was still unfamiliar to him. Mose wasn't one to go looking for a wife, but at twenty-two years of age he should be. His thoughts lingered for a moment on Elsie, then he quickly pushed away thoughts of her.

He hurried through the shop, hoping Joe wouldn't notice

him behind the forest of rockers and tables and chairs, heading toward the curing and painting area next door. He'd almost made it when he heard Joe call his name. "Mose, wait up."

Mose turned as Joe walked toward him. He looked a lot like his brother Gideon. Same dark hair and brown eyes, though shorter and skinnier. "Joe."

Joe offered his hand. Mose lifted his, which was a greater gesture than Joe could realize.

"The boss man just hired me." He was smiling from ear to ear. It wasn't always easy for daeds to let their sons leave the farm and take work in town, but it had become a necessity to make ends meet, at least for a short time, now and then.

"Congratulations." Mose couldn't think of much to say, so he turned to leave again.

"*Danke*. This is sorta like barn raisings and setting up Sunday church together."

He was making his point well, so Mose conceded. "*Jah*, just like it." He couldn't keep the sarcasm from his words. He started to turn again, but Joe continued.

"I'm not my brother, Mose." Joe gave him an even gaze.

There was something in his eyes—a hint of apology perhaps?— that raised Mose's respect for him a few notches.

"*Nee*, I guess you're not," Mose said in little more of a mumble, and then walked away. He and Joe had always gotten along, were tight friends since moving from Virginia. It was time to let go of the grudge. After all, Joe should not bear the brunt of what his brother had done. But Mose just wished he wasn't so stubborn.

Mose's boss waved him over, and Mose obliged.

His boss's son, a bright-eyed, redheaded young man, was standing beside him. "My son tells me he's ready to make those pieces of wood as smooth as you do, Mose." His boss grinned and tipped his head toward his son, whose passion shone in his eyes.

"Maybe I could come watch one day." The boy shrugged. "Just to get the hang of your way of doing things."

"I do it the old-fashioned way." Mose winked as if it was a

secret. It was just the right way of doing things. "I can teach you how." Mose moved away from the sander that was one of the many buzzing, pounding, and pulsating machines in the large work area.

"I can't do the magic like you can, Mose. But I'd be glad to clean up after you." Most of the workers knew the owner's son tried hard, but he just didn't have the touch or the patience to do carpentry. With his daed being who he was, the kid wanted to show him he could do the job.

But in truth, most of the English furniture wasn't the same as what the Amish made in his community, so it was harder to get repeat customers. Some of those places didn't care whether people came back. They were just glad to sell the junk in the first place. His boss was the exception.

"That's one nice chair, Mose. Somebody will be proud to own it." His boss walked closer and touched the wood for grooves. "Smooth as silk. Can't see a single screw hole, either."

"Sure would like to learn how to do that." The young man looked longingly at Mose's work.

"You can come and watch, and learn, anytime." Mose pushed his chair back toward the wall next to the others.

"See you tomorrow, Mose. Second shift. And thanks."

He preferred the first shift so he could still have a good part of the day to help his daed with his blacksmith shop. If he had a later shift, he'd stay overnight at the woodwork shop. His boss was good enough to set up a cot in the back room if Mose needed it. The shop was a thirty-minute drive by motor vehicle from his community, but a good two hours by buggy.

He walked through the large room that accommodated about six workers at a time, but there were only four working this shift. The noise of pounding hammers and saws made it hard to hear. Sawdust covered the floors, and sawhorses were set up at each station. Lines of tools filled one wall, and there wasn't a single window in the place.

The bottoms of Mose's boots scraped the cement as he pulled

the door handle. Sawdust floated in the air and tickled his nose with the sweet smell of cedar. He blew out a breath from his lungs as he opened the door and took in the fresh air when he stepped out of the shop. He missed working outdoors, but he was making a nice nest egg for himself, one he'd like to share someday.

The wind blew through his hair and reminded him again that he needed to find his hat or buy a new one. There was a place in town that sold them, but he hated to break it in, let alone shell out the money.

A slow smile took over his face as it came to him: the gusts of wind from the cars whizzing by the accident scene. His hat sailing away. He didn't remember retrieving it. Maybe it was still there. Or better yet, could the young woman named Abby have found it?

Maybe someone in town knew her. He would drive out to her place and see if she had it. He almost laughed at the fantasy. Not only were the chances slim that she even had it, but also from her demeanor, he doubted she would ever want to see him again. But he did wonder if she might have found it. Very likely he would never know.

Mose walked down the sidewalk looking for the shop, glancing in the store windows. He felt self-conscious not wearing a hat, but it wasn't as uncomfortable as if he were in the community. To the Amish, wearing a head covering meant obedience to God, and he appreciated the meaning.

Unable to find the shop, he stopped and looked for someone to ask. He knew to avoid the tourists. Although they knew the shops even better than some of the locals, they treated the Amish like celebrities. Some Amish didn't mind, but he found it annoying,

When he saw a young woman with long, blonde hair about Abby's build, he cleared his throat to get her attention "Do you know of a hat store around?"

"Yeah, it's at the end of the street." She pointed. "I'm surprised you don't know where it is." Her pretty smile told him she didn't mean it sarcastically, but he still felt a little sheepish. "I don't think I've seen an Amish without a hat."

He felt even more exposed after she made the comment. "I lost mine, and *I'm* lost, so I'm not doing too well." He grinned.

She laughed and held out her hand. This was the second time in two days a woman had offered her hand to him. The English didn't shake the way the Amish did, so it was more awkward than usual. "My parents own the pharmacy across the street."

Mose nodded. He'd never used the pharmacy, as his mammi made natural herbal medicines, but it was nice to know. "*Danke* for the directions."

When he pulled his hand away, he thought about how different it felt when Abby touched him, and it made him impulsively ask, "Do you know of a young woman by the name of Abigail, or Abby?"

She nodded. "Abby Barker. I went to school with her. She lives with her dad over off Old Mill Trail. Do you know her?"

Mose felt like he was intruding in Abby's life by asking, but he did need his hat. "She may have something of mine."

"Your hat?"

"*Jah.*" He nodded. "*Danke.*"

She grinned and turned away as Mose headed down the sidewalk to get his horse and buggy. Elam ran a restaurant in town and had room behind the building to board Mose's horse. Once in a while he'd catch a ride from someone who was coming into town. Sometimes Mose thought it might be easier to rent out a place for a couple months until fall harvest. But so far it was working out.

He whistled to Frank, his horse, and hitched him up. The area was small, but he had grass for grazing and a tub that Elam kept filled with water. The only problem was that Frank got anxious during the day with no work to keep him busy. He wasn't one for farm work as much as he was for pulling a buggy and racing. He was the fastest equine Mose had ever owned, and he'd raced him for fun. Sometimes he had an itch to take him to the local races, but it didn't set right with him to race for money.

Mose settled into the buggy and clucked at Frank. He was anxious to go, and Mose had to hold him back through town. He would let him run some, once they got to the highway. As he watched his nostrils flare, smelling all the scents his powerful nose took in, Mose started wondering how Abby's horse was doing. The injury hadn't seemed too bad, but he hadn't gotten a close enough look to know for sure.

Her daed was one of the most unfriendly people he'd ever met, but there was something about Abby that interested him. He just couldn't figure out what it was exactly.

He knew most of the signs along the highway, but he didn't remember seeing the one the girl had told him about. After going a ways from town he started to wonder if he'd passed it.

Well, then, maybe it wasn't meant to be.

The clop of the horse's hooves kept in beat as he stayed the course down the highway. He'd about given up when he saw the name of the country road. He hesitated.

Now what should I do?

He turned Frank onto the gravel lane. When he got up close to the farm, he stopped to study the place. It almost appeared deserted. The field was overgrown, and fence lines were down. The animals all roamed together in the general area that would usually be used to park buggies or cars in front of the house. He'd never seen neglect like this, and he wondered how the animals fared.

No sooner had the thoughts come to his mind than he realized he was being judgmental. It was a lot easier to run a farm when you had a community helping you tend to your fields and mend your sick animals. If it was only the two of them tending to this place, it would be a lot of work. He felt like rolling up his sleeves and diving in, but he knew with these two, he may barely get a *hallo* from one of them.

As he got closer, he wondered how much he really wanted

that hat, or if it was just an excuse for what he really wanted. He'd like to look in on the horse, but he also admitted that he wouldn't mind seeing Abby's pretty blue eyes again. Mose sighed and drove up in front of the house, hoping she would be the one to greet him, but as soon as he pulled in the reins, her daed came out the front screen door, which slapped shut behind him. Mose jumped down and stood at the bottom of the stairs.

Abby's daed stood at the top of the stairs, smoothed back his gray hair, and stuck a toothpick between his teeth. "You're the fella on the highway."

"*Jah*, Mose Fisher." He moved forward and lifted his hand to shake, but the man didn't move, just kept picking at his teeth.

Mose lowered his hand and stepped back. "How are the horses?"

"Fine." He moved across the porch. His tall but skinny frame towered above Mose. "What brings ya here?"

"Thought I'd check in and see how the filly's mending."

"Is that the real reason..." He stared down at Mose, taking his time to finish his thought. "Or did you come to see my daughter?"

Mose's patience waned. He could not recall ever being questioned like this before. He'd put up with rudeness from some of the merchants in town, but this was something different altogether. "Actually I was hoping one of you had found my hat."

Abby's daed frowned and studied Mose from head to toe.

"I lost it that day and..." He realized the man didn't care a single iota about the hat. He wanted to see Abby. "Sorry to have bothered you."

And with that he turned away and got into his buggy. As much as he wanted to see Abby again, wild horses would have to drag him back there.

∽ Chapter Five ∽

GINGER'S LEG WAS hot with inflammation. Abby fought back tears of frustration. She'd rubbed her down with liniment, hoping to increase circulation, but it hadn't helped. The only thing Abby had left was Epsom salts, so she filled a bucket with cold water, added the salts, gave it a stir, and hoped it would work.

While she waited, Abby changed out the shavings in the filly's stall with a different, softer kind to make her more comfortable. She stayed in the barn until she heard Jim drive off, then she took away the bucket and cleaned Ginger up and locked the gate. The horse looked out at the pasture, where Abby knew she wanted to be, but she couldn't take the chance of her getting too energetic and hurting herself even worse.

She walked toward her decade-old car near the house, keeping her fingers crossed. There was a fifty-fifty chance it would start. The door opened with a creak, and she jumped inside. Pumping the pedal once, she turned the key. When the engine sputtered and then sprung to life, she sat back and let out a long breath, grateful for the small favor.

Her friend Amy's parents owned a pharmacy, and they had a small selection of products that catered to horses. It might cost too much and not even work, but she was desperate. As she pulled away, she had the familiar fear Jim would drive up as she was leaving to go into town. He would wonder why she was leaving so early for work.

Every pickup that went by with a reddish tone caught her attention, as she watched for Jim, hoping he didn't notice her on the road. He never told her where he was going, so he could be anywhere. She was old enough to have her freedom, but too often she was too scared to take it. It depended on how bad his temper was on a particular day, how much work he left for her to do at the farm, and even whether her old car would start.

She relaxed a little after she parked, and then walked straight to the pharmacy and to the back of the store. There she found some wrapping and a few compounds, but she wasn't sure which one was best, so she went to the counter where her old friend Amy stood, smiling at her.

She returned the grin. "Hey, you still work here for your dad?"

"Yeah, in the summers I do. Going to college the rest of the year. I hear you're doing really well in the circuit with your riding."

"Yes, I just bought a horse that needs some good salve." Abby tried to act content, but she was too far away from any semblance of contentment to fake it. Her life wasn't anything like Amy's. "Which one of these do you recommend?" She held out the round containers.

"This one sells the most. That's all I know. I can ask my dad." She turned to the counter where the pharmacists were counting pills and filling bottles.

Abby didn't like to draw attention. She never knew whether Jim had cheated or caused any other trouble by his behavior.

"No, that's all right. I'll take this one." She set it on the counter and paid.

"I saw a guy who was asking about you the other day. He was Amish, kinda cute." She wiggled her eyebrows.

Abby startled. "What did he say?"

"He was looking for his hat." She shrugged.

"Is that all you know about him?"

"I think he may work in town, but I don't know where."

"Okay, thanks." She started to walk away and then stopped. "You didn't happen to see where he was coming from when you first saw him, did you?" Now she sounded like a lovesick school-girl, but she didn't care. He might be able to help her with the filly, and she'd lower her pride to make that happen.

"I saw him walk across the street from our store." She held up her hands as if that's all she knew.

"Okay, thanks again." Abby walked out onto the sidewalk and scanned the businesses across from her. There was a restaurant, a souvenir shop, and a furniture store. When she went in to work, Abby would see whether she could find out any information about where the Amish worked in town.

She tried not to get her hopes up. This wasn't a small enough town that it would be easy to find him. Did she want to? It wasn't an option. His handsome face couldn't make up for his pretension with horses, but Abby needed his help, and she admitted that he seemed to know horses. She looked at her watch. It would have to wait until after work. Abby liked to go early, as some of the children's parents who worked dropped them off before school started, and she didn't like them to be unattended.

As she drove down the street across from the pharmacy, she wondered where Mose might work. He was Amish, and figuring Amish make things, she decided to start with the furniture shop. As she entered, she looked around the place to see a nice showroom full of different pieces of furniture. She could hear the tools buzzing in the back room.

A clerk walked over and stopped in front of her. "Can I help you with something?" The young man was overly cheerful, so she thought she'd let him know right off she wasn't interested in buying anything.

"I'm looking for someone. Do you know a guy called Mose?"

His forehead wrinkled, and he nodded once. "He's one of our employees. Did you buy something he made?"

"No. Why?" This might be a good way to get a take on this guy. Like Jim said, being Amish doesn't make them perfect. She eagerly waited for his answer.

He frowned. "People come in and ask for him to make their furniture."

She was too surprised to comment but felt better already, hearing he did good work. "I found his hat." That was true, but she'd say anything to get him to step out of this shop right then.

He chuckled. "I wondered why he wasn't wearing one."

She smiled to be polite. "Can I see him?"

The man looked at his watch. "I'll see if he wants to take a break." He walked to the back door.

Abby waited, impatient. Watching people through the pane glass window as they walked down the street made her realize how isolated she was from people her age. She stayed at the farm unless she needed supplies or groceries or was at work, where she was almost exclusively with children. She didn't mind, but it would be nice to have company her own age now and then.

"Abby?" Mose's deep voice gave her some comfort.

She let out a breath. Skipping the small talk, she got down to business. "Can I talk to you?" She gestured to the front door with her thumb.

"Go ahead, Mose," the salesman encouraged with a smile.

Mose looked at Abby curiously and followed her out the door. "Are you all right?"

"I'm fine," she replied, "but the filly's not. Can you come take a look at her?"

He stuck his hands in his pockets and studied her. "You didn't want my help the other day. Why do you want it now?"

"You know horses, right?" Abby felt the tears well up and did her best to hold them back. She knew better than to look at him, or she'd cry for sure.

"You knew that then. What changed your mind?"

"She's not getting better."

He stood still, waiting for more of a reason. Abby couldn't blame him. She had been uptight and on guard when she met him. "Jim was there."

He nodded as if that was what he was waiting for. "I'll see if I can take an early lunch." He walked back in and was out again with the biggest lunch pail she'd ever seen.

She tried to walk as slow as Mose, but a sense of urgency kept her moving one step ahead of him. "The leg's twice as big as it was yesterday, and nothing I've done has worked." She told him everything she tried, and by the time they got to her car, she realized she hadn't given him a chance to say a word. "Sorry, I'm just worried about her."

"I understand. But rushing around isn't gonna help her any. She can feel your nerves. Then she'll get nervous."

These were things she knew but wasn't acting on. It was good to have a reminder. "I know." Then she mumbled under her breath, "I'm just glad I found you."

When he smiled at her, she felt a little more relaxed, like everything would be fine if she'd just calm down a bit. "I've seen horses heal from injuries like this, so I'm hopeful she will."

"Depends on what kind of fracture it is. If she can put any weight on it, it's probably an incomplete fracture."

"And that's good, right?"

He nodded. Like her father, he was a man of few words. She was used to filling the silences, and he didn't seem to mind.

When they pulled in to her farm, she felt the same embarrassment she always did when new people came around. It was in bad shape, and she knew it, but she submersed herself with her horses to escape from the way Jim let things go. She'd learned awhile ago that she could only do so much and that what she could do wasn't near enough.

She parked by the barn, not caring whether Jim noticed she'd driven someplace, and led Mose to the filly's stall. "In here."

Mose made his way to Ginger and let her get a whiff of his scent. Starting at her neck, he stroked with one hand all the way down to her injured leg. He knelt down and examined her, taking his time to touch each area.

Abby chewed her nails as she waited. "Well, what do you think?"

Mose leaned back and turned to her. "I think it's good to get a second opinion. It's hard when you've tried everything you can think of with no results."

"Is it bad?" She turned over the pail and sat next to him.

"I'm pretty sure it's an incomplete fracture, but I don't know for sure without an X-ray."

She felt a huge load lift from her chest. "Well, that's good news." She may have wasted money buying the compound, but she was relieved to hear his diagnosis of Ginger. "Should I use this compound rub?" She pulled it out of her pocket.

"Let me see." He held out a hand, and Abby gave the tin box to him.

When his hand touched hers, she felt the same warmth she had the day of the accident. His eyes lifted to hers, and he smiled before looking back at the compound. She did too, but her attention was on Mose.

"Ah-hum." Jim's shadow appeared next to her. Abby turned around abruptly, bumping the tub of compound onto the wood floor.

She stood. "When did you get here?"

Mose followed her lead, obviously not understanding the concern.

"The question is what is *he* doing here?"

"Afternoon, Mr. Barker." Mose offered his hand, only to have Jim ignore it.

Jim put his hands on his hips and waited for Mose to answer his question. She hoped Mose wouldn't tell him anything was wrong with the filly, when she'd told him the horse was fine. But even more she feared what he'd do about Mose being with her. If it would have been a guy from town, it might go better, but with an Amish man, there was no chance he'd let it go.

"Abby needed some help with the filly. Seems she has a fracture."

Abby let out a straggling breath.

Her dad looked straight at her. "Thought she was all right." He squinted, a sure sign he was mad.

"I didn't want to worry you, and it didn't seem that bad at first."
She was talking too fast, but she wanted to get the words out
before he blew up in front of Mose.

Jim's eyes shot over to Mose. "You know how to doctor a
horse?"

"I'm willing to try." Mose bent down to examine the leg again.
"The horse is young, so her bones are still growing. She's got that
going for her. There's no protruding through the skin, and it's not
in one of the larger bones. I think she'll pull out of it."

Abby held her breath and prayed—something she hadn't
done in a long time. It seemed forever before Jim responded. He
and Mose had locked gazes. At first Abby worried about Mose
holding Jim's gaze, but to her surprise, she saw one side of Jim's
lips lift as if he admired Mose's confidence.

He turned to face Abby. "When the money's gone, it's gone.
You understand?"

He knew her too well. As hard as she'd tried to hide how much
she cared about this horse, he could see through it. "I know."

"And I can't pay you either." He looked at Mose.

Mose shook his head. "No need to." And with that, Mose sat
back down on the pail and got to work tending the filly.

⌒ **Chapter Six** ⌒

MAYBE THIS WAS a bad idea, but Mose was determined to see it through. He second-guessed his plan as he drove up to Abby's farm the next day in a wagon pulled by Clydesdales and a horse trailer behind. It bothered him each time he set foot on the run-down piece of property. As he looked around, he tried to imagine what it was like in its heyday, which only served to make him feel worse.

The conditions at Abby's place were questionable at best, and if he was going to get that horse healed up, he had to work with her every day. He did worry that he wouldn't see Abby as much this way, but he felt it was best for Ginger.

When he jumped down off the buggy and turned around, Abby was standing on the porch, giving his rig a curious stare. To his surprise she didn't seem to mind that he was there. Her blue eyes twinkled in the morning sun, and her hair was in a braid down her back. He realized it had been a few seconds of silence. "Morning."

She nodded. "What brings you here this early?" She crossed her arms around her waist.

"Your horse."

As soon as he said it, Abby's face went rigid. Her eyes flicked to the trailer.

"How is she?"

"Not as good as I'd like." She narrowed her eyes with suspicion, but of what, he wasn't sure. He was still a stranger to her, but he'd thought she was beginning to trust him. Apparently not.

"I actually came by to see if you'd let me board Ginger for a while, but I can see you're busy, so I'll be on my way." He couldn't understand this young woman, and now he wondered why he should even try.

"You want to take a look at her?" Her strained expression caused him great pain, and he glanced over at the barn. Only when the horse was involved did she seem comfortable.

"Lead the way."

She took the stairs two at a time and walked with him toward the barn. He glanced down at her. "What's got you worried?"

"It didn't seem like much at first, but her leg is swelling again." She kept her head forward, her eyes on the barn just a few more feet ahead of them, still holding her guard. Her squinting eyes and stiff body language told him to stand back.

She opened the barn door and walked to the last stall. It was the largest, with an open half-wall to look out at the field where the horses grazed. Mose moved slowly, letting the filly take in his scent. The horse seemed to approve and dropped her head. He gave her a pat and slowly moved his hands down around the injured leg and lifted it for inspection.

"Well?" Abby's voice broke.

He stood to his full height to garner his courage. "I'd like to take her with me." He thought about talking her into it but figured his arguments wouldn't matter with her. She'd have her mind made up before he could get halfway through his spiel.

"It would be hard to let her go." Arms folded, Abby rocked back and forth slightly. "But if you think that's best..."

"*Gut.* I borrowed the horse trailer in hopes you'd agree. I'll give her a lot of attention." Mose hid his surprise that she'd agreed. Now he had to keep things moving along before she changed her mind.

"I know." She studied his eyes, as if searching for something— maybe thinking about letting the horse go or feeling remorse that she couldn't heal the filly.

That immediate response of trust gave him the confidence he needed to carry through with his promise. He cared for the horse and reminded himself that his motivation had to remain pure—it needed to be all about the filly, nothing else.

Abby helped him load Ginger into the trailer and stepped back. "Hurry and shut it."

"What's the hurry?" As soon as he spoke, Old Blackie nickered and walked toward them.

"These two are inseparable, but you don't need to take both of them, Wart has had to skip a few trips." As if to emphasize the point, Ginger whinnied her complaint being alone in a trailer without her companion.

Mose crossed his arms over his chest to let her know he felt strongly about what he was about to say. "I can't call that little guy Wart. Will Old Blackie work for you?"

Abby half smiled and nodded.

"Old Blackie is welcome to come along." He lifted his brow waiting for her permission. "They'll both do better if they're used to being together. Besides, these work horses of mine can pull anything."

"Are you sure? You're already doing enough."

Mose grinned. The whinnying and baying from the two horses would convince the most reluctant person to let them have their way.

Mose unlatched the trailer door. "I'm sure. Let's load him up." He couldn't help but smile as Old Blackie took his place in front of Ginger. Apparently size didn't matter considering Ginger was twice his size. In front of the rig the Clydesdales snorted and then settled.

"I don't even know where you live." She rubbed her arms and glanced at the trailer. "I don't know if I can do this."

"You can follow me if it will make you feel better." Mose hoped she would follow him, but all he got was a sigh.

"I'll see if my car starts." She walked over and flipped the switch.

Nothing.

Mose popped the hood. She tried to turn it over again, with

no luck. "I don't know much about cars, but it might be your battery."

"Well, that's just great." She pulled her hair back with frustration. "Can I ride with you?"

Mose hesitated. It wasn't proper for them to be alone together, but he had to admit it would be nice to ride with her. He couldn't say no. Bishop Omar may frown on it, but if it was for a good reason, Mose thought he'd understand.

Mose didn't blame Abby for wanting to see where her horse was going to be, so he made an exception, but he wondered how her daed would feel about it. "Your daed didn't seem too happy to see me the other day. I'd hate to upset him."

Her jaw twitched. "He didn't tell me you were here."

Her angry reaction made him wish he wouldn't have mentioned anything, but Mose wanted her to know that he didn't think her daed was too happy about his being around. He was glad to know that might be why she didn't respond to his visit, though.

"Daeds and their daughters." Mose smiled to minimize it.

She looked down the dirt road leading to her house before getting into the buggy. Her concern about Jim bothered him, and he wondered what she would be like if she was away from him and the worry that went with him.

"How long will it take to get there?"

"An hour or so. When do you need to be back home?"

"I don't. Jim's gone for the day and won't be back until late."

"Then why do you keep on the lookout?" He'd never seen a person so tense, worrying about what one person was thinking and doing all the time. He couldn't imagine what had happened between the two of them that she would be so worried or scared of her own daed.

She stared at him long and hard before answering. "Sometimes he surprises me."

He thought it was a fair question, but her reaction told him differently so he left it at that.

A couple miles down the road she let out a long breath and sank down into the seat. "So who let you borrow their trailer?"

"An Englishman who lives nearby. We do some farrier work for him in return."

"You're a blacksmith?" She raised her eyebrows. "I thought you were a carpenter."

"I do both. Everyone's a blacksmith in my family." Except for his older brother, Jake, but she didn't need to hear about that.

"How many are in your family?" She kept her eyes on him as he continued to drive.

"Three boys, my daed, and Mamm." He said it like it was no big deal, but he wondered how it sounded to her. That many guys around to shoe horses and tend to them if they were sick must sound like heaven.

"No girls?"

"Just my mamm, and my mammi lives in the *dawdihaus*." He smiled over at her. "Almost there."

Abby turned to see the entrance. She looked up at the sign with the community name as they entered, MEADOWLARK VALLEY.

"That's a little ironic, isn't it?" She finally smiled, and was even prettier.

Mose appreciated her recognizing the humor. He wondered whether many Englishers would understand it. Texas was primarily flat land, but because of the small hills on either side, they had called their land a valley.

The Yoders' bed-and-breakfast was the first building they passed by, and then the Bylers' store. The farms sprawled out north, west, and south of the community, going back far and wide.

"What is across from the store?" An area of land was dug up, with stakes creating four corners.

"We're building a school."

"Really? Will all of the kids go to this school?"

"Up until eighth grade." He looked over at her. "You seem surprised."

"I'm interested, because I'm a teacher."

"Now I'm the one surprised. I thought you were a horse trader. I guess I shouldn't have assumed."

"I do that because that's what I know, but I like to teach." She beamed when she talked about her job. "The state usually comes down pretty hard on schools that aren't government funded."

"The Amish used to have a difficult time, but a law was passed letting us off of some of the secular school requirements."

"What do you mean, 'a difficult time'?"

"If the kids didn't go to the public schools, they'd lock up their *daeds* until they would comply. They didn't think the Amish were educating the children."

"That's terrible. I hadn't heard about it. Did it happen awhile ago?"

"*Jah*, back in the seventies."

"Well, it's not that bad now, but you should be prepared, in case they start asking a lot of questions."

He grinned, enjoying her passion.

"Why are you smiling?"

"It's important to like what you do." Mose couldn't think of any better lifestyle than working a farm, and he was thankful that was what he was born into.

"These farms are so...nice." Abby looked closely at each field, windmill, and fence, commenting about each one and how well kept they were. "I knew you all moved here a couple years ago, but I didn't know how much the community had grown."

"Slow growth, but it's best that way." When they reached his farm, he clucked to the Clydesdales and they slowed to a halt. A barn and another large building for their blacksmith business stood opposite their large house. Mose pointed to a young man in one of the many fields. "That's my bruder. I'll try to spare you from his razzing."

"Where are your folks?" Abby squirmed a little, which made him grin. She was probably curious to meet them but not sure how comfortable she would feel, being an Englisher.

"Mamm's quilting, and my daed is probably keeping after my bruder."

As she stepped out and went to the back of the trailer to fetch Ginger and Blackie, she wondered if she was keeping him from helping with the farm. He got to the ramp and pulled it down for the filly. "She's putting a little weight on it." Abby urged her to move forward and smiled.

"She'll get there." He nodded toward Ginger with a confident smile. "I'll show you where she's staying while she's here." He went around the back of the barn, taking slow and steady steps so the horse could keep up with him. The covered corral was deep with wood shavings for the filly's comfort and sheltered from the other horses, with plenty of room for her to roam. The best part was the huge pasture Ginger could look out on.

"She might get a little jealous of the other horses out there running wild, but at least she has a *gut* view."

"She's in good hands here. Thanks." She wrapped her arms around her waist as if she felt vulnerable. "Mind showing me around?"

He contemplated the request. He had a sudden feeling she liked the farm more than most Englishers did. She understood the country way of life and lived it. She wasn't just a tourist curious about the Amish.

"There's not much to see, but sure, if you like." He threw the lead rope onto a hook on the wall and walked toward the barn door.

She followed him, listening as he described all of the crops they grew, horses they raised, and blacksmithing they provided for the community. Not only did Abby understand their ways, but also her comments told him she appreciated it. When he took her to the San Antonio River, she stopped and smiled. The wind blew her hair around her face as she looked from one horizon of the flowing water to the other. "This is a nice spot. I'd come here all the time, if I had the chance."

Mose stuck his hands in his pockets and took a little more time than usual to watch the water quietly flow downstream. "Guess I didn't think about enjoying it just to look at. I just think of it as a much-needed water source."

"I bet you grow good crops here because of it." When she turned his way, he enjoyed the smile that was still on her face. He liked seeing her grin, and he noticed again how attractive she was when she did.

"The water tables are pretty *gut* here."

"Do you miss living in Virginia?" She turned to him.

"I used to, but Texas has grown on me." He squinted his eyes, wondering how much he could ask her without her crawling back into her shell. "What about you? Have you been here long?"

"All my life. I don't have anything to compare it to." She took in a breath and closed her eyes. "Except here."

As he stood there with Abby, Mose tried to keep his thoughts centered. He'd been curious about her from the first time they met at the accident, and now Ginger had created a bond between them. He'd felt a tug from the Lord to help her, but whether He had an objective beyond that, Mose was uncertain. He hated to take her away from this small hill that showed the big countryside. It was nice to see her somewhat happy for a change.

"You're welcome to stay for the noon meal." He averted his eyes, not wanting to put pressure on her but wanting her to stay.

Her face went back into the frozen expression, the mask she used to protect herself. "I should get back."

Mose was torn. He wanted her to stay, but he knew he should keep his distance. He was unsure of what his role was and didn't want to get in over his head. "Maybe another time."

"I *would* like to see that blacksmith shop." She lifted her brows in question.

He grinned. He'd never known of a girl to be so interested in the trade, but he sort of liked the idea.

"What's funny?" She had that skeptical look on her face and seemed very curious as to why he enjoyed her comment.

"You don't always act like a girl." The minute he said it, he wanted to take it back. Thinking it was one thing, but saying it was another.

She folded her arms across her chest and squinted. "What does that mean?"

"I mean, you're interested in the same things I am." He could see the steam rising and waited for her to blow.

"Maybe it's strange to the Amish, but not in the real world." She started walking down the hill and over to the buggy.

Mose stood and watched her go. He thought about catching up to her and trying to get her to simmer down, but then he remembered who he was dealing with.

Why am I drawn to such a stubborn person? Then he chuckled as he followed at a safe distance. After all, he needed to drive her home. She was just as stubborn as he was, if not more.

⌐ Chapter Seven ⌐

AFTER HER VISIT the day before, Abby found herself looking forward to going back to the Amish community. There was a certain calm there that she didn't have in her own home. If Mose wasn't such a chauvinist, it might be a bearable place to live. He was probably raised that way, so she had to take him as is, but leaving no doubt she wouldn't conform to any of their sexist ways, even as a visitor. If that didn't work for him, she'd bring the filly home. But after that long silence of the drive home, she wouldn't blame him if she didn't hear from him again.

Abby got ready for the day and went to the kitchen to make breakfast. Jim sat at the table with a cup of coffee in hand as he did every morning and read the paper.

"Where's the filly?"

Abby stopped just for a second and then flipped a pancake. She calmed her breath before answering. "Her leg was getting worse, so I took her to a horse doc." She hoped that would be enough, but she wasn't counting on it.

"Can't afford a vet." He glided his eyes over to her and waited.

"It won't cost us anything."

She didn't know what his reaction would be if he knew Ginger was with the Amish, but he seemed to be okay with Mose, so she thought maybe she could tell him.

"People always want something, Abby."

That made her pause. Was Mose just being helpful because of his passion for horses, or was there an underlying reason for offering his help?

"Don't know how you paid for her in the first place. Now she needs a vet?" He was still staring at her. She could feel it, even though she had her back to him.

"She's with Mose."

His chair screeched as he turned in his seat. "The Amish fella?"

She turned to him so she could see his face, because she couldn't read his tone. "Yeah, he asked to board her so he could tend to her better." She walked over to the table and set the plate of pancakes in front of him.

"May as well have given him the papers to go along with her."

Abby felt herself ready to defend Mose. She hardly knew the guy, but what she did know, he wouldn't double-cross her. She grabbed a towel. "He's not like that." Now she sounded naïve, but it didn't really matter what she said.

"Fool child." He pushed off the seat and walked out. The screen door slapped shut behind him, and she heard his boots crunch against the gravel driveway as he walked to his truck.

Abby threw the towel over her shoulder and slid the plate closer before taking a bite of pancake. She'd become quite the cook, once her mom had become too weak to do much around the house and Abby had taken over. When she stood to clear the table, Jim's handkerchief fell to the floor. It was speckled with blood.

She stared, remembering her mother's symptoms when she was ill. This wasn't one of them. Abby tried to remember if she'd ever had this happen to her. Once when she was sick...drainage somehow damaged the membranes...she couldn't remember the particulars. It wasn't a worry, as long as it went away.

Abby cleared the table, feeling sudden regret for talking to Mose the way she had. Looking over that sparkling river had been the most enjoyable moment she'd had for a long time. The bitterness had come due to various reasons, but it was more than that. She had let it consume her. Abby wasn't the same person. She wanted to go back to what she once was.

She walked to her car and, thankful it started, made her way to Mose's community. Abby decided she would make every effort to drop her defenses, but she wouldn't be taken advantage of, either. She would prove Jim wrong about Mose, and maybe even the Amish.

As soon as she drove under the Meadowlark Valley sign, she relaxed a little, taking in the green fields of corn and cotton. Abby took her time and drove slowly up to the Fishers' place. She got out of her car, and with each step she took, Abby felt a little more anxiety. She hadn't met his family, and she thought it would be awkward if Mose wasn't there to introduce them. Then she heard his voice as he came up behind her.

"I didn't think it would take you this long." He jumped up onto the porch and sat down in a rocker.

Abby blinked twice, trying to be patient. She didn't want to sit down; she wanted to see Ginger. She let the air seep through her lips and sat with him. "How is she?"

"I've had a very *gut* morning." He paused, which she knew was just to test her patience. "With your horse."

"Really?" She turned toward him. "What happened?"

He rocked slowly. "I don't want you to get your hopes up too high, but her leg isn't as swollen, and she's putting more weight on it."

Abby leaned back, finally letting go of the tension. "So what do you think? Will she completely heal?"

"I can't promise you that, Abby. I don't think a vet could, either. She still has healing to do." His smooth and calm rocking was peaceful, and soon Abby was rocking in time with him. It made it easier to talk to him when their chairs were in sync. She felt like a little kid again.

"Why are you grinning?" Mose furrowed his brows.

"Am I? Well, Ginger, of course." She wanted to go see her, but she was content sitting on the porch for another few minutes. "So what now?"

"That's for you to decide. How is your daed with all of this?"

"He's not happy, but he isn't about most things." She didn't mean to share that much, but it was probably obvious.

"I'm sorry about that. Does he miss your mamm?"

Abby appreciated that he didn't look straight at her. It was getting personal, and she wasn't sure how far she wanted this conversation to go.

"My mom? Yeah. So do I." She'd lost the desire to share anything more and wanted to stop talking about her parents.

"I can't imagine what that's like for both of you." He said it like he was her best friend, knew the questions to ask, and let her talk.

"We'll be all right." Her protective armor was back on—safe, but a very lonely place to be. She stopped rocking, and he stayed put for a second before standing to lead the way.

"I think you'll see an improvement." He walked across the dirt driveway and to the barn where Ginger stood, nostrils flared, sniffing the scents around her. "Take a look." He bent over and touched the leg. Ginger didn't flinch or lift it up, a good sign.

Abby was pleased. She hadn't expected results this quickly. "What did you do?"

"Got her circulation going every few hours, walked her off and on during the day. And a few other tricks my mammi gave me."

Emotions of relief bubbled up and into Abby's chest. "It couldn't be that easy."

He shrugged. "You could probably take her home in a couple days, if you like."

As much as she wanted the filly home, Ginger seemed to be doing so well. She'd hate to see her relapse. "Maybe a few more days, if you don't mind me coming around all the time."

Mose looked down at the ground for a moment and then slowly lifted his head. "You're the one I'm doing this for. The horse just got lucky." He only looked at her for a second before shutting the gate behind him.

Abby was speechless and frustrated that she was so touched by what he'd just said. She couldn't remember the last time she had heard a kind word, probably from her mother. She realized she had no idea how to respond. But then, she didn't know how he meant it. Abby had come to loathe pity, and she definitely didn't need it from him. So she pretended he'd never said the words. "I don't need any favors. I can pay you for your time."

He shook his head. "Maybe what I said didn't come out right." They stood in awkward silence. "And I don't want your money."

"Let me know when you want me to pick her up." She mentally kicked herself even as she was speaking. Her pride kept rising, and she couldn't make it stop. He seemed to bring out her difficult side. She could hear him walking behind her to the side as if he didn't want to get too close, unsure of what she might say next.

Mose was silent as he walked to Abby's car and opened the door for her. "Thanks, Mose." She was too embarrassed to look at him. But when she did glance into his piercing blue eyes, Abby felt a knot in her throat. She didn't want to feel anything. Abby had learned to stuff her feelings. This was uncomfortable. She needed to leave, fast. She turned the key.

The motor groaned but wouldn't start. Abby groaned too and laid her forehead on the steering wheel. Without saying a word, Mose popped the hood and then walked away. Abby stayed in her car and watched him disappear into the shop and come back out with a hand generator.

Abby dug out her jumper cables and connected her end. The engine coughed but then started. Could she be any more in debt to the man? She'd rather walk than have him do anything else for her. What was his motive? Was he just a nice guy, or did he have another reason for always coming to her rescue? She couldn't imagine why he was so interested in her, especially with her behavior around him. He was just being a good Amish man.

He walked over to her window with the cables in hand. "You might want to keep these handy. I can follow you home if—"

She brought up a hand. "No, but thanks. You've done enough already."

He stared into her eyes for a moment. "It's just the Amish way."

She tightened her lips together and nodded as she drove away. If she didn't care about him, why did that comment sting her heart?

⌒ **Chapter Eight** ⌒

WHY DO YOU care so much about this horse?" Joe asked, clearly irked at being roped into fetching a horse instead of his original plans of going fishing.

"It's lame, and the owner's done everything she can to mend the filly." Mose watched Joe's eyes dart over to him. "So I brought her here for a while."

"She? Are you interested in the horse or her?" He frowned. "And who is it, anyway?"

"I'd be so bold as to match this horse against Frank." Mose figured that would get Joe's attention, and it did.

"I never thought I'd hear you say that. She must be something." He stacked the buckets and headed for the barn door. "But who's the owner?"

"She wants her back, so I need you to go with me. Claude's gonna pick me up with his trailer."

Joe stopped and stared at Mose. Riding in a machine with that kind of power was a rare experience.

"All right, under one condition." Joe opened the door and stood in the way so Mose couldn't get out. "Tell me who owns the horse."

Mose hesitated. "The person in that accident."

"*Ach*, I see."

Mose looked down at him. "It's about the horse."

"Whatever you say, but I've gotta get back. Some of us have to work." He grinned, and they walked out together.

"You mean, go fishing." Mose grunted, wondering whether he was doing the right thing, but he'd given her his word that he would see after Ginger for just a couple days, so he needed to follow through. Besides, it was a sure way to see Abby again. He had to get his priorities straight. But then, all it took was a little time with her, and he was questioning what the attraction was. She was salty or bittersweet, but deep down, Mose had a hunch Abby could be attracted to the right person like a bee to honey if she'd drop her guard.

Mose was readying the horse when Joe came back in. "Henry said he got a call from your driver. He's running late."

Mose blew out a breath. Abby wouldn't be happy—which wasn't anything new—but this time it fell on him. He could hitch her up to his trailer, but the truck was faster and a better ride for the horse.

Joe leaned against the barn door. "What are you gonna do?"

Mose looked at the horse and then at Joe. "Go fishing."

Joe clapped his hands. "Now that's a plan. You know I really didn't want to go, but I do want to see her in person."

"I haven't even let her meet my bruder, so why would I let her see you?" Mose's brother would tease him until the cows came home for bringing an English girl into the community. Because Abby was so touchy, Mose made a point to come and greet her before she could get to the house, and he made sure the barn and shop were clear before she went in. It was a lot of stress that he thought a couple hours of fishing would take care of. He'd deal with Abby later.

He and Joe had each caught a fish or two by the time Abby's car came down the driveway with a dust cloud floating behind. He expected her to be upset that he hadn't taken Ginger to her, so he prepared himself and kept on fishing.

Joe glanced over his shoulder. "Is that her?"

"Who else would be driving a car?"

"And driving like a madwoman." Joe squinted up at Mose. "Were you supposed to have taken her the horse already?"

Mose looked up at the sun directly above them. "Guess it is noon."

When Abby saw them, she parked and made her way down to the pond. "Catch anything?"

Mose didn't know whether she was being friendly or sarcastic, so he thought he'd just give an honest answer. "A couple."

She came closer and looked over the pond. Tall grass bent with the slight wind as dragonflies flew by. "This is a good size fishpond. I bet you've caught some big ones in here."

Joe and Mose looked at each other. Joe stood and wiped off his hands on his pants. "I'm Joe." He stuck out his hand and pumped hers. When she made a face at him, Joe explained. "We just shake once, kinda hard, and that's the end of it."

"Oh, interesting." She seemed sincere, and Mose was beginning to enjoy the interaction.

"Mose tells me you have a horse that's gone lame." Joe studied her intently as he waited for her answer.

"She was bad off for a while there, but Mose has done a good job with her." Then she smiled. Mose hadn't seen but small hints of a smile from her, so he leaned back and enjoyed the transformation. "She's only been gone a few days, but she seems to be better."

"*Nee*, I doubt it was Mose. The horse just needed a place she felt peaceful in. Makes a difference with animals—the stress level and all."

Mose watched Joe talk, giving away his secrets and flirting with Abby. If he had feelings for her, he'd be bothered by it, but since there was nothing between them, he sat back and listened.

Abby hadn't said anything after Joe's last comment, and Mose realized how Joe may have overstepped his bounds. Abby's farm was the most uncomfortable place Mose had ever been, and that was no lie. The thought had crossed his mind, but he was preoccupied and didn't think it through. There was more needed than just a calm setting, but Joe was right about that.

"Mose." Abby was talking to him.

"*Jah*, sorry." He snapped back into the conversation. "Do you want to get Ginger ready to go?"

She scanned the tranquil body of water in front of her and looked at Mose's pole. "I suppose so."

She looked at the bubbles that came popping up, the water lilies that fish liked to hide under, and the direction the wind was blowing.

"Do you want to throw in a line?"

She shrugged, but when he handed her his pole, she admitted, "I haven't done this for a while." She tightened the line and threw her hand back, holding the pole, then flung it forward to cast a perfect line.

Joe and Mose stared at one another. "*Gut* cast."

"Nice pole." She kept her eyes on the tip to see if there was a nibble.

Mose grinned at Joe, who was smiling too. "Made it myself."

"You're pretty serious about this." Mose picked up Joe's pole and jerked on the line.

"I used to fish with Jim when I was little." Her wide blue eyes moved across the water, catching every movement.

"How little?" He had a hunch she'd kept it up longer than she let on.

She glanced at him. "From kindergarten to...middle school."

He grinned. It was nice to hear about better times between her and her daed. They sat in silence, and after awhile Mose began to wonder whether Joe was ever going to talk. He was never this quiet.

Abby suddenly yanked on the line and pulled. The pole was bent almost in half, and Mose wondered whether he dared help her. She was an independent one, and he didn't know when to be a gentleman and when to let her take the lead.

"Ya got it?" Joe moved forward, probably struggling with the same restraint Mose was.

"No, this must be a big fish." She wrinkled her nose and used both hands to reel in the fish. Colorful scales lit up in the sunlight each time the fish jumped.

Mose pulled on the middle of the rod, and together they easily plucked the large fish up and out of the water. "It is!"

They had him pulled up to the tip of his tail when the rod snapped in two. Abby lost her balance, grabbed onto Mose, and they fell back, landing on their rumps. He pushed himself up, but not as quickly as he meant to. Mose was glad nobody had seen that fiasco.

"Are you all right?" Joe stood above them.

She chuckled. "Yeah, I'm fine." Her pants were grass-stained on one knee and her hair had fallen out of the clip, but she wore a wide grin and her face glowed.

Mose shook his head. "Remind me never to take you fishing again." He helped her up, and she brushed herself off. Her smile quickly faded, and her eyes misted.

Mose came to her side. "Are you hurt?"

She let out a long breath. "No. I just realized how long it's been since I laughed."

When he saw her in this vulnerable state, all of the emotions Mose had locked up inside stormed out like a twister, swooping down on him. He'd only known her for little more than a week, but the connection between them was like nothing he'd ever felt before. He had no idea what to do about it.

She was English, and he was Amish.

~~ Chapter Nine ~~

BBY PARKED AT St. Phillips Episcopal School and hurried through the Texas heat to the front door. The blast of cool air instantly refreshed her. She waved at the secretary in the office on her way down the hall to her classroom. She taught English as a second language, so the kids came to her for help with whatever communication issues made them struggle. A few more days of summer school, and she would have too much time at home with Jim.

When she was young, she had wanted to go to school there. Abby's family didn't attend church, and she wanted to have what some of her friends talked about, like a loving God who forgave you when you made a mistake and cared about you unconditionally. She couldn't get her head around the concepts they talked about. They seemed to have something she didn't.

Visiting Mose's place had created an awakening in her. Mose and Joe both seemed to have that same connection with what they believed in, but they didn't have to say it. It shone through in their actions and the way they treated others. Abby wondered when she'd see him again, now that she had Ginger and Old Blackie back home and her leg was improving by the day. It hadn't been that long since she'd seen him, but it seemed like it.

As the children began to enter the building, Abby took out the lesson book that had the schedule of students she'd be working with for the day. The agenda was condensed in the summer classes, so if a child missed a day, it meant a long day was ahead.

"Buenos dias." Manfred sat down at a desk next to her. The room was small but sufficient, because she didn't teach to a full

classroom. Abby felt it was more comfortable to work together in a smaller area.

"Good morning." Abby enunciated the words so he could understand them.

Manfred smiled a toothy grin and attempted to mimic the words. "It is hard to say the *morning* word," he said with a thick Hispanic accent. His dark hair was shaggy and uncombed. His dark brown eyes showed his emotions no matter how hard he tried to hide them.

"Then that's the one we will work on the most." She smiled and heard him groan.

Ada ran in, breathless and rosy-cheeked. She gave Abby a big smile as she sat next to Manfred.

Esta came in right as the bell was ringing. She wore the traditional plain clothing of the Amish. "Good morning, Ms. Abby."

"Very good," Abby encouraged, but she also knew not to overdo the praise. Manfred wasn't learning English as well as Esta and was easily discouraged. But Abby was glad the Amish children took to English quickly. Even though she took some German in high school, she knew how to teach Spanish better.

Esta's wide smile told Abby she knew she'd said the words well. She tucked her skirt under her and sat next to Manfred, facing Abby. She was pudgy, and the way she carried herself was more mature than the girls two grades ahead of her and made her seem older than her eight years.

"We are going to find out what our names mean." Abby opened a book and searched for her name.

"I think I know mine!" Ada leaned forward in anticipation, and Manfred scoffed.

"What's wrong?" Abby looked at Manfred. He was the overly emotional one much of the time, but she'd thought this would pique his interest. "Don't you want to know the meaning of your name?"

He shrugged, so Abby found the page with her name and began to read. "The name Abigail means *God Is Joy*." Abby stopped, stunned by the words. The significance of it seemed too far from reach. She hadn't practiced her mother's faith since she passed away, but it fit with what she'd been thinking about when she came to work. *There are no coincidences,* she could hear her mother say.

"Ms. Abby?" Ada's voice brought Abby back, and she realized they were staring, waiting for her to continue.

She looked at each of them for a quick moment and then settled back into the conversation. "You see there, it's nice to know what's behind our given names."

"Mine is *Star,*" Esta stated as she sat up in her seat and waited.

"Let's see...*Noble.*" It was almost fitting, if Ada would keep it in check for Manfred's sake. Abby wished she had prepared by looking up the meanings before they'd come in.

"Really?" Her eyebrows lifted, and her smile was luminous. "I thought of a lot of things, but not noble." She beamed and rested her cheek in her palm.

"Now for yours, Manfred."

He crossed his arms and laid his head down on them. "Do I have to?"

Ada snapped her head over to him. "Why wouldn't you want to know?"

He shrugged and peeked over his arms at Abby.

"I bet it will be something great!" When she turned to his name and saw what it meant—*Little Warrior*—she decided to change it a little. "Listen to this...the name Manfred means *God's Little Warrior.*"

Ada sat straight up and frowned, and for once she was speechless.

Manfred sat up and smiled. "Does it say that?"

Abby showed him and hoped he didn't see the added word. If so, it was still worth a try.

The bell rang and they left, only to have another three children come in. The numbers continued to increase until the last bell rang.

Normally she would be thinking of what to make for dinner, but Jim had been spending more time away. Sometimes she started to worry, but whenever she asked about him, he would get irritated. He never answered, so she left him alone and enjoyed more freedom. Abby hadn't seen any more symptoms like she had that one day, so she figured it was a one-time thing, but she knew he wouldn't tell her if it was anything more. He wasn't one to go to the doctor before he absolutely had to.

As she said her good-byes, she started to think about Mose. He came to her mind more often than she knew what to do with, and she had stopped trying to push him out of her thoughts. He was there whether or not she wanted him to be. But what good did it do? With Ginger on the mend, she had lost her connection with him.

After work, on her way out of town, Abby paid more attention to the fields and the farmers working them, especially the Amish farmers. Their life seemed similar to hers in many ways, living off the land and raising livestock. They both had jobs to subsidize their incomes, even though their first priority was living the country life. But there was more to it. They lived in a community, and the more she saw the benefits of it, the more she envied them for having the support they offered one another without hesitation.

As she drew closer to the turnoff to her farm, she wished she had somewhere else to go, even to run a chore, but she couldn't think of anyplace. Halfway down the lane she remembered. Stopping in front of the house, she went to the closet in her room and moved back the laundry basket next to Mose's hat.

As she picked it up, she started to feel a bit of guilt. He surely needed it, and he may have gotten another by now. He might think it strange that she'd kept it for so long, and she wondered why she had. As she walked back out to her car, she threw her cares to the wind, refusing to let herself second-guess her decision.

When she came to the familiar bend in the road to Meadowlark Valley, Abby slowed to a crawl. She suddenly felt she was trespassing. Not that they never had visits from the English, but she just felt uncomfortable, not having been invited.

As she drove by the community store, an older woman with graying hair stopped sweeping the porch and waved at her. She stopped, thinking the woman wanted to tell her something, but she turned back to her sweeping, so Abby kept going down the narrow road leading to Mose's place.

She'd passed by three farms when she finally found the Fishers' farm. Maybe she was partial, but their place seemed to be the best groomed. She wondered how common it was to have three boys to help with a single farm and blacksmith shop.

"Afternoon."

Abby turned abruptly to see Mose. "Are you busy?" She glanced at the tool in his hand and the soot on his cheek.

"Never too busy for you." He stared at her for a moment then turned away as if he felt her discomfort at his words. It caught her unaware. Mose was anything but a charmer, but his words had flattered her, and she didn't know how to respond.

Abby touched her forehead to gather her thoughts. She was a little embarrassed having shown up at his place when he would be working.

"How's Ginger doing?"

"She's improving, thanks to you." She looked up at him then, tempted to look into his eyes, but knowing better. "You should come and see her sometime."

"I'd like that."

The moment was awkward, and once again Abby was too distracted to remember why she'd decided to come. Abby scanned the area. "This farm seems larger than most others."

He hadn't taken his eyes from her, and still didn't as he talked to her, as if fixating on her every feature. "Just one that's bigger, the Yoders' place. You'll drive by it on your way out."

"I'll be sure and look for it." She twined her fingers behind her back, deciding she couldn't stand the tension any longer. "I had a reason to come here."

"You don't need a reason." He nodded to the blacksmith shop. "You said you wanted to see the shop."

She smiled and followed him into the building. Dust motes danced in the afternoon sun. The smell of grease and mist of hot water bit at her nose, and metal shavings glistened across the floor. "Have you been working in here?"

"*Jah*, just finished fitting some horseshoes." He showed her their antique tools and others that they'd made themselves. "That's the *gut* thing about being a blacksmith. If you don't like the tool, you change it and make your own."

When Mose smiled at her, a piece of her heart melted—a sensation with which she wasn't familiar—but she instinctively pulled back her emotions. Her guard rose up to a level that made her feel safe again. His kindness was creating that feeling, and she didn't know what to do with it. She wrapped her arms around her waist.

"Your hat."

Mose turned to her and tilted his head to the side in question.

"I have it. I've been meaning to give it to you, but I keep forgetting." A part of her didn't want to give it to him. It gave her some sort of security. Why, she wasn't sure, but now that she'd said it, she had to return it to him.

"How did you end up with it?" When Mose smiled, she felt a little better about having had it so long. She should have known he wouldn't be upset, but it was what she was accustomed to with her father.

"That day of the accident. I found it on my way to the truck, and I've been holding on to it for you. It's in my car. I'll get it for you if you'd like." She grinned as if to make light of it, but for some reason, it really wasn't a lighthearted matter to her.

Mose shrugged. "No need. My grandmother made me a new one." He straightened, as if regretting saying the words. "She's handy at wheat weaving."

"Your *mamm*?" she guessed. She was familiar with Pennsylvania Dutch but could understand it better than speak it.

"Close…mammi." His eyes lit up as if he enjoyed her attempt at using his language.

Her eyebrows lifted. "I can make sense of it in my head, but I don't feel like I say the words right."

"That comes from being around it. The more you hear people talking, the better you'll get a feel for it." The way he said it, as if she was going to be among the Amish, made her realize that would be something she would like to do.

"I have to know some German for my students."

Mose's eyes narrowed in on her. "That's right, you teach Amish children. Remember the land I showed you? They're having a ground-breaking ceremony for the school later today, as a matter of fact."

"So, all of the Amish children will leave the schools in town?" She was disappointed to hear the news. She enjoyed teaching a variety of children with all different needs, and she appreciated the demeanor of the Amish students.

"*Jah*, the city comes down pretty hard on us, making sure we're following all the rules and whatnot."

"They're making sure the children get the education they need."

"It's more than that. There's one guy from the state that comes around and checks up on us. He either doesn't like his job, or maybe it's just the Amish he doesn't like."

She wondered whether it was the same guy who came to the school where she taught. Abby had heard him saying some comments regarding the Amish and how they shouldn't be allowed to homeschool, didn't pass code, had bad documentation, and so on, but she didn't know how much was just him.

"Hopefully that will all change soon, when the kids move to the community school." She feared he'd be harder on them once they all left the public and Christian schools. She knew a few people who didn't appreciate the Amish, and that inspector was one of them.

Mose started for the door.

"Where are we going?"

He turned toward her. "To the ceremony."

"Is it okay if I join in?" She was right behind him, surprised that she was suddenly so excited to see some people throw dirt on top of more dirt and announce the building's purpose.

"Of course." He waited for her and held the door open. "Follow me."

They took the buggy without the top on, which was more sun than Abby wanted, but she didn't complain. When they got to the site, Abby was amazed at the turnout. It looked as if the entire community was there.

Mose walked beside her, guiding her to a spot so she could see and greeting others as they made their way through different groups of people.

"That's Minister Miller." Mose pointed to the tall, skinny man holding a shovel and a Bible.

"It's *gut* to see so many here. I promise I'll get you home in time for supper." Minister Miller choked out a rough chuckle. "The passion we have for our children is the driving force to build this school. We have leaned on *Gott* as to if this was His will, and through His provision our community has agreed to school our children here among us in a nurturing environment."

The women fanned themselves and the men wiped their brows. Abby appreciated the good behavior of the children, from babes to young adults. Everyone remained respectful and quiet as the minister spoke.

"We will build a Christian foundation with the values of our people and pray for teachers who are obedient to *Gott* and will equip students to serve Christ, their families, and impact the world." The minister handed the shovel to another older man with a long white beard and large belly. He scooped up the dirt and flipped it over, sprinkling it on the designated area.

"Who is that man?" As Abby watched his deep blue eyes and ruddy cheeks, she formed a favorable opinion of him.

"That's the bishop, a *gut* man." Mose whispered in her ear, creating goose bumps down her neck.

When the ceremony was over, Abby turned to Mose to thank him and tell him she needed to leave, but instead he took her hand. "I'd like you to meet the minister and deacon." He introduced her to a number of people whose names she tried to remember, but there were so many, she finally gave up.

"Bishop Omar." Mose called to him, and the rotund, engaging man quickly made his way over. "This is Abby. She works at the Christian school in town."

"Well, I'll be. You may be able to teach us a thing or two about running a school!"

"I'd be willing to help."

He gave her a mischievous grin and reached out his large, weather-worn hand.

When the deacon shook her hand, Abby instantly knew she would like this man, and she thought he felt the same.

Chapter Ten

WHY THE CHANGE in your trade?" Mose's daed, Eli, stared at him intently. His brown hair was grayer and his midsection was filling out, but he worked like a horse, taking great pride in his farm and sons who worked it with him.

Mose took his time to respond. "Just thought it might be *gut* to try something else."

"You've been tending horses all your life without even knowing it. You wanna be a blacksmith, carpenter, *and* horse trainer?" His daed leaned against the anvil in the middle of the shop. "What's the real reason?"

Mose knew when he was beat and let it spill out. "The owner of that horse that was lame wants to train the filly." He figured fewer words were better and stopped there.

"You mean that pretty young lady who was at the ground breaking?" One side of his lips lifted.

"*Jah,* she's the one." Mose automatically crossed his arms over his chest. When his daed's grin widened, Mose added a little more. "How did you know about her?"

"In a field full of Amish she stood out a little." He smiled so big, his teeth gleamed at Mose.

Mose had hoped he'd kept her out of sight from any of his family—not an easy task. "She needs a horse trainer, and I can train horses," Mose said matter-of-factly.

"You're a carpenter, son. You can work a horse and shoe one, but your gift is working wood, not a filly."

The double meaning made Mose pause. Abby would hate that innuendo. He sighed. Maybe he was being too ambitious. If so, it would be obvious to Abby as well. He wasn't much of a romantic, but his efforts in caring for her horse may have worked to get her attention, and that was enough.

"I've done some thinking on that too." His boot dragged along the worn wood floor. "I'd like to set up a woodworking shop here."

His daed pushed up his bottom lip. "Here on the farm?"

"I get less than half of what customers pay, and they request me. And I could work year-round planting and harvesting." Mose noticed his daed's head nodding and knew he agreed.

"Makes *gut* sense." He glanced around the shop. "We can make a place for you." He held up a finger. "But I still need your help with blacksmithing until your younger bruder sharpens his skills."

Mose grinned, elated that he could do what he had a passion for and stay in the community doing it. "I won't miss that drive every day into town."

"Frank won't either. You're wearing that horse down." His daed wrapped his arm around Mose's shoulders as they walked over to their work at hand.

Mose examined a crooked old horseshoe, deciding if it was worth repairing. "Another *gut* reason to stay put."

"I'm gonna miss your expertise in shoeing the horses."

Mose chuckled. "Any other ways to make me feel guilty?"

They both laughed quietly, the same laugh all the Fishers had. When they were together, it was a cacophony of different sounds, from the mature and older to the adolescent whose voice was changing. Mose had always been amazed at his mother for putting up with them when a wrestling match broke out or there was a battle for food at the dinner table. She had taught them to be respectful, and his daed told them to be chivalrous.

"I miss Jake." Mose didn't know where the words came from, and once he said it, he wanted to take them back. His daed slowed his movements, avoiding Mose's comment. "Sorry, shouldn't have brought him up."

"It's best that way."

Mose was the eldest brother only because his older brother

had left the community. It was difficult. Mose kept it in most of the time, but sometimes he wanted to talk about Jake to make him seem real. It was almost as if he didn't exist. That made Mose uncomfortable. He knew it was the Amish way, but there were times when Mose questioned it.

They dove into their work, and soon his brother Chris was at the door, telling them to come in for supper. His bowl-cut hair was a bit too long, and his big blue eyes seemed to twinkle with mischief.

The smell of fried chicken drew Mose in as they walked in the door. Their home was larger than most and was sparsely decorated, not only because of the Amish way, but also because Mamm didn't see the sense in doing much with a brood of boys who wouldn't appreciate the effort. Still, Daed had made a point to make her a hand-engraved chest for the sitting room, among other crafted gifts arranged throughout their home.

Once Mamm was seated, they prayed silently and waited for her to start passing the food. One chair was empty—Jake's. Mose noticed her staring at the seat next to her more than once each time they sat together for a meal.

"So, how was the day?" Daed looked at each and waited for a response. Their silver forks shimmered in the gas lighting as the guys shoveled the food into their mouths.

"Caught me a bullfrog," Chris boasted. His blond hair and blue eyes fit in with the rest of the crew, with the exception of his father, who had brown hair and eyes and stood taller than the rest of the family.

Chris grunted his approval, and Mose smiled, remembering what it felt like to catch a big old frog.

"What did you do with him?" Mose knew the answer but wanted to hear him say it.

"Let him go." Chris nodded his head three times quickly. "Maybe he'll let me catch him again if he knows I'll set him free."

Mamm grinned and glanced at Mose. "I hear you were with a young lady here the other day."

Mose stopped chewing and looked over at his daed, who continued to eat as if he hadn't heard her. "*Jah*, I was."

"Is she English?" Mamm didn't look up from her plate.

"*Jah*." Mose didn't feel the need to explain. He knew the situation he was in, so as far as he was concerned, he and Abby enjoyed each other's company, and that would be it.

"How did you meet her?" Mamm slowly cut her chicken as she waited.

"Her filly injured its leg, and I helped her with the healing." A tinge of irritation slipped up his back. As much as he liked being with his family, something growing in his mind made him want to be on his own. He was well over the age most married, so it was time. And when he really thought about it, he didn't like answering questions about things he wasn't sure of. He didn't want to be reminded of his feelings for Abby.

Mamm opened her mouth, but Daed intervened. "Mose has decided on something."

Mose regrouped and switched to the new subject his father had so cleverly diverted him into. "I've decided to set up my own shop."

Chris's eyes widened. "Can I help?"

Mose wanted him involved, but not with the equipment that could get him hurt—at least, not right away. "*Jah*, you're *gut* with curing and painting."

"That's exciting news." Mamm's hesitant reaction let Mose know she wasn't done talking about Abby. The last thing she would want was an English girl in her life. It had been done in the large community they came from in Virginia but was swallowed up by the amount of people there. The couple kept to themselves more than most, only seen at Sunday service or other mandatory events. They were not shunned, because the wife joined the church, but they were never fully accepted either.

Mamm stood and started in with the dishes, giving Mose a chance to slip out to the shop and start arranging tools and utensils to one side of the room. As he worked, separating the blacksmithing from the woodworking, he found that he couldn't keep his mind from wandering back to Abby, filled with thoughts of another way to see her once he stopped working in town. But then, she didn't seem to go anywhere much. Then he thought of a way. His hat.

⌒◦ Chapter Eleven ◦⌒

JIM WAS GETTING worse. And his insistence that he didn't need to see a doctor was grating on her. His obstinacy made her back off, even though she knew that was exactly what he wanted her to do.

"You didn't eat much breakfast." Abby took the plate from the table and set it on the counter.

"Wasn't hungry. You don't cook like your mother." He grumbled, but she heard him loud and clear.

"I do the best I can," she said under her breath, sure he couldn't hear her.

"You been seeing that Amish man?" He kept his eyes on the newspaper and sipped his coffee.

Abby was caught off guard by the question.

Why is he asking, and did he know I've been with him?

"The community had a ground breaking for their school."

"What does that have to do with you?" His voice grew stronger with each word.

"I was there to take him something, and since I'm a teacher, they thought I'd be interested."

"You teach people who can't speak English. Your mother was a *teacher*, went to school, got the certificate."

His mood was more foul than usual, and his barbs stung. She was tempted to correct him, to say how things really were, but she held back. "We didn't have the money for me to go to college."

He stiffened and turned to her.

She quickly thought of something to say that would dampen his obvious anger at her comment. "But I still got a good job, thank God."

His eyes narrowed. She felt so much anger from this weak and frail man. "God has nothing to do with it or anything else."

Abby's defenses went up. She didn't understand her mother's faith much more than Jim did, but she felt a prick in her heart each time he degraded her mother's beliefs. "That's not what Mother believed. She read the Bible and tried to live her life by it."

He pounded his fist on the table. "That book is what took your mother from me. She became one of those zealot born-again Christians."

Abby's heart pounded with fear. She didn't dare talk back to him, but what he was saying wasn't true, and it was too important to remain silent about. "You didn't share her faith. That's not the same as leaving you."

He raised his hand, the same position she had seen before as he bent over, holding his arm up high, reaching for the sky, before he hit her mother. She shielded her face with her hands and closed her eyes. Her hands wouldn't protect her, and to cover her eyes was cowardly. But she didn't want to see it coming, his fist balled up so tight his skin turned white.

"Humph." He dropped his arm and walked away with slow strides to the door and let it close after him with a *slap*!

When she heard the door shut, the pulsing in her head slowed to a normal pace. She had wondered whether it would ever come to this—passing along his physical abuse from her mother to her. She knew what followed. It was only a matter of time. He'd threatened her before, but never raised a hand to her. All she could do was be compliant, but Abby wasn't very good at that. She spoke her mind to most people, but not to Jim. This was a good reminder of why she didn't.

Abby cleaned up on autopilot, methodically got ready for work, and left without paying attention to any other housework that needed to be done. Sometimes she wondered what it was like for Amish women. They helped each other do their daily chores, something Abby didn't like to do, but it would be much better to have others to share the load. They probably became fast friends, as well. Friendship was something Abby gave up a long time ago. Her home life was too unpredictable to invite anyone over. Her parents hadn't invited others over, either. The older she got, the more she knew why. Her father was a controlling, jealous man. He had loved her mother but hadn't let her live a full life. Distrust created a holding pen for her and for Abby. The only way to hide the dysfunction was to hibernate on their farm. It was bearable up until her mother died. Now Abby felt she was serving a sentence, with locks and shackles confining her into a solitary existence.

She drove slowly to school, though she felt she should be speeding because of how late she was going to be. At the school the secretary waved her into the office. She didn't have time, but she couldn't say no.

"Morning." She tried to sound much more cheerful than she felt.

"There's someone to see you." The secretary's round figure and bouffant hairdo fit her unique personality.

A chill went down Abby's back as she worried that it was Jim. She chided herself.

He's never come here before.

"Where is he?" Abby turned and began to breathe again when she spotted Mose sitting in the waiting room next to the office.

He smiled and gave his hat a tap on the brim. He seemed perfectly at ease. When a little girl walked by him, she giggled and told him she liked his suspenders.

"What are you doing here?" Abby asked with more of an authoritative tone than she meant.

"That's some greeting." He frowned.

She let out another breath to regain a more gentle composure. "Sorry. It's been a rough morning."

"I can see that." When he stared at her with his head cocked slightly to one side and no expression on his face, Abby knew she was being analyzed. But she was too worried trying to act like everything was fine.

"Did you come to see me?"

What other reason would there be?

She instantly felt stupid for asking, but it was just going to be that kind of day.

"Came to get my hat." His blue eyes twinkled slightly as he said it.

So there was another reason—the same excuse that she had used to visit him the other day. They seemed to have found a mutual way of keeping in touch. Thank goodness for the disappearing hat. "Looks like you have another one."

"*Jah*, can't go without one where I come from."

"So, you didn't come to see me?" She sat next to him and glanced at the secretary, who was enjoying the conversation.

Mose moved forward. "Well, *jah*, that too."

The bell rang, and she stood. "I have to go to my class."

Mose wasn't in as much of a hurry as she was, obviously used to a slower pace. "Mind if I see how you work?"

Abby was genuinely surprised. No one had been interested in her job, except her mother. But even with her, it helped pay the bills, and that's what was always on her parents' minds. She looked over at the secretary.

"I'm not gonna screen him. He's Amish." The secretary grinned, showing a crooked front tooth. "I know where to find you." She pointed a finger at him.

Mose smiled at her, then stood and followed Abby. "Must be the hat."

"Yes, it seems to serve a lot of purposes." She grinned. It felt good to be playful with someone. Abby kept the grin as they walked to her room, where Manfred sat waiting. His eyes lit up when he saw Mose. Having no father figure in his life, Manfred obviously longed for the attention of a male figure.

When Esta walked in, she stopped and stared. "Mose?"

"*Jah*, thought I'd learn something new today."

Esta chuckled. "I never thought I'd see you here."

He bent over and spoke softly. "Neither did I."

She grinned and took her seat. Some of the younger Amish children needed assistance with their English once they started school. Esta was one of those few.

Mose held out his hand to Manfred. The boy's eyes widened as he gawked up at him. Mose was tall and had a muscular build that might be intimidating to a little guy like Manfred, but his warm smile seemed to make him relax. "*Gut* to meet you... Manfred, was it?"

"Huh?" Manfred lifted his hand and frowned at the one pump hand shake of the Amish.

"*Gut*, is 'good' in German," Abby explained to Manfred. "Let's do some reading. Take out your books."

"Aww, can't you read to us first?" His doe-brown eyes captured her as usual, and she agreed to read one chapter of *The Giving Tree*.

Mose leaned against her desk and rested his hand on top of the old piece of furniture. She started to read as usual, but she began to feel Mose's gaze as he stood behind her. An awkward sensation came over her. Grateful to have a picture book, she moved the chapter along quickly and then asked the children to continue taking turns until the story was over.

When the bell rang, the girls thanked Mose for coming, and Manfred tried out the Amish handshake again. "I think I got it."

"*Jah*, you did. You have a strong grip."

"Got two older brothers, but you know what that's like." He gave Abby a wave as he walked out the door.

Abby turned to face Mose. "Quite the character, isn't he?"

"*Jah*, but there's something about him..."

"He has a difficult home life. But Manfred is fortunate enough to have a benefactor who pays for him to come to this school."

Mose frowned and stood tall. "What do you mean by difficult?"

"Their family can't make ends meet. His parents work the fields taking what work they can, but it's not enough to live on.

Social service got involved, and the children are split up in different foster homes."

Mose flinched and let out a long breath. "That's a sad story."

Abby couldn't help but smile. His concern warmed her heart and brought her one step closer to him. "You really took to little Manfred, didn't you?"

Mose shrugged and put his hands on his hips, seemingly a bit embarrassed. "And your reading. I didn't know you did voices."

She smiled slightly, now the one embarrassed. "Habit, I guess."

They stood silently for a moment, which seemed much longer, until he finally spoke. He watched a couple of students come in and take a seat, and then turned back to her. "I guess I should be going and let you get back to work."

"Thanks for stopping by."

"Still didn't get my hat."

She chuckled. "Guess I'll have to bring it to you at work."

He pointed at her with the rim of his hat. "See you tomorrow, then."

She nodded and watched him leave. They may come from two different worlds, but she felt more of a connection with him than any other person she knew.

Seeing Mose had started Abby's day out well, and it continued that way until she got home and Old Blackie came running out of the barn with his tail between his legs.

As she drove up to the house, she saw Jim's truck had taken out the top two stairs of the porch. The barn door was open, and any horses, cows, or donkeys that were kept in the barn were out wandering the grounds. Abby let out a sigh that almost turned into a sob, but she wouldn't go there. She needed to take care of this, whatever it was Jim was up to.

It was Friday, so she knew where he'd been. Two or more days a week, now, he'd come home barely able to drive. As she walked to the barn, she prepared herself for the condition he'd be in as the bubble of fear and anger moved up her throat.

The whinny of a horse caught her attention, and she ran the rest of the way. She pushed through the barn door and followed the squealing sound of a horse. She knew it was Ginger and heard Jim growl at her so loudly her eardrums vibrated. The next sound brought her to a halt. A gunshot.

Tears flooded her eyes. Her vision blurred as she ran to the last stall. Ginger pranced around, her white eyes filled with fear. Another shot went off and hit the ground, causing Jim to fall back against the wood planks behind him. He slid down, landing on his rump, his breathing labored and legs sprawled out in front of him.

Abby reached out to grab the gun, but he dragged it out of reach. He pushed her away, but he was too weak to hold her back. She lunged for the gun again and ripped it out of his hand. The alcohol had taken his strength, giving her the advantage. She stood and looked down at him and felt hate like she never had before.

"Where did you get the money for this horse?" He slurred the words and rolled his eyes at her, trying to focus.

"What?" Abby scoffed, unable to comprehend how he had the gall to ask anything of her after putting all three of them in danger. "What are you doing?"

"I'm puttin' her down." His thick tongue made it hard to comprehend, but she understood, only because the words fit him so completely. "You used *her* money." He pointed to Ginger pacing around the far side of the stall. "Don't lie; I talked to the horse trader you bought her from." He sat up, stared at her, and then stood. He bent over with his hands on his knees. "You spent that on this." He threw out a hand and stood up.

He was regaining his faculties. That scared her. He wasn't in his right mind, and he was angry and violent. She wanted to run, but it would be the tiny mouse running from the crazed cat. She'd seen what he could do, and she wasn't brave enough to try to outwit or run him. So she stood there waiting for his next move.

She jumped when he took his first step forward. "Darn you and this horse." He pushed past her, turning her sideways as he hit her shoulder with his.

Abby made sure he was gone before going to Ginger. Her leg was just as bad as on the day of the accident. Who knew how long he'd been in there tormenting the poor animal. Abby sat down against the stall, staring as Ginger tried to walk on three legs. She took the bullets out of the gun and lifted one of the planks in the wall.

She placed the gun in the wooden hiding place. Abby hoped she'd never have to use it.

~~ **Chapter Twelve** ~~

BUDGET HAD LIMITED the new shop to only five stations—one for each piece of machinery. Mose was using the saw, his daed next to him with the shaper, Chris handled the jointer, and next to him was the planer. If Jake were home, he would be on the jointer, with Chris on the planer, but Mose didn't want to think about Jake; it only made him angry. The mortise machine held the bits together and finished the job. The curing and painting would need to be done, as well. There wasn't enough space for all of them to be in there together at one time, so daed took Chris with him to the blacksmith section of the shop.

"I'd like to make this place bigger, but it would cost money we don't have." His daed let Chris pick out horseshoes and gathered the nails needed for shoeing the five horses in the corral.

"No hurry, Daed. I've still got to finish up my two weeks' notice at the shop in town. Once we get some customers coming out this way to fill furniture orders, we'll have some cash to expand." Mose watched Chris smooth down a piece of wood with precision. He seemed to be in his element when working with wood. This would be a good chore for them to do together.

He hadn't seen Abby for a couple of days and wondered why she hadn't come to the shop. He didn't care about the hat, but he appreciated its purpose. He had an unsettling feeling whenever she was away too long. Her daed concerned him. Something wasn't right, but he wasn't sure what it was. She didn't share a lot about herself, and especially about her family. He couldn't help but wonder why. He didn't think badly about many people, but he couldn't help having doubts about Abby's daed.

He pulled his saw through a piece of hickory wood with ease using the tool he'd bought and repaired, costing half the cost of a new one. The process was so familiar, his mind wandered. Maybe the silly hat had outworn its charm. When Mose remembered her reading to the students and how little Manfred struggled, he appreciated the work she did. A thought tumbled into his brain.

She could help us with our school, like the bishop suggested.

They would build the school the same as a barn raising, so it wouldn't take long. They didn't usually build in the Texas summer due to the heat, but it needed to be done, and it would take half the time due to the size.

"Daed, did they decide on a day to build the school yet?" Mose hoped it was soon, as he'd heard it was. It couldn't be soon enough for him.

"Day after tomorrow, so make time." He brought his hammer down on the smoldering horseshoe, working out the bent metal.

"Can I try, Daed?" Chris watched with fascination, reminding Mose of the time he first shoed a horse.

"*Nee*, son. Watch and learn first." Daed wiped his forehead and banged on the stubborn metal.

When Mose saw Chris's face drop, he thought of something to cheer him up. "The coming-of-age ceremony will be soon, won't it, Daed?"

Chris's eyes widened. "When?"

Daed grinned mischievously. "Are you ready for that? It's a big responsibility to say you're a young man."

The service would go forward as usual, but there would be a special time for the boys around Chris's age to be recognized. Mose suddenly thought it would be something Abby might like to experience. Then he shook his head. Everything seemed to lead back to her, and it worried him. They were separate, living different lives. He would have to force himself to concentrate on the work at hand.

"Mose." Chris was watching him, waiting for him to answer something that Mose hadn't heard.

"Sorry, what was that?"

Chris shook his head and pointed to the piece of wood Mose was working on. When he looked up, his daed was grinning. Mose had cut the piece lengthwise instead of across.

Mose took off his work belt and walked outside, taking in the humid heat that was so thick he felt he could touch it.

His daed was close behind him. "What's on your mind, son?" He rolled his fingers to rid them of the metal shavings that had collected on his hands.

"Something that shouldn't be," Mose blurted out, and then regretted it. He didn't need to be told. He just couldn't stop the irrational thoughts.

"If you're worried about the shop, we'll get it going in due time." Daed rested one hand on his ever-growing belly and hooked the other hand around his suspender.

"It's not that. I hadn't planned on quitting my job in town until I know it's all gonna pan out." He let out a long breath that felt as heavy as the hot air.

"What is it, then?" They both stared at the many acres of cotton.

"It's hard to explain." He could hear his daed's advice without even telling him. He knew the answer; he just didn't want to face up to it.

"There are plenty of nice girls here, you know."

Mose whipped around to face him. "I'm not interested."

"That's what I hear." Daed finally looked him in the eye.

"How do you know?"

"I'm not a fool. I was there once."

Mose shook his head. "Not in the same way I am."

"I'm pretty sure I was. Sweetest girl I ever knew was English."

Mose about jumped out of his suspenders. "Why would you mention that?"

"You know why."

Mose swallowed hard. He hadn't realized how obvious he was when it came to Abby.

"We are a small community, but there is another one right close to town that we commune with." His forehead wrinkled in question. "Just do what's right." And with that, he walked back into the shop and shut the door.

What did that mean, "do what's right"?

He knew nothing could ever come of him and Abby's relationship. He didn't need to be reminded.

He kicked the dirt, walked back in, and spent the rest of the afternoon making a fine rocking chair for his first customer, Abby.

Chapter Thirteen

IT HAD BEEN eight days and counting since her encounter with Jim, which was also the last time she saw Mose. She purposely made stops at places where Mose might be—the furniture shop and the place he boarded his horse in town, even the hat store to find out whether they had seen him.

I'll just have to drive down to his community. She wondered if he was upset with her, but she couldn't think of anything that would cause him to be.

As the children left for the day, she noticed Esta walking down the hall in front of her. She'd been tempted to ask her about Mose, but she wanted to keep it proper, so she didn't put her on the spot.

"Have a good evening, Esta." A cordial way to let her know she was there. "And tell Mose hello for me."

Esta stopped, so Abby did too. "You probably see him less now that he doesn't work in town anymore."

"He left the furniture store?"

"*Jah*, he's opening up his own shop at his daed's place, next to their blacksmith shop."

"Oh, I didn't know."

Is he deliberately trying to stay clear of me? She was thinking too much. "I've missed seeing him." That much was true, and she hoped Esta told him so.

"He asks about you too." She smiled and waited for her response, which Abby tried to make as subtle as she could without appearing to be too interested.

"I'm sure we'll see each other soon." She smiled and walked away, wondering in what way he wanted to know about her. Common curiosity as to whether he was really interested in her?

Abby shook her head. This was silly. She would just go out there and see him so she could find out for herself.

On the way home she felt like a schoolgirl going to see her beau. She acknowledged that it was a crazy notion, but that was how he made her feel. As she turned into the driveway by their home, she noticed the house was dark, with the exception of the kitchen, where a dim light let off a faint glow. She had done her best to avoid Jim, and it seemed he had done the same. He hadn't gone near Ginger or anywhere else around the farm, which meant not tending to the chores either.

"Jim?"

There was no answer, only the sound of snoring, but it didn't come from his bedroom. As she peered around the door, she saw he was sitting in a chair with his head down on the table. Her first thought was his health. She took quick steps to his side.

When she tapped him on the shoulder, he didn't respond, but the snoring stopped. Abby shook his arm, and he slowly lifted his head. He turned to her with eyes squinted and hair askew.

"Twenty-five years today," he mumbled through the alcohol fumes.

Puzzled, Abby drew her eyebrows together for a moment, and then she understood. "It's your wedding anniversary."

He swore at Abby and pushed her away. "Leave me be."

Anger flared up in her for only a moment. Abby couldn't ever imagine her mother treating her this way. If the roles were reversed and her mother was still here, she would never be so harsh. How could two people be together who had nothing in common but their daughter? A fleeting thought wrestled its way up into her mind.

Why couldn't it have been him and not her?

Her instant guilt created surprising compassion for him. She reached for him again, trying to comfort him, but he sat up, his eyes wild as he glared at her.

"Go away," he slurred, his head bobbing.

"Let me help you," Abby pleaded with both disdain and

heartache. This man was so hard to love, but he was her father, faults and all. She had to forgive.

"I'm fine." The heavy breathing meant he may lash out again. This time he would be angrier. She remembered seeing her mother trying to deal with him, and it had never gone well for her.

"You don't have to go through this alone." She waited for an answer, but none came, so she took his arm to lift him up. He roused but wasn't fully aware until he clutched his stomach and grunted with pain. His face twisted and turned red.

"What is it?" She first thought if might be his heart, but when she saw spots of blood on his sleeve, she didn't know what it was. She panicked, grabbing the phone instinctually.

"No!" He yelped and let go of his abdomen, catching his breath, and wiped his mouth. "No doctors."

Abby kept dialing, but her fingers shook, and she had to start again. The next thing she knew, she was on the ground. She landed on her back, feeling unbelievable pain shooting across her face. The phone slid to the other side of the room, but she couldn't stabilize her thoughts enough to get to it.

Abby heard the chair screech back and watched his feet coming toward her. Pushing herself up with both hands, she lifted her head to see him come closer. Abby knew she should run, that he had hurt her and might again. But what her brain told her, her body couldn't do. So she did the only thing she *could* do—pray.

He stood above her with hands balled into fists, breathing heavily. She didn't dare look him in the eye. She knew every movement that would set him off. Speaking would bring on the worst retaliation. She waited silently, holding on as long as she could, until he finally left. The sound of his boots drifting away brought back her sanity one step at a time. He paused once, causing her breath to stop, but she let it out when she heard the front door open and then shut.

She collapsed onto the linoleum floor and sobbed, letting the tears flow freely that she hadn't let go since her mother's funeral.

The memories haunted her of how her mother had made this house a home, and how different it was now. It was no longer safe.

Garnering her strength, she forced herself to her feet, letting the throb on her cheek drive each step forward. There was no telling what he might do in his condition, and Abby didn't want to find out. She made her way to the front door. All lights were turned off, so she could see far into the pasture and to the road. His truck wasn't there, creating conflicting emotions. She wanted him gone so she could leave, but he probably shouldn't be driving.

He wouldn't listen, anyway, and I'd get slapped again for telling him.

The creak of the screen door pierced the night and made her wince as she stepped out and slowly let the door shut. There was no turning back. She knew Jim well enough to know this was unforgiveable. She couldn't leave and expect to be accepted back. But guilt plagued her. He was ill. There was something very wrong, and she was leaving.

Once in her car she was so anxious Abby froze when she turned the key. The engine of Abby's car groaned but wouldn't start. She sat back, listening for every car that went by, hoping each time it wasn't Jim. She tried the engine a couple more times, and it finally sputtered into action. But her confidence wavered as to how much longer it would continue to keep running.

Abby watched the sun descend as she slowly drove away and wondered what could ever bring her back to this place. There were no good memories left, and Jim had crossed a line. The only thing she cared about was Ginger, but she didn't have the vehicle to take her. At the moment she could only think of herself.

Headlights in the distance danced between the oak trees. Her stomach dropped as she strained to see the pickup drawing near. With great relief she watched it turn away. When she got to the road, she stopped, not knowing which way to go. To the right was town, and to the left was Mose. She'd never felt so alone.

Maybe that was why it had taken her so long to leave. Jim was all she had, and whether he cared or not, Abby was all he had.

She turned left. Just seeing Mose and having him to talk to

was enough for her to lower her pride. She might later regret it, but she didn't have another choice, and maybe he could help her save Ginger.

The drive helped settle her nerves, but the throb in her cheek grew worse and her neck was sore. The pounding intensified in her head like the beating of a drum. When she pulled in, she saw stacks of lumber on the land where the school was to be built. It was the only good feeling she'd had all day, seeing their work about to be done.

Dim lighting shone through the windows of the farms she passed. Some had candles shining in the front glass panes. Abby was used to the quiet of the country, but here it wasn't somber; it was peaceful.

When she got to Mose's place, she was surprised to see more lumber by the blacksmith shop. A lot went on in this little community. As soon as she turned down the lane, someone came out the front door and stood on the porch. Abby couldn't see the man's face, but due to his height and build, she thought it might be Mose.

He stuck his hands on his hips and walked to her car to greet her. As soon as she turned off the engine, a loud popping noise burst from under the hood. She stepped out and took a couple steps away in case there was another explosion. Mose grabbed her hand and pulled her away.

"Are you all right?" When he looked at her cheek, his demeanor changed from question to concern as his brows drew together. "What happened?"

Abby realized by his reaction that it must look worse than she thought, and she instinctively touched the area that hurt. She shook her head, not wanting to explain such a horrid thing to such a gentle man. She fixed her gaze on Mose's fists as they tightened and released.

"You don't have to explain. I think I understand." He turned his head away, obviously wrestling with what to say, so she said it for him.

"My dad." Abby didn't know why she called him that. He was Jim to her. She never called him dad to his face. For so long she'd felt nothing but disdain for him until that strange moment of compassion that filled her heart...right before he hit her. The anger on Mose's face brought out long buried emotions of her own. It was hard enough to admit you'd been abused, but admitting it was by your own parent made it even harder.

"I'm sorry." Mose stepped back from her, his gaze probing hers. Then he reached up and slowly took Abby's hand away from her face and held on to her. "What can I do to help?"

His empathy broke the barrier she'd created to keep her emotions tucked away, and she let a tear fall and then struggled to regain control. "I just needed to get away for a while. But the animals...I'm worried. I need to make sure they're safe."

He nodded. "You're welcome to stay as long as you need to, Abby."

Abby didn't know what she was doing there, but it felt safe, and she didn't want to leave—at least not tonight. "Can we just sit down for a minute?"

"We can sit on the porch."

When she didn't reply right away, he offered another idea. "Or we can go into my shop."

Abby glanced at the shop and then nodded. She didn't care where they went, as long as she was with him.

∽ Chapter Fourteen ∾

HOW COULD ANYONE *do such a thing, and to his own daughter?* Mose's first impulse would've gotten him arrested if he'd acted on it. He'd never felt such malicious thoughts toward another human being. But what he felt right now toward the man who'd wounded Abby needed to be reined in before he did something he would regret.

He took a couple of deep breaths and let them out to hold back the words he wanted to say but that would only make Abby feel worse.

Watching the clouds churning in the wind, he tried to settle his anger, but they created the opposite effect, identifying with how he felt.

She looked over at him as they walked into the shop. "Are you okay?"

"*Nee*, this is wrong." He pulled up a bench for them to sit on.

"I knew this would be upsetting, but I didn't know where else to go." She looked down at her hands where they lay in her lap. Her face was drawn and white except for the bruise that made Mose angrier each time he looked at her.

"You knew you'd be welcome here." He questioned how much to say. This was her daed, one told by God to respect. But how could someone respect a parent who hit them? "You can stay with us tonight if you're comfortable with us males in the haus."

She looked at her car. "I wasn't planning to, but I don't have much of a choice."

"I can ask another family, if you'd be more comfortable." He wanted her to stay with him. He didn't know how far Jim would go, but he wanted to be there for her if he was so bold as to come to the community.

She turned slowly to face him. "I came here to see you."

The feeling in his chest caused a sensation he wasn't accustomed to. His attraction to her when she was bad-tempered was nothing compared to how he felt now that she was so vulnerable. "I'm glad you did."

She leaned forward and placed her chin in her palm. He wanted her to tell him what had happened, but worried he might say or want to do something he shouldn't. "Do you want to talk about it?"

Abby shook her head, and her body went limp.

She must be exhausted. "Let's get you settled in for the night."

She looked out the shop window, then to the dark house. "I don't want to bother anyone."

"Everyone's ready for bed. We get up early around here." He forced a smile. "But you can sleep in." He thought he'd offer that so she wouldn't have to worry about anyone seeing her, more so her bruise.

"Okay. Thanks, Mose." She lifted herself up off the bench and followed him to the door. "Is it nice to have your own shop?"

Her question surprised him. The shop was the last thing on his mind, which was strange because it was all he had let himself focus on when he'd spent time away from her. "It is. I'll show you around tomorrow, if you like."

He'd tried to take his daed's advice, and he'd done pretty well staying occupied, but there wasn't a day that went by he didn't think of her. And now *Gott* had brought her to him. There was a reason, and his daed couldn't deny it.

When they walked into the house, Mose hoped no one would be around, but his mamm greeted them as soon as they walked in. Abby turned her bruised side away, not wanting to look at his mamm straight on. "Mamm, this is Abby."

"Hallo, Abby. I've heard Mose talk about you." Mamm was the same height as Abby, and when their eyes met, there seemed to be a connection. They took an extra second to study one another before Abby finally spoke.

"He does?" She tilted her head, hiding the bruise, but Mamm ignored it.

She turned to the kitchen. "Come with me, and I'll make us something."

"*Nee*, Mamm. She's tired." Mose tried to swiftly divert her, but Abby followed and sat at the table.

Mamm turned on the gas stove to heat up leftovers from supper. "I hear you're a teacher."

Abby looked at Mose, who quickly defended himself. "My daed saw you at the ground breaking." He didn't want her to think he was telling everyone about her. They were nothing more than friends, and she just happened to be English.

"I'm not a certified teacher, but I help children to speak and read English." She inspected the plate of food Mamm gave her, and Mamm offered one to Mose. He took it but had no appetite.

"She's very *gut*," he said without thinking. "Is the summer session over?"

Abby nodded. "I was looking forward to having the last few weeks to work Ginger before school started again."

Mamm continued to busy herself in the kitchen, but he knew her too well. She made it seem as though she wasn't nosey, but Mamm was getting a lot of information. "You've seen her teach?"

"*Jah*." That's all he'd tell her. But then he worried about Abby. She seemed to be comfortable talking to Mamm, and he hadn't told his family anything about her except what his meddlesome daed had figured out.

"You should stay tomorrow while our school is being built." Mamm put the pan away and scrubbed the already clean counters.

Mose was about to protest and get Abby out of the awkward situation of saying no when she spoke up.

"I'd like that." She continued to pick at the food on her plate and politely refused when Mamm offered more. The dark rings under her eyes grew darker, and her eyes shut once quickly.

"Let me show you to your room." Mamm motioned for Abby to follow, which she did, with Mose close behind. They went to Jake's old room and showed her around. "If you need anything, holler. The men in this haus don't hear a thing, so don't worry about being quiet."

When she was told she would need to go outside to use the bathroom, as they didn't have plumbing, she paused. "I hadn't given this much thought until right this moment," she said, but she was too tired to think much about it.

Mamm closed the door to her room, ushering Mose along with her. He regretted not having a chance to tell Abby good night. Maybe it was silly, but he wanted her to know that he was right across the hall.

"She's fine." Mamm clasped his upper arm and walked him to his room. "You're a *gut* man, Mose." Then she slipped into her room without a sound.

At times, he felt his daed had married an angel. She never passed judgment and always waited patiently for an explanation. She didn't offer advice unless it was asked for. Her counsel was sound, and there was no condemnation.

When Mose walked out of his bedroom the next morning, he wondered what the day would be like. There would be lots of looks and, later, questions—not only because she was an English woman, but also because her bruise would be obvious. To his surprise, when he walked into the kitchen, Abby, in plain clothes, was making cheese biscuits with his mamm.

The dress was a bit large, but not so much that it looked bad. Abby's long, golden hair was down, hiding her face. Having figured out what was going on, he walked in to say good morning. "What's for breakfast?"

They both turned to him at the same time, but Mamm spoke first. "Eggs, biscuits, and bacon. Your daed and bruder just finished."

Mose looked out at the sun and realized he'd slept later than usual, which he never did, but he couldn't sleep last night, thinking about Jim, trying to fight off the bitterness he felt toward the man. He imagined Abby had gone through the same sort of battle. "How are you this morning, Abby?"

He meant that in many ways. She must be torn about what had happened to her. He'd heard victims of physical abuse have remorse after the incident and even blame themselves. He hoped she'd stay strong and not go back until Jim worked things out.

"You slept in." She brought over a plate with extra bacon and smiled when their eyes met. Her bruise had gotten larger and darker.

She touched her cheek, so he quickly averted his eyes. He searched for words but found none that would reassure her.

His mamm lifted her head toward them and pursed her lips in thought, then grinned, making Mose wonder what he could say that wouldn't give her false assurance.

Abby rubbed her cheek as if she could brush it away, then winced.

"I'm sorry." It was all he knew to say.

"I'm fine." She walked over and sat next to Mose, and they ate together as Mamm cleaned up the kitchen. "Let me help?"

Mamm shook her head. "*Nee*, you finish your breakfast.

Abby stood and took her plate to the sink. "I'd like to help."

Mose was glad to hear it. Helping with chores was the Amish way, and her upbringing was showing through. Watching them work together stirred something in his gut. He wasn't sure where this would lead, but at the moment he knew they needed to get back to her farm and get Ginger as soon as possible. "Are you up to going to fetch Ginger?"

"Her and Old Blackie if you don't mind." She tried to smile, but she flinched when it got to the bruise.

Mose just grinned his answer. The little guy had grown on him, and Abby knew that he couldn't say no.

Chapter Fifteen

MOSE WATCHED ABBY tinker with the tools in the shop. He could tell she was used to being busy. It was also a little awkward to have her living in his haus. With anyone else it wouldn't be an issue, but his feelings for her were growing. He just didn't know how apparent it was. "It would be nice for you to feed and water the horses while you're here."

She nodded in agreement. "I need to make myself useful. Everyone around me works, so should I. I just don't know where my place is." She leaned against a workbench and looked down at her boots.

Thinking of ways to keep her there seemed to be his latest selfish desire. But he also was worried for Ginger's welfare, along with the rest of the livestock at her daed's place. He knew it was always on her mind too.

"I've been worrying about Ginger since I left." She ran a hand over the horseshoe she'd been fingering. He didn't miss the opportunity to tell her he felt the same about Ginger. Getting Abby out of harm's way was first and foremost; if she was ready to go back, he was ready too.

"Let me know when it's the right time for you to go." He sounded knowledgeable but didn't fool himself. At least his comment was somewhat impartial.

"This has never happened before. I didn't think he'd hurt me the way he did my mother." She averted her eyes as she spoke, something unusual for her. Abby was very direct, looking a person in the eyes, almost defensive at times. But Mose felt from the first time he met her that that was a cover for her hurt and insecurities.

"Jim hurt your mamm?"

She nodded. "A couple of times that I know of. He stopped when she got sick."

He scoffed unintentionally. "But now he's started again."

Her eyes softened with pain, and she looked down at her shoes. "Something's wrong with him."

"*Jah*, and until he's gotten help, you should stay away."

"No, it's more than that. It's his health."

Mose tried to feel empathy for this man, but he couldn't get there. Not yet. "That's no excuse."

She turned away from him, looking out the only window in the shop. The metamorphosis was somewhat like a butterfly returning to its cocoon. She took a rag and began cleaning the tools—something that actually needed to be done but that Mose tended to put off until they were unmanageable.

"I apologize if I said something wrong."

I should keep my thoughts in my head, where they belong.

She shrugged. He hated it when she did that. The gesture meant she'd closed down and would disengage him until he could break down the wall again. "How about we take a drive and haul Ginger and Old Blackie back here?"

She stopped and turned abruptly toward him. "But we don't have a trailer."

"We'll borrow Ira's again. He'll be happy to help us out." He smiled slowly, waiting for her reaction before he felt he'd accomplished what he set out to do, which was to make her smile. It worked.

"I'd like to use Jim's, but he keeps it under lock and key." A glint of anger shone in her expression, but she moved forward and was out the door before he was.

"Hold your horses." Mose teased at her enthusiasm. "I don't want you to be disappointed if there's a glitch."

She slowed and listened. "Like what?"

"Ira might not still have the trailer. It was originally borrowed from an Englisher. There could be something that needs fixing.

85

Repairing it is the agreement we have with the Englisher who lets us borrow it. And even if we do get everything we need, your daed might be there."

Abby lifted her eyes to his. "I'm aware of that." Her eyes flashed, and she was moving forward again. "But I'm willing to go if you are."

By the time they hitched up the Clydesdales to the wagon and made it over to pick up Ira, Mose was sure Abby would make this work even if every possible scenario that he'd described happened.

Ira came out to greet them and meet Abby. "What happened to him?" she asked, noticing he compensated fairly well for missing a leg.

"He lost it to an infection that spread and almost killed him. But he rejoiced over his loss, saying that's why *Gott* gave him two—so he'd appreciate the one."

She grinned as he helped her step down from the wagon.

"Well, aren't you a dandy sight to see." Ira didn't lean to the side as she expected; he stood as straight and tall as Mose did, eye to eye with him as they talked.

"*Hallo*, Ira." She held out her hand, and he gave her the one-shake Amish pump that Mose expected she was getting used to.

"I hear ya have a couple of horses that need a ride." He motioned to her.

"Thank you for letting us use the trailer again. I'd like my horses close by."

"Special 'uns, huh?" He squinted one eye like Popeye.

"Yes, very much."

"Needs some training, though. And Ira's the man for the job. He has an instinct like nobody else." Mose shook his head as if he couldn't believe how talented he was.

Abby's eyes lit up into a vivid blue. "I'd like to see you work with her."

"Then that's what we'll do." Ira looked over to Mose for reinforcement.

"Sure. We'll bring her over here for you to take a look at her." He knew his daed would want them to be chaperoned and thought he'd ask, knowing he'd done the right thing by trying. "You wouldn't happen to be up to taking a ride to Abby's place, would ya, Ira?"

Abby's eyes caught Mose's. He'd have to explain to her at some point, but for now, this is what he needed to do to make it right.

"Need a chaperone, eh?"

Abby kept her gaze on Mose, but her features softened with the knowledge Ira so quickly offered.

"My daed would appreciate it."

Abby smiled now with clear understanding as she stepped up into the wagon. It took a few minutes to hitch the trailer to the wagon, which Mose did mostly by himself. But Abby seemed so taken with Ira, he didn't mind. Besides, once Ira started talking horse training, Mose was pretty much left out of the conversation. The Clydesdales plodded along without complaint, but when they got close to town, Abby got fidgety.

When Mose put his hand on hers, Ira leaned back in his seat and kept quiet, which Mose knew was difficult for him.

When they got to the last country road before town, Mose slowed the horses. "We're almost there. Are you sure you want to do this?"

"This is the third time you've asked me, and the answer is still the same." But when she didn't see her dad's truck and exhaled, he knew differently. She was scared to death, and deep down, so was Mose. Someone like her dad was unpredictable, but that wasn't what Mose feared. He didn't know if he could keep himself from what *he* might do. He'd never felt true hate like he did with this man, and he'd been diligently praying for discernment and forgiveness for his thoughts.

"It seems pretty quiet." Abby's eyes swept over the farm and what she could of the house. But with her dad's truck missing, he felt they were safe. He didn't want to worry about Ira being out and about, so he'd have him stay put.

"Do you mind staying in the wagon, Ira? This will just take a minute."

"I don't mind waiting."

Mose smiled at the old man. His balding gray hair and pot-belly only made him more likeable than he already was, but Mose didn't want anyone to know more information than necessary. "Give us a holler if you see anyone pull in."

"Sure. Glad to help." He leaned to one side of the wagon, his head bobbing. Mose figured Ira would be taking a nap by the time he and Abby returned.

Mose parked by the barn and backed in as far as he could, to Ginger's stall. "How does she look?"

When he didn't get a response, he walked over to see the horse. Ginger's leg was swollen again, but what was worse, she was without food and didn't have much water. Mose's first reaction was anger, but when he saw tears on Abby's cheeks, they washed the rage away. He opened the gate and harnessed the horse.

"Open the trailer door, Abby."

She startled at the sound of her name and did as she was told. Ginger stumbled, but with some coaxing, slowly lifted each hoof and forced her body forward. Abby murmured comforting words to the horse as she got her settled in the trailer. She moved stiffly as she made her way to the wagon.

They repeated the process, and soon Blackie was by Ginger's side.

"Let's take a drive around the place to see how the other animals are," Mose suggested, feeling more secure about it with them all mobile and able to leave quickly if needed.

The barnyard looked much worse than the first time he'd seen it. "With the pond and a large enough area for grass, the animals must do okay on their own."

"It's what they're used to." Her tone didn't sound convincing, but he didn't read anything into what she said right now. There were probably a lot of emotions stirring around inside of her. He didn't want to overwhelm her. "Ready to go?"

"Yes, more than ever." She kept her eyes forward, looking at the road until they got to the highway. Then she sat back and relaxed.

Mose's two best Clydesdales made pulling the trailer seem effortless as they clomped down the road. The time would go a little faster with the two strong animals leading the way. Abby was as jumpy as a rabbit, constantly looking over her shoulder.

"Abby, even if we do run across your daed, there's nothing he can do with me by your side." He patted her tense shoulder and thought back to when he'd first met her. She had been so strong and forceful. But this Abby was transparent. All of her fears and worries were out there for him to see, making her completely vulnerable. She looked over her shoulder again. "We've come this far. I don't want anything to stop us from getting Ginger out of here now."

They were silent for a while, until a pickup came up behind them. Abby discreetly watched it as the vehicle passed them, then she looked away.

Mose tried to look into the truck, but he couldn't see through to the driver's side. "Was that him?"

"It might have been, but I didn't look." She glanced over at Mose. When the truck was farther down the road, she let out a breath. "Do you think I'm being ridiculous? It's not even his color."

"*Nee*, but you can't live in fear."

"It's not that easy."

"That is the way of the Amish. We've been persecuted for centuries, and still are, but with a different sort of persecution."

Her brows drew together as she stared at Mose. "I did hear about some young men who were threatening a young woman from your community a while ago."

A flash of Elsie's face brought the whole incident back to him. She had been harassed by a group of Englishers for months. "*Jah,* but our vow of no resistance kept her from telling anyone until it got out of hand and the authorities got involved."

"Have I met her?" The way Abby looked at him, it was as if she knew there was more than what he was telling her. Maybe it was obvious. Maybe he was still sensitive about the way things had turned out with Elsie.

"*Nee*, it's awkward for me still, sometimes. She married someone else."

She took her time in responding, digesting his meaning. "Oh, I'm sorry."

"Don't be. It's all for the best." And when he looked at her, he honestly felt, for the first time, that what he said was true. Despite the barrier between them, Mose couldn't help the way he felt about her. He would enjoy the time they had and be grateful for it—even if they'd never be together.

⌒ Chapter Sixteen ⌒

WE HAVE A school to build today."
"It only takes one day?" Abby looked from Mamm to Mose. They both nodded. "It's hard to believe."

"Come and see." Mose stood and took their plates to the sink. "Are you coming later, Mamm?"

"*Ach*, yes. I'm bringing my sweet potato pie." She smiled at Abby. "You two go ahead."

Mose felt Abby's discomfort, but he knew she'd find the process interesting. Most English did. As they walked to the buggy, Mose took off the top and then offered his hand to help her up, but she climbed in before he had a chance to assist her. She apparently wasn't one that wanted coddling, but he thought she might enjoy letting someone care for her, once she learned to trust.

"Is it going to be awkward?" She kept her eyes forward and wore a frown. He couldn't tell her; she would just have to see if she would be accepted.

"*Nee*, it's not usually like that here. We had some trouble with some English young men, but once that was ironed out, some visit now and then." He wanted her to look at him, just once, and smile. She was prettier when she did, and he wanted her to be content. He realized that was what he wanted most for her. There was so much to Abby that she held inside, understandably so, but no matter what happened between them, he wanted to see her happy.

When they got to the site, Mose felt a little guilty for not getting there at dawn with the rest. They had three sides of the frame up and were working on the beams. Every able-bodied male was there, ready to help with whatever needed to be done.

Mose parked the buggy and tried to get to Abby's side before she got out, but once again she beat him to it.

"They've gotten a lot done already."

"*Jah*, it will be finished before dark." He walked her over to where the women were preparing the food. He knew the person he wanted Abby with and walked straight over to her to avoid too much conversation from others. "Rebecca."

She pinned her brown hair and secured her kapp as she turned around to see them. "Mose, we were wondering where you were." She gave him a teasing smile and then turned to Abby. "*Hallo*, you must be Mose's friend."

Abby's face softened, and the start of a smile rippled across her lips. "Yes, I'm Abby."

"Becca is with Joe, if you remember him." Mose was sure she would after their day fishing together.

Abby's grin spread at hearing the name. "Oh, yes. I accidentally went fishing with him and Mose."

Becca chuckled. "So I heard. I admire you trying your hand at it. I've never quite seen the fun in it." She put her hand on Abby's arm and led her away from Mose. Abby turned back once and smiled at him.

With Abby in good hands, Mose went over to help saw the wood. He would do more of the detail work once the building was finished, but for now, he was one of the fastest to get the posts and beams cut to the right measure.

As the morning went on, he looked from time to time to find Abby, and each time she was helping the women or chatting with the others, mainly Becca. There was no one better she could be with. Rebecca had a big heart and a gentle spirit, one he felt Abby had as well, but she had been on guard so long, she kept her feelings deep inside.

"*Hallo*." Chris plunked down by Mose and watched him work. "Can I help?"

"*Jah*, you can, by meeting my friend Abby." Mose pointed to her where she stood with Rebecca and the bishop's wife.

Chris moved the blond hair from his eyes and turned his head completely around to see her instead of getting up to look. "Is she from the other community?"

Mose grinned. She did look the part with the plain clothes his mamm had given her to wear. "*Nee*, she's English."

Joe let go of the lever on the generated powered drill and looked at Mose. "She's getting on well with Rebecca."

"Who wouldn't?" Mose said sarcastically, but he meant it in a good way. "Will you see if she needs anything?"

"Is she nice?" Chris jumped up as his blue eyes grew larger.

"She's very nice, and she likes children."

Chris smiled, seeming to like the idea.

"She's a teacher," Mose added, and watched his smile slip away. "A fun one."

"How do you know?" Chris folded his arms across his chest, challenging Mose.

"I went to her school one day to see her teach. Esta likes her." Mose looked at Joe, who stared at him in surprise.

"*Ach.*" Chris shrugged as if that made everything all right. He walked away, and Mose shook his head, wondering when he was going to stop.

Joe jumped down and took a step closer to Mose. "What are you thinking, my friend?"

Mose couldn't read his expression but trusted Joe wouldn't judge him. "I'm keeping my head about things." He didn't look Joe in the eyes, worried he might see more than he wanted him to.

Joe shrugged. "It's not the worst thing that could happen."

Mose wasn't sure what Joe meant by that, but didn't know if he wanted to, so he didn't answer.

"You've pined over Elsie for too long. It'd be nice to see you happy again." Joe grabbed the drill and jumped up to the beam he was screwing in.

Mose hadn't expected that. The lecture about settling down, *jah*, but not that he was unhappy. He hadn't realized he was, it'd been so long. He felt like a hypocrite for thinking only Abby was. They were quite the pair.

But was Joe saying what Mose thought he was? That it was okay to have interest in an Englisher? He hadn't let himself think about it, expecting too much grief, but maybe he was wrong about what might be accepted within this community. It wasn't as conservative as the one in Virginia, but something on that level would be more than even Mose could pardon.

Abby watched with fascination as the men set up the beams that outlined the area where the schoolhouse would be. They had finished building the frame and now stood in a line, each holding a section. The crew chiefs stood across from them at the opposite end.

The chief counted, *"Ein, zwo, drei!"*

They lifted the frame together, and men at the platform up top took hold of it and put the frame into place, ready to be nailed down. They did this with each side, creating a skeleton framework of the building.

The women took glasses of lemonade to them halfway through the morning, but the men didn't stop working, and the women kept busy preparing the food and quilting.

"Would you like to take Mose some sweet tea?" Rebecca handed her two glasses without waiting for her to answer and started walking toward them. "You seem amused."

"I've never seen anything like this. An entire schoolhouse built in one day?" Abby looked at the tea and was suddenly thirsty. It was dark, brewed to a deep brown.

"Jah, the barns take longer, but they're usually done by the time the sun goes down too." She raised a glass of freshly squeezed lemonade. "Thirsty, Eli?" She asked an older man, who smiled and took the glass.

"Danke." He took a sip. "You must be Abby."

A rush of heat slipped up Abby's neck. He intimidated her for some reason, even though he was friendly. "You're Mose's father?"

"*Jah*, and proud to be. He's a *gut* son." He narrowed in on her bruise, downed the rest of the drink, and stood. "Back to work."

Abby floundered with what to say but didn't want the moment to slip by without saying something more. "Thanks for letting me stay at your home."

"*Wilkom*." He smiled and went back to his work. No one took breaks that she could see. They drank plenty, but nothing seemed to stop them from keeping on task until the work was done.

There was a slight breeze, just enough to give some relief against the blazing sun overhead. As the women walked along, Abby felt eyes on her. She didn't know whether she liked being known as the young woman staying with Mose's family, but then, what would she expect? Abby handed a glass to one of the many men with beards that didn't touch over their upper lip. Rebecca had explained this style meant they were married.

Abby looked around at all of the men. "I've wondered why there are no mustaches."

"That goes back to the Civil War when the Amish refused to fight. The army men grew mustaches, a symbol of valiance that we don't share," she said it boldly as if not to be questioned, but Abby had no intention of doing so. She was just curious and found herself wanting to know about their culture. This group of Amish were of the few who moved to Texas from Virginia and had only been in the area for a couple of years. She didn't see much of them, so this was all new to her.

Rebecca bumped her arm and motioned to where Mose was working, digging a hole for the beam to be inserted. "He's one of the few who does the joinery and doweling of the beams. He's quite the craftsman."

Abby was impressed, even though she didn't know exactly what Becca meant. She watched him work as Abby walked closer to hand him the drink she held. "Mose." When she called to him, the men close by slowed their work to glance at her.

Mose climbed down and took the drink. *"Danke.* I hoped you'd bring me a drink."

As he took a long swig, Abby stewed inside at his comment. It was the same type of arrogant comment she'd heard him say before. She tried to let it pass and forced a smile.

He downed the entire drink and then thanked her again. "Are you okay?" He looked at her sideways, seemingly unsure of what she might say.

She shook her head. This was his way, his people. She should keep her opinions to herself, but she didn't know if she could.

"Abby, I want to know if something is bothering you. Is it your daed?" His eyes closed as if to soften saying the word. But now that he had, her mind went to Jim. She wondered what he was doing and whether his health was better. But after he had struck her, Abby wasn't sure what she should do.

"I do wonder about him, but no, it's not that."

His brows went up in question.

"Okay, I'll tell you. I'm not comfortable with the roles of men and women here, and what you said just now..." When she heard herself saying the words, Abby stopped and thought about how different it was here. They each had a role to do, and by doing their parts, they came together as a whole. It was different here than it was where she came from, and Abby knew she had a lot to learn before judging what went on in Mose's community.

He shook his head. "I didn't realize—"

"I know. That's why I shouldn't say anything." She glanced around and realized she was taking him away from his job. "You should work now."

"Jah, we'll talk later, then?" His forehead wrinkled as he waited for her answer. His concern shone through, and that was all that she needed to know—that he honestly couldn't understand.

"No, we don't need to. I've said enough." She pointed to the beam he'd been working on.

"Hey, I'm Mose's bruder Chris." He stuck out his hand. "I've heard a lot about you."

Abby looked at him and smiled. She recognized that he was a little slow for a boy his age. "That's not fair."

"Why's that?" He stuck his hands in his pockets.

"I haven't heard about you." She took in the blond hair and blue eyes so similar to Mose's.

He hit one fist against another and tried to look mad, but he didn't pull it off. His pudgy cheeks and frown made him laughable. "Mose didn't tell you about me?"

"Maybe he was saving the best for last." She tried to make him feel better, but it didn't change his mood.

"Have you met Zake already?"

"No. Is he a friend of yours?"

"*Jah*. He's older than me, but we act the same about a lot of things." He nodded with a serious expression. He seemed wise beyond his years, which made Abby smile. She'd had students who acted older than they were, but some couldn't be taken seriously. "I gotta give this hammer to my bruder. He's sure picky about his tools." He shook his head with a grin. "Wanna go with and meet Zake?"

There was no way possible she could say no to him and stood to follow his lead. "I'm right behind you." With that prompt he gave her another grin and marched forward.

"I think I should tell you that my friend is special." He slowed and squinted one eye against the sun and closed the other. He was very serious, so she responded in the same manner.

"I work with all kinds of children who have different ways of dealing with things that are a little easier for you and me." She watched as he stuck out his bottom lip and studied her.

"*Jah*, just like that."

She nodded at his understanding and then looked ahead to see a lanky young man walk over. "Is that your friend?" Abby nodded her head toward him.

"*Jah*."

"Should we say *hallo*?"

Chris grinned at her using an Amish word. "Sure." He led the way and stopped just short of stepping on his friend Zake's shoe. "This is Mose's friend Abby."

Zake robotically lifted his hand to shake hers. His face was without expression, and he wasn't about to drop his hand until she shook it. Abby wasn't comfortable with the greeting but knew enough not to reject his offer. His grip was tight and he made only one pump, then smiled quickly and pointed to a sawhorse. "Gotta work."

She couldn't help but smile at his serious expression. "Nice to meet you. Work hard."

He nodded and walked slowly to his station, along with the other men.

"He doesn't talk much, but he liked you." Chris squinted his eyes to show the seriousness in his words.

They walked slowly back to where Mose was working. "Thanks for introducing us, Chris."

She watched as he stood on his tiptoes and stretched his arm up to Mose. Abby could hear Mose telling him something, and then Chris climbed up a few rungs to hand off the tool to him. As he did, Chris looked like a smaller version of Mose.

As the sun slowly drifted down on the horizon, the food disappeared, tables and chairs were put in wagons, and the pounding of hammers slowed to a stop. Everyone slowly left, one after another, until all that remained was the new schoolhouse.

Abby walked closer to admire the building that was built together in one day's time, from the ground to a completely constructed building within a matter of hours. Although it was raw, with coarse wood sides and no windows cut out yet, or a door, it was a beautiful little old-fashioned schoolhouse.

She heard someone walking up behind her and turned to see Mose admiring his work.

"What do you think?" He didn't take his eyes off the structure.

Abby's eyes roamed from top to bottom, in awe of their handiwork. "It's perfect."

When she turned to him, he was smiling. "It does give a person a sense of accomplishment."

Now that the day was done, Abby felt out of place again. She didn't have a home to go to like everyone else. She let out a long sigh, wondering what in the world she was doing there. Abby never thought she would be living in an Amish community, but there was something else. Abby felt a closeness to God here. Maybe because of their ways—helping one another, praying, and simplicity of life, or perhaps it was that she was still enough to feel Him near her.

"Why the long sigh? Are you tired?" Mose was regarding her intently. His eyes were fixed on hers as she turned to answer him.

"No, just appreciating the hard work that went into this. You were in demand. Becca said you're one of the best at what you do."

Mose shook his head. "I don't like to be compared like that, but I am handy with wood."

"Does modesty come with being Amish?" She smiled.

One side of his lips lifted. "I suppose so." He picked up a wooden box with tools and walked with her to his buggy. "Mamm will have something cooking at home, if you're hungry."

As Abby climbed into her seat, she was suddenly famished. "She made a good breakfast, and her macaroni salad was delicious."

"Cooking for four boys and my daed has kept her busy." He grinned and slapped the horse's hide with the reins to start him moving. "Get along, Frank."

Abby chuckled. "Frank?"

"*Jah.* Ya don't like the name?"

She shook her head. "I just haven't ever heard of a horse being called Frank before. It sounds so...human."

"I heard the singer once on a radio in town, so I decided to name my next colt that was born, Frank."

She paused, putting the pieces together. "Are you talking about Frank Sinatra?"

Mose's eyes lit up. "That's the one." Then he lowered his voice.

"But it may be frowned upon to listen to other music than what we sing in the *Ausbund*."

"Oh." She didn't know what that meant but assumed she should keep that to herself. She asked questions about building the school that Mose was happy to answer, and they were soon at his house. Only a sliver of sunlight shone over the horizon, burning yellow and orange colors across the sky. She wanted to work with Ginger every day but didn't want to bother anyone about her. Everyone here was doing more than they should for her already. Abby was just glad that she didn't have to face Jim and that Ginger and Old Blackie were being cared for. Once Jim was thinking straight, he'd think about the money, and at the very worst, he would sell Ginger, though it hurt her to even consider such an action.

Abby stayed seated in the buggy as Mose stepped down and grabbed his tools. She took in the clean air and the quiet that made time stand still. There was no urgency or stress, only a peaceful place that surrounded her soul.

When she looked over at Mose, his arms were crossed as he leaned on the buggy door. "Enjoying the view?"

"The land seems to go on forever out here." Most of the ground she'd seen in Texas wasn't picturesque, but this place, with the manicured fields and white clapboard houses, was as close as she had ever been to any real beauty. "I've never been outside of Texas. Have you?"

"Born and raised in Virginia. Went to Haiti to help build a haus after the hurricane." He walked over to her side and helped her down. She admired him for doing mission work overseas, something she'd never considered.

"That was good of you." She wanted to say more, but he seemed embarrassed by her appreciation of his work. "You aren't proud that you helped others in need?"

"*Nee*, that's considered prideful." He kept his eyes to the ground as they walked up the stairs to his home. The extra-long porch held a number of chairs and a porch swing.

"You're a very humble people." She meant it as a compliment, but judging by Mose's expression, she worried it didn't come across as the accolade she meant it to be. "I meant that in a good way."

Mose opened the door for her. "*Danke*, but the praise goes to the Lord."

Abby was thrown for a loop again, slowly catching on to the ways of these simple but genuine people whom she had a growing respect for.

⌐ Chapter Seventeen ⌐

BEFORE DINNER MOSE'S daed excused himself and asked Mose to sit with him so they could talk. Abby seemed comfortable in the kitchen with his mamm, so he took slow steps behind his daed, wondering what was so important. His daed plopped down in his chair in their family room.

His mood was serious, and he didn't waste any time getting situated. The second Mose sat down, he started in. "I'm not going to pry—what's happening with Abby isn't my business—but it's not right that she stay here, Mose."

Mose was in a tough place between what to tell his daed and how much to protect Abby's privacy. His daed obviously knew Mose had feelings for her to be bringing up the issue; he wished it wasn't so apparent. Her safety was more important than how he felt. "I know, but I can't send her back home."

His daed gave him a long look, and Mose hoped he wouldn't ask him to say more, but he understood Daed's concern. "It's nothing that would be putting us in a bad place if anyone knew about it, but out of respect to Abby, I'm going to leave it up to her as to what she wants to share."

Daed's face turned to concrete. It was their way to help someone in need, but to carry one's burden, it was best to know the hardship. Harboring someone for the right reasons was acceptable, but foul play could put them in a bad place. Abby might be open and willing to share her plight, but that was up to her. From what he'd seen, she and her father kept to themselves, accepting no help from anyone. This was probably difficult for her to be in an unfamiliar place with people she didn't know and carrying her cross alone.

Daed sat back in his chair and looked into the dark fireplace. "You're a wise young man, Mose. I trust you know what's best." He rubbed his trimmed beard. "The bruise worries me, though. Whatever or whoever caused it, I hope you're taking care of." Daed's eyes were still and intense as he stared at Mose.

"I worry for her too. But just by being here, she's in a better place." He grinned. "She liked seeing the school go up today."

Daed grunted a laugh. "Is that so...well, that's *gut* to hear."

"She was even interested in our blacksmith shop and my tools." Mose tried to curb his enjoyment, but a smile snuck up that he couldn't hold back.

"Well, now that *is* something." Daed chuckled.

Mose shook his head at his father's ribbing. "It's not every girl that would ask about things like that."

Daed let out a long breath. "*Nee,* but she's been in a different way of thinking that's not our way."

Mose didn't like the words, but he knew his daed was right. But the more he thought about it, the more he realized maybe her different way of thinking was what attracted her to him. And that wouldn't go well with his daed.

"Even something as simple as tools and a shop?" He was hanging on to hope that his daed may let this pass.

"It's nothing to concern ourselves about. She's a visitor, and that's how we'll handle things."

Mose breathed a little easier.

"One thing though. You've been alone together quite a bit. I know you're older and you both have reason to go into town, but try to have someone around."

Mose nodded, but he thought it was unnecessary. He wasn't one to take advantage of a situation, and his daed knew it. But he didn't want the deacons making a fuss about it. "I'll drag Chris around with us."

Daed chuckled and then became serious again. "She'll be leaving as soon as it works out for her to go, *jah?*" He held Mose's gaze.

"*Jah*, I'm sure she will." He turned away to leave, but then stopped and looked back at his daed. "What if she stayed?" It was a fool thing to ask, and as soon as he said it, he wished he hadn't. Was it that he didn't like his daed deciding things for him, or did Mose really want her to stay?

Daed's head shot up. "What are you thinking, son? She's English." There was no humor in his daed's face, but there was a warning. His entire expression, from his narrow eyes and wrinkled forehead to his tight lips, cautioned Mose to tread lightly.

"Nothing. *Gut* night." Mose felt irritation flutter up into his chest. He was a grown man, and if he wanted to get some answers, he could go to the minister or bishop. He knew how his daed felt, but that was because he felt responsible about the situation.

Mose walked out the front door to let off some steam. The stars were big and bright in the Texas sky. He took in the fresh air and let out the tenseness in his neck.

"Pretty tonight, isn't it?" Abby's voice startled him, and she laughed when he turned around quickly. "Sorry. I thought you knew I was here."

Mose put a hand to his chest and searched out her silhouette through the darkness. "I thought I was alone." He moved closer to the porch swing and sat with her.

"Do you want to be?"

He looked into her face, not wanting the same feeling to rouse him when he searched her eyes. But it did, so he turned away. "*Nee*. Since it's you, I don't mind the company."

"Is everything all right?"

"*Jah*, why do you ask?"

"I could hear you and your daed talking."

Mose whipped his head her way. "You heard us?"

"I wasn't eavesdropping. We were making dinner, and I heard your voice is all."

Mose was never very good at hiding his feelings, but he tried his best for her sake. He didn't want her to feel unwelcome, but

Mose had just found out she was. Then it dawned on him what she'd just said. "You and Mamm made dinner?"

She pushed off the wood floor with the tip of her shoe and let the swing sway slowly. "*Jah*. It was nice to make something different. Jim always wanted the same thing."

"I didn't know you cooked."

"I didn't until my mother got sick. Then I learned real quick."

He knew her daed was a controlling man, so she probably hadn't had much choice but to take up her mamm's chores. Then a speck of hope sprung up—she had learned to be domestic. She probably did much the same duties his mamm did. She lived on a farm, so the outdoor duties were familiar to her too.

"We should eat before it gets cold." She stood and reached for Mose to help him up. When he grasped her hand, it felt so familiar, he pulled away, not wanting the connection, knowing he couldn't have what he really wanted.

When she turned to him and smiled, Mose sighed.

Daed is probably right—I'm grasping at a whole lot of straws.

～ Chapter Eighteen ～

AFTER ABBY HELPED Esther with the breakfast cleanup, she went to find Mose. He'd told her he needed to ask her something, and she'd been curious all morning as to what it was about. She found him on the front porch, rocking slowly as he looked out over the many acres of corn.

"*Danke* for helping Mamm in the kitchen." His smile was weak, but his words were genuine.

"You're welcome." She smiled and considered his thoughtfulness since telling him how she felt about the unfair treatment between men and women. He was so oblivious, she felt badly that she'd even mentioned it. It wasn't the same as it was in her world. They had a different understanding that she was oblivious to. Abby would be more careful to be considerate of these people and respect their ways while she was there.

Mose stared at the wood planks under his boots, seemingly deep in thought. She was about to ask him if he was all right when he finally lifted his head and spoke. "Do you feel comfortable staying here, Abby?"

She hadn't expected the question, so she took a minute to answer. "Your family makes me feel at home, but I wonder if they are uncomfortable with me here." She had an idea of where he was going with the conversation and thought she'd make it easier on him. "I've been thinking a lot about what my choices are and what I should do next. But I like being here and learning this lifestyle. Everyone is very kind, and the amazing thing is they don't question me; they just accept me without knowing why I'm here."

He smiled as she shared her thoughts and seemed content to

hear them. "It's *gut* to know you feel that way. You don't hesitate to jump in and help. Everyone appreciates that."

"It's the least I can do. I want to earn my keep, maybe with the new school."

Mose slowly lifted his head and caught her eyes. "Now that would really be something, to have a bilingual teacher..." His eyes shifted away, and he was silent.

She felt his heavy heart and began to worry he was going to tell her something bad. "What is it, Mose?"

He moved forward in his chair and folded his hands together. "Would you like to stay with Becca and her family?"

His eyes were pleading with her, but she didn't know why he seemed so worried. "Why do you ask?"

"It might be more appropriate for you to be with more women than men." He cracked a smile, an appreciative gesture on his part.

"I'm fine with that." Abby knew she was welcome but felt a little awkward, even though Becca wouldn't let her feel that way. She would need to confirm the plans she'd been making. Only a few weeks, and school would start. She had to have her arrangements in order before that.

"I'd prefer you'd stay here. I still worry for your safety." He almost looked sad, but she sensed a touch of anger.

She put her hand on his. "It's a good idea. You know how I enjoy Becca. And if her family is anything like she is, I will appreciate my time there even more, especially if I can help at the school."

He searched the field as if looking for something out among the green waving leaves on the tall stalks. "I'll be checking in on you often."

"I would expect nothing less." She smiled and stood. "I'll help you with the milking." She was getting the hang of how to milk using the gas-generated pumps. Using them made the job go much faster, but they had a lot more Holsteins than she had on her farm, so it took awhile before all of the heifers went dry.

"I'd like that." He stood with her and finished the rest of the chores before they rode over to Becca's in the buggy. "We'll stop in and see if Joe wants to join us. He'd probably like to see Becca."

"That's fine. Does he know we're coming?" She was still getting used to their casual ways and liked Joe, so she was happy to spend more time with him.

When Joe came moseying down the path leading to the main road, he hopped into the buggy with ease and sat down between them. Mose shook his head and tried to ignore him, but did seem to relax once Joe was with them.

When they reached the door, it opened with Becca there to greet them. "Come in. You're just in time for the noon meal." She clasped hands with Joe as they walked to the back porch, where her dad sat with a couple other young men, and Mose followed.

Becca grabbed Abby around the waist, leading her into the bustling kitchen. Abby had never seen so many young women in a room cooking, chopping, slicing, and baking. "Mose, Daed is doctoring a lame gelding in the barn."

"I'm on my way." He smiled at Abby before he turned around to leave.

The energy in the room was electric, and Abby relished it. A bowl of bread dough was the only part of the meal unattended. "Do you want me to roll out the dough?"

"*Jah*, please do." Becca went back to her station, chopping vegetables.

The girl next to her, who seemed a little older, smiled, but didn't stop working. "I'm Arianna. I hear you're a teacher."

"Yes, I teach in town."

"I've taught my siblings a lot, taking some of the load for my mamm."

"I'm sure she appreciates your help."

"There's some flour in the canister there." She motioned at the glass container half full of white flour. "And Mel has the rolling pin."

And on it went, until the meal was prepared and all of the family finally sat down together and had a time of quiet prayer. Abby was so distracted with remembering their names, she caught herself running through them during prayer.

The family passed around healthy portions of food, conversing all the while, most of it all at one time. Becca was next to her, for which Abby was grateful in case she forgot which face went with what name. When Abby forgot the youngest sister's name, Becca asked everyone to say their names. By the time Abby met all of Becca's family, she felt she should go around again so she could remember everyone. All six girls and three boys, including Mose and Joe, sat at the kitchen table with Becca's parents, sharing the meal. Then it was time to clean up while the boys did evening chores.

When all was done, Mose and Abby went out on the front porch to talk before he left. He was quietly studying her. She couldn't see his eyes in the dark night, but she felt his stare. She hoped the evening together made him feel better about her staying there. The more she thought about it, the more she felt it was best and was glad he'd suggested it.

"It's as if the Troyers have another daughter. You fit right in."

"Once I got their names memorized. I've never been with a family that big." She had known the Amish had large families, but actually experiencing it firsthand made her realize how different it was from her own quiet home.

"Mamm always wanted more children, but couldn't."

That felt a little awkward, and Abby searched for something to say. "Maybe she'll have a lot of grandbabies."

"I hope to have a big family." Mose was staring at the field again. Only the silhouette of tassels was visible as it swayed against the moonlight.

Abby grew more uncomfortable with the conversation and was glad to see Becca and Joe walk out the door. "Come sit with us."

Abby felt better with Becca with them. She figured it was frowned upon to be alone together, even though she noticed they seemed to be more lenient with her, maybe because she wasn't Amish.

"We should go." Mose and Joe stood and thanked Becca for the meal. "It's always good to see you, Becca, and your family." When he turned to Abby, his expression softened. "Let me know if you need anything. I'll be back around tomorrow."

"She's fine, Mose." Becca gave him a gentle push to the stairs. "You'll be seeing her soon enough." She pecked Joe on the cheek and giggled when he blushed.

Mose took one last look at Abby before descending the stairs, climbed into his buggy, and left. She felt an unexpected loneliness even though she was at a house full of people.

Becca settled in beside her and grinned. "We won't have long before someone comes out, so tell me anything from the heart now."

Abby chuckled. "This is so opposite of how I grew up; it's wonderfully crazy."

"And that's *gut, jah?*" Becca was honestly asking because she didn't understand the word. "*Narrisch?*"

"Yes, *narrisch*, crazy." They both laughed about the language barrier and because they were exhausted. "It's a lot of work to be Amish." They both giggled again and then enjoyed the quiet.

"Do you like it here, Abby?" Becca asked seriously, so Abby answered in the same way.

"I didn't have any idea how it would be, but I do. It's somewhat like living on a ranch like I grew up on, but this is so much more. It's a good way to live." Abby sat back in her chair and suddenly felt so tired she didn't want to move.

"*Gut*, so maybe you'll stay?" Becca was truly asking, which surprised Abby. It wasn't that easy, and she knew that as well as Abby did.

"Why would you ask me that?"

"It suits you." She smiled. "Tell me about the English way."

Abby was still digesting her words about her fitting into the Amish life. Some of it was familiar to her, but there was so much more she didn't know. "The bad part is that it's fast. And people don't know each other. We buy expensive things that we don't need. There's a lot to do, but people seem bored. The good things are that you can have a meal within minutes. You can travel the world in just hours. You can talk to most anyone anywhere. And there's a lot of variety. Everyone's different."

"Everyone is different here too."

Abby rolled her head to the side against the top of the chair, too tired to lift her head. "Hmm, I guess that's true, but you can't tell by looking."

"You don't know unless you can read a person's heart."

That made Abby pause. Becca's insight made her think about things she hadn't before, and she liked the challenge. "I suppose you're right."

"I'd like to visit the English world some time."

Again, Becca surprised her. There was so much more to her than most of the other Amish she'd come across. "You could stay with me."

"*Jah*, I'd like to go to Africa to do mission work."

She couldn't picture little Becca in another country. She was only a year younger than Abby even though she was mature and responsible. Abby couldn't imagine why she would want to spend time someplace when she seemed so happy here. But Abby didn't believe she would be allowed to go, anyway. "Can you leave the community like that?"

"The Mennonites frequently go on missions."

"I've heard that, but I didn't know the Amish went with them."

"They don't usually, but I've made an effort to connect with a group not far from here."

"That doesn't sound like something you would want to do. You seem so content here."

"I want to explore the outside world, be an example, living as a Christian in places where they don't know the Lord."

Abby couldn't help the jolt that caused her body to move back in the chair. She'd heard of the mission trips and seen pictures on the TV, but she never thought of actually going and doing something to help those in need. For Mose and Becca to be examples of what it means to live a Christlike life in the outside world was amazing to Abby. They were both so bold and brave, as if it was just the next thing to do.

"That's amazing. Even if you may not see it that way, I certainly do." Abby couldn't imagine an Amish person living out their faith in the English world, even in a small town like Beeville. If anyone asked her about her religious beliefs, she wouldn't know what to say. Where did these people's confidence come from?

Becca shrugged and stopped rocking. "Can I ask you something personal?"

If it was anyone else, Abby would have felt uncomfortable, but she trusted Becca. She trusted many people here—strange, since she'd only recently met them. "I suppose."

"You don't have to answer. What brought you here?"

Abby realized how much better she felt over the past few days not living in her "real" life. Her cheek was starting to lose the black and blue color that seemed to be an explanation in itself, but this was Becca, so of course she would tell her.

"Things haven't been so good since my mother died."

"I'm sorry, Abby."

Abby thought she might offer condolences and tell her own experience with a loss, but Becca quietly waited for her to continue.

"It's been hardest on my dad, Jim. He hasn't been the same since Mom passed away, and I get the brunt of it."

"Is he responsible for the bruise?"

Abby hadn't thought of it that way—that he was the one accountable, not her. "Yeah, I guess so."

"I'm glad you came here." Becca's warm smile made Abby feel the same acceptance she'd felt from nearly everyone she'd met since being there, only Becca's meant more.

"I wish it would have been for a different reason."

"What else would have brought you here? It's all *Gott's* plan.

It's just hard for us to figure out what needs to happen to get us where He wants us." She clasped her hand on Abby's.

"How do you think that way?" Abby tried to wrap her mind around the way Becca thought, but she couldn't get there. Completely trusting God with the good things was easy, but not with the hard stuff. It didn't make sense to her.

"Put *Gott* first." Becca sat back in the rocker, and they gazed up at the stars. Abby didn't know how to get to where Becca was. But she would sure like to have that steadfast belief in something.

⌒ Chapter Nineteen ⌒

NOW THAT ABBY was at Becca's place, Mose found himself visiting there more than he ever had, and he'd never spent so much time with Joe. The girls were polite, and there were so many of them that it didn't appear that he was there just to see Abby. A different Troyer sister (or daughter) answered the door each time. He and Abby usually sat on the porch and talked, or if she was busy with chores, he would help just so he could to spend time with her. He was getting in deeper each time he saw her, but he couldn't stop himself from wanting to be near her.

After feeding the livestock, they walked and talked until they got to the Troyers' house. Abby took a seat on the porch swing. She always did, and Mose was careful to sit on the rocker, although he'd have preferred to sit on the swing with her. He loved to study her face as she told him about the garden she was helping Becca with.

She reached for a tin pail that she'd placed beside the porch swing. She held it out to him. It was full to the rim with three kinds of fragrant berries.

"The berries are ripe for picking, the blackberries and blueberries are good, but the boysenberries are wonderful. Taste one."

"Which one's which?" He studied them but wasn't sure if he even liked boysenberries. His mamm was partial to blackberries and occasionally blueberries.

"A country boy like you doesn't know which is which?" She grinned, obviously enjoying having knowledge he didn't. She picked out a berry and handed it to him. "Try it."

The minute he saw it, he remembered why he wasn't familiar

with the purplish-looking berry. They were tart. He popped it into his mouth and swallowed before the flavor could spread across his tongue.

"You don't like them, do you?" She sat quietly and waited for his reply.

"*Nee*, not really." He wished for a strong taste of tea but toughed it out instead.

She laughed, and that made him smile. "You're a good sport."

He turned to her in question. "That's *gut, jah?*" Abby took her time looking at him before she answered, as if seeing him for the first time. "Yes, it's good."

"Is there something wrong?" He worried there was a berry stain on his chin or a seed stuck in his teeth, and he wiped his face with his hand.

"You're so handsome and kind. Why aren't you married like most of the young men your age?" She continued to stare at him, making him uncomfortable—especially with her question.

"I've been told that I am too particular or difficult, depending on who you talk to." He could tell her he had found someone, but that person was her, so he thought he'd turn it around. He knew her society waited longer before they married, and he wondered why. They seemed to be noncommittal and spend time with many partners, making it difficult to decide who a person should end up with. "Why haven't you?"

Her smile disappeared, and she looked to the wood porch beneath her feet. "After my mother died, I thought I should stay with Jim. He took her death very hard. I don't think he'll ever stop mourning the loss." She looked away, suddenly withdrawn and serious.

"It's hard for me to have any sympathy for him, Abby." He stopped, even though he wanted to go on. But he didn't want to push too far or say too much. "But then again, it's hard to see things from the outside in."

"Yes, it is." She stood and gave him a weak smile. "I should help prepare the noon meal."

He reluctantly stood with her, wishing he would have listened more and said less. "Forget what I said. I don't know what you've been through."

She looked up at the miles of crop that was the lifeblood of their community and gazed down at her boots. "You're right. It's hard when you detest someone you live with. People don't understand the unreasonable way families can be, even if it's hurtful."

A chill went through him even though the temperature had reached triple digits.

"Everything you said was true." She gazed at him with sad eyes. "I just wish it wasn't." She turned away and walked to the door, letting the springs pop as she opened it. He heard everyone of them as they snapped back into place. He wanted to tell her he shouldn't have brought it up, but the words never made it past his throat.

He stood on the porch for a moment after she left, kicking himself for saying too much, or speaking the truth so close that it hurt. Either way, he'd lost her again. He took two steps at a time, wanting to leave quickly. Making himself busy was the best way to let it go. At least, that was how it usually worked for him if he'd had a hard day. But this was full of emotions that he hadn't felt before and sure didn't know what to do with.

As he tapped Frank on the hide with the reins, he told himself not to think back on what he'd said. Right or wrong, it was over, and they'd move on from there. Actually, she was the one who needed to. There would never be a "them." He'd keep his mouth shut from here on out and let her do the healing on her own.

Tomorrow the community planned to put the final touches on the schoolhouse. That might be a good way to lift Abby's spirits. He'd call for her tomorrow morning after the chores.

As he pulled onto the gravel road leading to his home, Mose noticed his daed walking down the rows of corn closest to the house. He bent down and rubbed the soil between his fingers. That wasn't a good sign. They'd worked on just the right mix to add nutrients to the soil, and after the first year of experimenting, they thought they'd found the right formula.

Mose pulled the buggy around to the barn and unharnessed Frank, then led him out to pasture. He could tell by his daed's face there was something wrong. "What is it?" He shouted loud enough for his daed to look up, but he didn't greet him or wave him over as he usually would.

"Weevils."

It was all he said, and all he needed to. The beetles could kill an entire cotton crop and then go into the next because freezing temperatures didn't last long enough there to kill them off. With the mild winter the spring crop would come early.

"We're gonna have to rotate the crop so they don't spread," Mose offered, thinking out loud.

"That, and spray the eggs that are nestled in the cotton balls." Daed looked over the acres of cotton plants and let out a frustrated breath. "Hopefully we caught it soon enough."

"Thank *Gott* our corn is growing strong." Mose tried to think of more positive thoughts when he saw the etched lines of worry across his daed's brow.

"*Jah*, it would take a mighty strong storm to ruin the rest of our crop." He slapped Mose on the back and guided him to the house. "*Gott* won't give us more than we can handle."

"Remember that when we're spraying those weevils, will ya?" Mose hoped he'd find the humor in his words and wasn't disappointed when Daed's lips curled upwards.

"You've been gone a lot lately." His daed gave him a sideways glance.

"*Jah*, helping Abby settle in over at Becca's place."

"That's *gut* of ya, as long as you don't get your hopes up." Daed averted his eyes and said no more, but Mose didn't want to discuss it any further. "I trust your judgment on this, son."

Mose didn't want to hear it—not after the way he'd parted with her—but his daed was waiting, so he tried to think of something that would reassure him but also be honest. "She's my responsibility while she's here, Daed. I hope you understand."

Daed grunted and stuck out his lower lip in thought. "I suppose."

He didn't need to know that Abby meant much more to him than that.

~ Chapter Twenty ~

WHEN ABBY HEARD Becca come in from milking, she felt instant relief. She hadn't been to church since she was too young to remember. There wasn't a question as to what to wear, but she didn't know their customs and worried she might do or say something wrong.

Becca tapped on the door. "Are you dressed?"

"Come in." Judging by Becca's expression, Abby looked as miserable as she felt. "What's the service like?" She squeezed her hands together, waiting for Becca's answer.

Becca put her palms over Abby's. "You don't need to do anything. We have visitors from time to time. No one expects them to know what to do."

Abby felt a little better already—Becca had the gift of providing comfort—but Abby couldn't believe there wasn't anything she needed to know. "I don't want to make a mistake. Mose said there was a special ceremony today."

Becca sat on the bed and pulled Abby over to her. "It's for the young boys, sort of like a coming of age, an observance. When the boys reach maturity, they are brought in with the men and are able to do certain chores they weren't big enough to do before." She shrugged. "And that's about it."

"That sounds easier than I thought." Abby was glad to have Becca to help her. She was so patient and helpful with Abby, it made her wonder whether she was like that with everyone. "How do I look?"

The bun she attempted to pin together was a bit wobbly, but she hoped it would stay in place. She was still getting accustomed to the dress. She was used to jeans and boots, so this was an adjustment.

Becca took her arm and led her down the stairs. "How are you feeling today?"

Abby absently put a hand to her cheek. "Numb. I think it's easier that way, for right now, anyway." She thought of Jim often, but that brought back the pain, both physical and emotional. So she pushed away the thoughts. Something about being in the community melted away the anger she carried around. Resentment of her family life and Jim's inability to be a father to her had hardened Abby, and now, looking back, she didn't like herself much either.

"There's not a wrong or right feeling." She squeezed Abby's hand. "I'm glad you're here." Her soft brown eyes made the words feel genuine and warm. Abby felt a lump lodge in her throat, but she didn't want to get emotional, even for a good reason. If she started, she wouldn't be able to stop.

"We're all going together." Becca hurried out the door. "Mose doesn't like to be late." Becca climbed up with Joe in the front seat, and Mose helped Abby up into the back with him.

It was plenty warm with the top off, and Abby saw they had one but didn't use it. Wearing a full-length dress was much warmer than the shorts she usually wore. By the time they got to the church, Abby was starting to sweat. She was glad when they got to their destination, but to her surprise, it wasn't a church. "Are we stopping here first?"

"*Nee*, we take turns having church in our homes. Our hearts and minds together as one is the embodiment of the church."

Abby still didn't completely understand, but she followed Becca into the home and sat with her on the left side while Mose and Joe sat on the right. The boys then came in their Sunday best and beamed when they took a seat in the men's part of the room. She searched for Chris and soon found him by his dad.

Becca took out a singing book that had the word *Ausbund* on the front. They sang in German, so Abby listened to Becca's pretty voice as they sang song after song. Abby wondered whether it was because there was a ceremony that they sang so many. The minister talked for what must have been two hours. She squirmed in her seat and bumped into Becca once trying to shake her foot from falling asleep. After announcements and the recognition of the boys who were now young men, they got up and took the benches outside.

"Is the service over?" She whispered in Becca's ear as everyone began setting up for the noon meal.

"*Jah*, now we share a meal together. Come help me." Becca used the word *help* as if it was a gift, and she was special to be asked. Abby couldn't imagine anyone saying no to anything Becca requested.

Mose and Joe helped arrange the benches and tables while she and Becca brought over a whoopie pie, slices of ham, and tea. Abby looked down the tables covered with more food than she'd ever seen.

Mose came up to Abby and held her hand, which shocked her, but then she felt Becca's hand slip into hers and realized they were about to pray. There had to be over fifty people there who stood shoulder to shoulder in a circle around the bountiful provisions. When Abby opened her eyes, she wondered how they had all fit in that house.

"Hungry?" Mose, her man of few words, asked, and he handed Abby a plate.

"Even if I wasn't, there's no way I would pass this up. I've never seen so much food."

Mose grinned as he filled his plate. Abby followed Becca, and they found a place to sit with the women. She glanced over at Mose more times than she should have, but half of those times he was looking back at her. She saw him go up for more food at least twice. Abby hadn't ever eaten so much and rarely had any dessert, but she tried Mose's mother's whoopie pie and something called a shoofly pie.

"I'd like you to meet someone." Mose guided her over to a

group of older men and women who were having a leisurely conversation on the porch to stay out of the sun. "This is my mammi and dawdi."

He said it with a smile, almost proud. Abby knew how special they were to him. She was different anyway, being English, but it was something more than that with Mose. She just wasn't sure what that was yet.

"It's nice to meet you." Abby wasn't sure what else to say but quickly found out she didn't need to say anything.

"So you're the one little Chris's been talking about," his dawdi said in a loud voice.

"You look just like Esther said." Mose's mammi elbowed his dawdi. "Doesn't she look just like Esther said she did?"

"What?" He looked at his wife, waiting for her to repeat what she'd just said.

Mammi leaned in closer to him. "I say she looks like Esther said."

Dawdi shook his head. "*Nee*, she doesn't look anything like Esther."

Mammi waved a hand at him in frustration. "*Ach*, goodness. Come sit down."

Mose smiled and sat on the stairs next to Abby. "I don't know why Mammi even tries to get him to hear her."

"So will you be staying here for a while?" Mammi asked, but Dawdi was oblivious she'd said anything.

"Yes, just until I can get some things sorted out." Abby wanted them to know as little as possible about her circumstances; she knew they would begin to wonder, and she would have to be prepared with the right words eventually.

Dawdi scanned the area. "This is *gut* land we come up on down here. *Gut* crop of corn the bishop has coming in." They all looked out over the many acres of green corn leaves waving in the slight wind. The other elderly who could hear him nodded or grunted their appreciation of the healthy field of corn. "And it's so peaceful you can hear the corn grow."

Mammi chuckled. "You can't hear much of anything, especially corn growing."

"Come again." Dawdi leaned closer to her.

She didn't try to answer, just pecked him on the cheek and then leaned back in her rocking chair.

The bishop popped the screen door open and laid his eyes on Abby. "*Hallo* there, Mose...and Abby, I believe." He sat on the top stair with a little effort and then glanced at the two of them before speaking. "So how are you liking your visit here so far?" His twinkling blue eyes, chubby stomach, and gray hair made him appear to be a rosy-faced elf. He wasn't terribly short, but more so than Abby.

"I'm finding that it's more interesting than I'd thought it would be." She didn't want to feel like a tourist or even a guest. Abby discovered she'd much rather be treated like a relative or visiting Amish from across town than the Englisher who was visiting for a time.

"We're glad you're here." He rubbed his long, gray beard. "In many ways, actually."

Mose turned to face the bishop with full attention. Abby felt a protective guard from Mose when others addressed her. She wondered why. Was there something being talked about or decided about her being there?

"The new school is an exciting addition to our small community. Did you enjoy watching it being built?" She couldn't help noticing how his red lips contrasted with his snowy white beard when he spoke.

"I was amazed at how quickly yet well it was built. I've never seen a group work together so symmetrically. The children seemed excited about their new school." Abby couldn't hide her enthusiasm for both the schoolhouse and the unity of the people who made it happen.

"I noticed that as well. They seem to be glad that they're together instead of separated in their own homes." He scratched his beard.

"I think they learn better when they can share their ideas together and have others to socialize with," she said with conviction that surprised her. She'd never complained about her job, but neither had she thought about actually liking her work. It helped pay the bills and paid her better than most places of employment would, but in talking with the bishop, she realized she liked it more than she was aware of.

"I wonder if you might be interested in helping with some of the course work. Just to get things started." It was more of a suggestion than an invitation, making it easier to decline, but Abby was flattered that he considered her able to help with such a project.

"Well, I don't know how much I can assist you, but I'm willing to do what I can."

He frowned. "I hear you teach at the Christian school in town. Is that so?"

"Yes, I do, but I'm certified in ESL, not as a full-fledged teacher."

His eyebrows drew together and he shook his head once as he dismissed the importance of credentials. "A piece of paper is less value than a caring heart."

Abby searched Mose's face to get a read on his thoughts. He smiled slightly but didn't say a word.

"I don't know how long I'll be here, but I'll do what I can."

She thought about what the bishop was asking. There had to be mothers who knew how to teach their children in the way they were used to. There were surely differences between the way she knew how to instruct them. Then she thought about the one-room schoolhouse. She was used to working with students two or three at a time, not an entire school. Despite the differences, she had never been so eager to start a project like this. It fit her to the brim. There was nothing more she wanted to do with her time.

"*Gut! Danke*, Abby. *Gott* does work in mysterious ways, does He not?" Mose winked at her and stood to respond to one of the elders. Judging from the way the elder glanced over at her a couple of times, the bishop must have shared the news with him.

The pressure continued to mount, and Abby wondered what she'd gotten herself into.

When they started talking about the three days of wet weather they'd had again, Mose excused himself and Abby, and they snuck away. "The bishop is a *gut* man. If you decide any differently, he'll understand." He grinned.

Abby was so relieved, she felt her shoulders sink. She was encouraged by his faith in her, but it was nice to hear those words from Mose. "Why are you smiling?" She noticed a slight dimple that she'd never seen before.

"He likes you."

She looked back at him where he chatted away with a group of men. "He seems to like everyone."

Mose looked straight into her eyes. "But there's something more about you."

She walked quietly for a moment, reflecting on his words. "I think you're partial."

"*Jah*, but so is he."

⌒ Chapter Twenty-One ⌒

WE COULD TRY it." Abby tilted her head to examine Ginger's injury. "Still a little swollen, though." The filly had acclimated well to Ira's place when she was there, but now that she had returned to Mose's place, Abby could see that she had not healed as well as they'd hoped. Abby's daily regime of walking Ginger and applying Epsom Salt had helped; now they'd find out how well. Old Blackie ran around the outside of the corral, stopped, and then started in again as they worked.

Mose glanced over at Ira to see if he agreed, then up at the unusually dark sky.

"Still may be tender, but this horse wants to work."

Ginger snorted and dug at the ground with her injured leg as if to show them she was ready.

Mose nodded. "I guess she's telling us something."

Chris walked in. "Whatcha doing with Ginger?"

"We're trying to decide if Ginger is healthy enough to work."

"I seen her running and stop short of the fence when she needs to get her energy out." He stuck his hands on his hips like his big brother.

Abby cupped her cheek in her hand. "Well, we can go easy on her." She stood and smiled at Mose, who was already grinning.

"Grab the lead rope, Chris."

He beamed, hurried to the tack room, and then returned with the rope and a harness. "How's this?"

Ira examined the lead. "The lead rope is *gut,* but why do you have a harness?"

Mose chuckled. "He's been practicing dressing up the harnesses."

Abby shrugged. There were so many things for her to learn in their culture, she'd started leaning on Mose to explain as they went. With each new custom she encountered, he'd tell her what it stood for and why they did it. She was always amazed at how they had a purpose for everything they did. Nothing was happenstance or without meaning.

Chris caught the nonverbal communication between them and jumped in to explain. "A harness is a kind of tack you put on a horse to pull carriages and wagons and stuff. Oxen use a yoke. But that's not what this here is." He held it up, but it was heavy for his small frame.

"Ira will help you with that, Chris. I'm gonna work Ginger and see how she does." Mose patted his back to nudge Chris in the direction of the tack room.

"Are you ready for this?" Mose asked Abby.

"She's probably more ready than I am." Abby gestured to Ginger. "There's something about Ginger that I can identify with more than other horses we've had. I guess that's why she means so much to me." Abby didn't want to say all she was thinking, but this filly was everything women in the modern world want to be—independent and strong both emotionally and physically.

Mose stiffened, and she realized the pressure she'd put on him. "Sorry. I'm not usually this sentimental, but she's special...for a lot of reasons." Abby stared at Ginger and wondered how an animal could have such an effect on her. "You two will do great together." And that she truly believed. Between Ira and Mose, she was in no better hands.

"I'm gonna forget everything you just said with no disrespect. If I don't, I won't know the first thing to do with her." He shook his head and grinned.

"Yes, go. By all means, just do what you normally do." She laughed at herself, but she had so much invested in this horse in many different ways. She couldn't help the emotions Ginger brought out in her. Her way of thinking was so different from the way they lived, it was no wonder Mose didn't understand. And even if he did, he probably wouldn't be comfortable with it.

Abby dropped her arms over the fence, and Ira did the same. Chris climbed up and sat on top to get a bird's-eye view.

Mose stood in the center of the corral as Ginger walked in a slow circle around Mose as he toyed the end of the rope attached to a halter. Abby leaned against the rail, watching stock-still. Ginger started trotting and snorting. Her muscles tensed as she tossed her head, a full mane flopping over her large brown eyes. Mose toyed with the rope, turning his back to the horse. Ginger's ears twitched, and she turned toward him, taking a step closer.

"I didn't know you were a horse whisperer," Abby said softly as Mose took a step closer to her.

"Just want her undivided attention." Mose turned sideways and held out the halter. Ginger pawed the ground, put her head down, and took slow steps over to Mose.

"Are you going to halter her?" Abby was less patient than the horse. She knew Mose understood. She had high hopes for this mare. He did too, for her sake.

"If she lets me. I'm not a pushy guy." He shrugged a grin.

"So I've noticed." She rested her palm in her chin and watched Ginger sniff the halter and Mose slowly place it over her head. She'd been through enough trauma to be temperamental, but she conveniently cooperated.

He repeated his command. "Walk." Then he gave the command, "Lope," but the horse stumbled on her bad leg and didn't increase her speed.

"Reverse." He only had to say it once. The horse turned on that command and ran in the opposite direction. Mose had to raise his hands up to get her to turn around. She never went faster than a walk and continued to cater to her bad leg.

The other horses in the pasture stood and watched. Each time the other horses heard Mose yell the commands, they playfully jumped and took off running in the wide, open field next to the barn. Mose continued until Ginger came to a stop and lifted her leg. Then he took her to an empty corral and walked over to Abby. His shirt was drenched in sweat. He removed his hat and raked his fingers through his wet hair and then walked over to the first corral, where Abby was sitting on top of the fence.

He shook his head back and forth until his hair lifted into slight curls around his head and face, and then turned to her as he placed his hat firmly on his head. "What are you smiling about?"

"I've never seen anyone fix their hair like that before."

"That all depends on how hot you get." He grinned.

"How do you think she did?" Abby didn't see the enthusiasm in Mose that she'd hoped for. If he thought she did well, he would have said so right off. And Ira had been too quiet.

Mose wiped the dripping water off his forehead. "I'd have to work with her again before I knew for sure."

She touched his arm. "Do I need to ask Ira to get an honest answer?"

He stared at her and let out a short breath. "She caters to the bum leg." He hadn't taken his eyes off hers. "That might not change."

The look in his eye made Abby wonder whether there was any reason to keep on hoping. But when she turned around and saw Becca, she took it as a sign not to give up.

As if sensing Abby's worry, Becca stopped and took in the atmosphere, then focused on Abby. "Is this a *gut* time to take a break?"

"Yes, Becca. It's always good to see you." Abby went to her side and walked down the dirt floor of the barn as they talked.

"So it didn't go well with Ginger?" Becca glanced over at Abby.

Abby shook her head. "I had a feeling it might turn out that way. She might just be a companion horse, but I'll take it. At least she's still alive." At that moment seeing Ginger and Mose in that corral, something clicked. The acceptance of what Ginger was, and now is, was sealed. There was something freeing in knowing and moving on from there.

"*Jah*, that had to have scared you and her into appreciating you're in good hands here." She shook her head. "I thank *Gott* for both of you."

That put the situation in place for Abby. No, Ginger would never compete in shows or win ribbons, but they could be together, just in a different way.

Becca picked up the pace. "A few of us are making engraved music pages."

"I don't know what that is." Abby didn't much care but wanted the diversion, and it looked like something Mose would like.

"I'll teach you. It's easy. They're beautiful to display in a home."

Abby hadn't seen many decorations in anyone's house, so she wanted to see what was acceptable. "This might be just want I need right now." She turned and waved to Mose. She was a little abrupt, but Abby knew he'd understand. He had been the one who encouraged her to be with Becca from the beginning, and she was so glad he had.

His smile back to her was one of reassurance that her absence was acknowledged and that he understood. "I'll be in to help."

Abby turned to Becca. "What did he mean?"

"We need help creating the blocks before we can etch them onto the wood."

Abby nodded, finding herself tickled that Mose would be there with them. "He doesn't mind being amongst a group of women alone?" She teased.

"Not if you're one of them." Becca smiled, and Abby tucked her arm under Becca's, feeling this was the sister she'd never had. What would it be like to have a community full of young women who rallied around one another, worked together, and grew their families collectively?

When the rain started, they ran to Becca's home. Her mamm greeted Abby with much the same kindness as she did Becca. "Have you made a music wood engraving before?"

"No, I'll watch you."

"*Nee*." Becca handed her a block of rough piece of wood. "You'll learn better by doing with Mose here." She went to a shelf where a dozen or so wood blocks of the same size were stacked neatly like a tower of Lincoln Logs.

"You've made all of these?" Each block had been sanded, engraved with a music verse, and cured. Abby looked at the titles of the songs she'd heard the children sing at school where she worked.

"Pick out the one you like."

Becca decided on "Amazing Grace," and Abby chose "Jesus Loves Me." The song always sounded so tender when the little ones at school sang the tune. Thinking about it made her miss teaching. The principal knew she was having personal problems at home, though she suspected he had an idea something was wrong even before the incident with Jim happened. The bruise kept her away from the school, at least for the summer. She hadn't given school a second thought until now.

It was quiet until Becca's sisters came in one by one and filled the kitchen. There was rarely an idle moment in the Troyer house. If it wasn't cooking, cleaning, or doing laundry, it was making crafts. Abby asked questions, and they readily offered their help, but with each of them came their personal opinion on how to do the etching, and some preferred to stain the wood darker than others. Each personality shone through in how the girl created the craft.

When Mose came in, Abby's heart jumped when his eyes met hers. He was surrounded with questions and requests from each of the sisters wanting his help. Abby waited patiently, taking her time rounding the corners of the block and then sanding it down. There was something soothing about the process that calmed her nerves. Some opted for a tablet of wood made into the complete song, chorus and verse.

"They're nice, aren't they?" Becca gestured to the pieces of flat wood twice as big as the blocks. Then Becca looked to where Abby was looking and poked her in the side. "Mose distracts you."

Abby felt her cheeks heat and turned back to sanding. "I like to watch him work."

"*Jah*, I've noticed." Becca grinned and checked Abby's work. "It's improving, but if you don't stay focused, you won't get it done until tomorrow." She shook her head at Abby.

"I'm trying." She held tight onto the wood and sanded harder.

"*Jah*, but now Mose is distracted."

When Abby looked up, he was walking toward her. "How is our new student doing?" He took the piece of wood from Abby, and she realized how unevenly she'd sanded it.

"I guess I need to pay attention." She shrugged at the divot in the wood.

"I can even it out for you." He took a large piece of sand paper and rubbed the wood until it was an even color. "There, better."

She admired the way he carefully worked on each area until it was perfect in her eyes. "You are very intense when you are working with wood."

When he handed her the smooth wood, their hands touched, sending a shock of energy through her. She watched his face and wondered whether he felt it too. By the way his eyes poured into hers, she felt he had.

A sudden sense of apprehension overtook her, and she turned around in her chair. "I need to get some air." She jumped up and walked out the door. The rain drizzled on her as she walked down the stairs and into the tall stalks of corn. She got lost in them as she faced her emotions.

She heard someone behind her—Mose, or maybe Becca— but she didn't hear anyone calling, so she kept going until the crunching of the ground was right behind her. She turned and looked up at Mose. He wiped his brow and stopped when she turned around.

"Where are you going?"

"I just needed some space." She looked everywhere except into his eyes. If she did, the truth would come out, and she couldn't let that happen. There was no point.

"Tell me what's wrong." He said it with such force she almost thought she had to answer, but she didn't. She couldn't tell him about her conflicting emotions.

"It's nothing I can talk about, Mose." She looked toward the unending rows of corn and then back to Becca's home. It was such a dreadful metaphor of her life—either going forward alone to live in a void that she was blindly walking through, or going back to people who live by their faith. She wouldn't bring Mose into it. That would complicate the decision she had to make.

"It's as if you suddenly get upset when kindness is given to you." He continued to stare as she turned to him; it was as if he would understand when he could study her eyes. "Or is there something else?"

She was sure he felt the connection between them, but they both skirted around it. And she wasn't about to be the one to bring it forth. Considering the circumstances, she hoped he wouldn't either. "None of this matters." She started walking back to Becca's, not wanting to risk saying something she couldn't take back.

"There's obviously something wrong. But if you don't want to tell me, at least—"

"Abby, Mose!" Becca's urgent voice was faint but growing closer.

"We're coming!" Mose yelled from behind her.

"Where?" The shrill emptiness in Becca's words were so unlike her, Abby couldn't help but worry. She came down through a couple of rows over.

"What is it?" Abby asked as soon as she saw Becca's blue dress through the green leaves surrounding them.

"A hurricane." She put a hand to her chest to catch her breath. "It's already hit Corpus Christi."

~~ **Chapter Twenty-Two** ~~

MOSE MET WITH the elders and Minister Miller as they gathered together at the Zooks' home to discuss the impending weather. The mood was tense. This storm could destroy their entire crop with one blow. They studied the latest weather update and waited for Rachel to bring them news. Her daed was the only one with a phone.

Mose stood with a few others in the large foyer. "This is out of our hands."

"*Nee*, it's not possible to protect our fields," David, one of the deacons, threw in.

Minister Miller gave them all an encouraging smile. "We will do as always—pray for *Gott's* provision."

The front door opened and Rachel rushed in, holding out a piece of paper to whoever would take it, and then bent over to catch her breath.

The bishop read it quietly. "There has been flooding along the banks of the Rio Grande over the last few days. Four and a half feet, and it's forecasted to remain high for several days. They are bracing for more rain and possible flooding. River flood warnings have been extended. Some homes will have to be evacuated." He paused and looked down for a moment, almost as if in prayer. When he raised his head he said, "And Henry is missing."

"Do we know how much time we have?" Joe spoke more to himself than anyone.

"Says they've gotten almost a foot of rain a day." Rachel blinked back her tears and dropped her head.

David looked down in thought. "We can make a dam around the haus closest to the river, fill up our seed bags full of sand."

Abby quietly walked in with Becca and listened to the rest of the conversation. Mose worried for Abby's safety while she'd been in the community, but now he felt it more than ever but for a different reason. If the weather moved this way, there was a possibility people could get hurt, but there was no chance he would let that happen to Abby. He would see to it that she was by his side through the entire ordeal, no matter what Abby, her dad, or anyone else had to say about it.

"Becca, let Joe take you to your family. Abby, come with me." Their expressions changed from concern to surprise at his direct words, but they listened, and that was what was needed at the moment. He kept her next to him as they continued to brainstorm. "We need to gather supplies and food."

"*Jah*, and have a warning so we know when to evacuate." Bishop Omar paused. "We're used to tornados, but this is something different altogether. Our cellars won't help us now. Where's the highest ground?"

"Over by the Bylers' store, and the new school. The hill they're on may help some." Eli shrugged.

"Gather together all the supplies you can at your homes, and start making that dam. Don't know if it'll help, but it's worth a try."

Minister Miller let out a long breath. "And if Henry is found, ring the bell."

"What about the livestock?" Abby asked, causing all eyes to focus on her.

Mr. Yoder didn't even pause. "Bring 'em to my place if you don't have a *gut* holding pen. We'll make room."

They dispersed and made their way to prepare their families, but Mose kept Abby close as they left, not caring what the others might be thinking. The one thing Abby needed most was to feel safe, and he would make sure he provided that for her. "You've got Ginger on your mind?"

"I can't help it." She stepped quickly to keep up with him, but he couldn't slow down. There was too much to do with little time.

"Most of them are in the same spot as you are, some more so." He went over to help her into the wagon, but she waved him away, understanding the urgency.

She looked up into the dark, foreboding sky. "How did this come on so suddenly?"

"It's either drought or rainstorms down here in the south. Being close to Beeville, you probably have a better idea of what's going on." Mose glanced at the dark rolling clouds and felt the need to outrun them, to get to his home before they took over the sky.

"I haven't missed much since staying here, but a television with the Weather Channel would be nice right now." The wind slapped long strands of hair against her cheeks as the horse raced down the dirt road. A swift downpour would turn it to mud in no time. Pelts of rain slowly spread throughout the plains and made its way into the buggy. Although the windshield helped them from getting drenched, it made their vision difficult.

Mose looked over at Abby's hands, white-knuckled against the black cushion she sat on. The wind increased in velocity, seeming to push the buggy from all sides. When they pulled up to the house, Mose got up close to drop Abby off.

"I'm going with you." Abby didn't even blink, keeping her gaze on him until he gave in and clucked to the horse.

When they pulled up, he jumped out of the buggy to open the large wood doors. The drops of water hitting his bare skin began to sting when the big gusts of wind started up. He looked around, wondering how much they could fit in the area that now seemed much smaller. It would be a crowded place once all of the animals and equipment were brought in.

Abby stepped down and went to check the livestock. They were wide-eyed and pacing. So were the other animals in the stalls. "Do we have room for the others in here?" She was already starting for the barn door when she asked.

"The horses will come back if we let them go. We need to keep the smaller livestock in here." Abby didn't hesitate as he'd expected. Growing up in the country must have taught her that you can't be partial when it comes to the animals. He had learned early on that you had to do what was best for the whole, not the few.

Abby didn't hesitate to help Mose set up makeshift corrals to get as many sheep, cows, and pigs as possible in one enclosed area. They just had to hope the chicken coop would stay intact. Once they got tubs of water for them, they moved on to the horses.

Abby went to the larger ones first and let them out. Mose hurried to let out two others that would lead the way for the others. Once Frank got a feel for the weather, he was full of energy and took off running out in an open pasture. One followed, and then another, until together in a herd they ran out of sight.

The wind was gaining strength. Mose put a hand on a wooden post to steady himself and beckoned for Abby to follow him to the house. Rain pelted down on them and stung like tiny pebbles shooting their skin. He put a guiding arm over her shoulders so she could put her head down against the driving storm.

Once they stepped onto the porch, a loud crack filled the air, and a lightning bolt hit the ground behind the barn. Abby clapped her hands over her ears and closed her eyes. The sulfur smell carried over their way, working their senses into overdrive.

"Let's go inside and check on everyone," he yelled over the overwhelming downpour. He followed her in and shook his head like a dog shaking its wet fur. "*Hallo!*"

Chris came running, carrying his boots. "Can I help?" He looked at Mose with hopeful eyes.

Mose pointed to his boots. "You're not going out in this." Mose wasn't as patient as usual, but there was no time for discussions.

"I'm tying up the stuff outdoors that might blow away." He dropped his boots, ready to put them on. "I wanna help."

"Then I'll take you." He turned to Abby. "I don't want you to be alone."

"I'll look for your mother and stay with the women."

He was hesitant to accept her offer, knowing how she felt about being equal, but that was just not the way it was done in the community. Maybe she was beginning to understand that.

"Daed already put some stuff up, but then he left with the men." Chris stopped and stared at Mose. "He said I could help."

Mose doubted it, and would talk with his brother about being truthful later, but if Chris wanted to try and stand the weather, Mose would let him. "We'll be back."

"I'll double-check the house. I already see some things I could tuck away somewhere."

She walked away before he could answer, grateful that she had a good mind about her. He was pretty sure his mamm hadn't had time to prepare much food, but just in case the waters got high enough, it would be helpful to have Abby pack a few special items away and gather together some provisions.

"Let's go." He put a hand behind Chris's head and led him out into the coursing storm. He stopped once to nod to Abby. She glanced at him and motioned for them to go.

Mose took long, fast strides and pulled him along. He pushed Chris behind him as he opened the barn door, in case the wind whipped it open. Once inside, Mose grabbed some rope and a small ax. "Let's go. Ready?"

Chris nodded quickly. "*Jah*, can I carry the rope?"

"Don't lose it. You'll need it to tie down the furniture." Mose reluctantly handed it over to him. Normally he wouldn't mind the loss of a piece of twine, but not this day. Time was of the essence. Their boots sank into three or more inches of water as they hurried to where Chris was working.

They went from chair to table, or anything in the yard that they could lift, and tied it to a large oak tree by the house. When they were finished, Chris's face reddened as he tried to move a bench from the garden. Mose grabbed it and dragged it to the large truck and tied it to the tree, then turned to see a bloody cut on Chris's arm. "You can't do everything. You need to know how much you can handle and ask for help."

Chris handed him what was left of the rope. "Are we done already?"

"*Jah*, let's go. Our safety is more important." Mose knew Chris was frustrated he hadn't gotten to do much, but it was a good lesson to learn, and there wasn't a moment to waste. Mose wished he'd had some of the men to help—he could have done more with the extra muscle—but there must be a bigger demand somewhere else in the community.

"Abby, are you here?" Mose looked to the top of the stairs and motioned for Chris to stay put then went into the kitchen. When she wasn't there, he began to wonder whether she'd met up with the women and left. She'd started upstairs and would have worked her way down and into the kitchen. He looked around the area. Some crumbs, bits of cut-up vegetables, and open cabinets meant she'd gathered provisions.

"She's out there."

Chris's voice startled Mose. "I told you to stay put."

"You were taking too long." Chris followed Mose out the door to where Abby was pumping water into canisters. Without a word they helped her until all of the containers were full.

"*Gut* thinking," Mose told her as he gathered as many bottles as he could. Chris and Abby filled their arms and headed back to the kitchen. Mose kept his eyes on the skies. It had gotten darker within just the few minutes they were at the water pump. "We need to go. Now."

Mose pulled on Chris's arm and ran to the barn with Abby close behind. "Get in," he told Abby and Chris.

"It's getting worse, isn't it?" Abby looked up at the swirling gray clouds as the rain pounded on the windshield.

"*Jah*, we waited too long." Mose kicked himself for trying to do too much, but he was also frustrated that at least his daed hadn't stayed and helped him finish with what needed to be done.

"Why do you look so mad?" Chris's question just made him angrier, so he didn't answer. The steel wheels slid in the muddy road. Mose moved the Clydesdale closer to the side of the road where there was more gravel.

They turned off onto the dirt path leading to the bishop's home as the thick mud sucked the wheels into the muck. The strong horse grunted through it, but then stuck fast a few feet farther. "We'll walk the rest of the way." Mose jumped out and unhitched the horse to let him find cover. Then he helped the others walk through the downpour.

When they got to the Zooks' home, Chris rushed to the door, but Abby stopped on the porch steps and put a hand on Mose's chest as he was turning to leave again. "What's wrong?"

"We usually help each other out, go from haus to haus to help until every farm is prepared."

"I'm sure there's a reason why everyone is here instead." Wanting to help, she went up the stairs to the house.

He followed her, prepared for anything. "*Jah*, we'll find out soon enough."

Chapter Twenty-Three

THUNDER GROWLED AND the rain pelted them more heavily as they walked into the Zooks' house. When they got closer, Abby saw Eli in the kitchen with a circle of men. The women were huddled together talking in hushed tones.

Abby stepped closer to hear what the women were saying and then went over to Mose. "Everyone's upset."

"About what?" Mose glanced down at her.

"I heard the name Henry."

Eli turned to them. "*Jah*, he's gone missing."

Mose frowned with worry. "How do you know? He could be out on his farm."

"*Jah*, no one's doing what they normally would, so it's hard to know what to think. A group of men are out scouring his place right now."

"Let me know when they need another man." Mose and his daed embraced, which was touching. She couldn't remember the last time she'd had any type of affection, especially from her own father.

Mose caught her gaze. "It's scary, I know. But hopefully we'll find him and this flooding will come and go quickly."

"I hope you're right. I should find Becca." She glanced at the room full of men and pointed out a flash of some blue and black dresses in the kitchen.

Mose looked reluctantly at Becca and then back to Abby. He took both of her hands in his. "I know you won't like this, but I'd prefer if you'd stay with me until this is over."

She opened her mouth to speak, and he held up a hand to stop her. "We don't know what to expect, and if something happens to

141

you and I'm not around, I'd never forgive myself. The way I see it is you're in my care until you work things out with your daed. Until then, you're with me." His face was firm, unwavering as he looked her in the eyes.

"That's fine." She met his gaze.

"That's it? You're not going to protest?" He turned his head to the side and studied her.

"I'm agreeing with you, Mose."

"*Jah*, I know. That's what's got me confused." He rubbed the back of his neck and waited to see whether she would change her mind.

"Have I been that difficult?" Abby waited to hear his opinion, though she thought she knew the answer.

He nodded. "But you seem to be coming around. And so am I." He grinned.

She tucked her arm under his and walked to the kitchen then let go. "I know."

He stopped at the door before leaving. "I'll be back. I want to check in on a few things."

As he turned to walk away, he looked down as if thinking hard about something. She watched him walk away, and as she started working in the kitchen, she caught him staring in at her. She tried to ignore him and stay on task but had to admit she liked the attention.

The women bagged sandwiches, cut up fruit and vegetables, and put jugs of water in bags to be given out to the men working. Some were making a barricade to stop the water from flooding their homes and ruining the crop, but most were searching for Henry. Abby couldn't imagine that many men couldn't find him. And she found herself praying constantly for Henry's safety, as well as Mose's. Even if she wasn't exactly sure how God fit into her life, she hoped He would protect them.

Becca handed her a dish to dry and peeked into the other room. "I think he's leaving."

"Who?" Once Abby's thoughts came back to her, she realized what Becca was implying.

When Becca turned around to where Abby was looking, Mose happened to walk by and came to the door. "Mose."

"I'm going to take my shift at Henry's."

"What's the latest on the weather?"

"No sign it will let up. The river's flooded by his farm, which makes it more difficult."

"I hope you find him and come back quickly." She smiled at him, and he nodded and then walked away. "Be careful."

His response was a gentle grin, and then he was gone. Abby couldn't stop her feelings for him from growing. As much as she'd tried, something like this broke down all of the walls and brought them closer. It was beyond them, something that threatened everything in life all at once. With no certainty of what the outcome could bring, even a stubborn soul like hers was brought back to the place it ought to be.

"Abby." Becca touched her shoulder. When Abby looked at Becca, she put a hand to her lips. "*Ach*, my." She grinned. "Whatever are you going to do?

"What do you mean?" Abby knew exactly what Becca was referring to, but she wasn't ready to talk about it. She was as over her head in her feelings for Mose as the water that was rising in around her.

"I won't force you to face the reality of what's going on, but you'll have to sooner or later." Becca shook her head and handed Abby another plate.

"This isn't the time." Abby felt selfish worrying about her own situation when she thought about Henry and his daughter, Rachel. "Where's Henry's daughter?"

"Rachel's at their farm. She's with Elsie, her good friend, and her bruders, probably a haus full, by now."

She grabbed a handful of bags and opened one for Becca to put in a sandwich and water. "What about her mother?"

"Her mamm passed away."

"That must be hard, being the only female in a house full of young men."

"I wouldn't know." Becca grinned.

Abby could empathize with having only a father. She had wished for another sibling, thinking it would fill the void somehow when she lost her mother. But this was a terrible way to lose a parent. The unknown alone would always haunt a person. Abby felt a sudden urge to talk with Rachel.

Why would Rachel want to hear from someone who doesn't even belong to the community?

"It's amazing to me how you are all here for each other when something happens, good or bad."

"I've never known any different. I can't imagine it any other way." She put away the dishes with Abby and gathered the food and water together to take to the men. "I'll go with you to Henry's." Becca bent over and brought out a big and one smaller basket.

"Is that where Joe is? I haven't seen him." Becca and Joe seemed to be a perfect couple, but Becca was independent, and that kept her separated from him at times, as if she didn't want to get too close. She admired Becca for keeping true to herself but hoped they would end up together.

"*Jah*, I have to keep an eye on him. I think Rachel has taken a liking to him." She lifted her eyes to meet Abby's. They filled the baskets with the food and drink, and then each took one to carry to the buggy.

"Henry's daughter?" She watched Becca nod and was torn as to how to feel. "I suppose it may be awkward around her, knowing how she feels about him."

"*Nee*, I know my Joe. He'll be kind to her, and that's what she needs about now." She turned to see the women packing up and getting ready to go pass out food and water. "Let's go."

They both grabbed as much as they could carry and climbed into Esther's buggy with her and the boys. Chris sat with arms crossed, pouting because he wasn't out with the men working or searching.

"You are as soggy as a wet mop," Esther teased.

"I'm old enough to help, Mamm." Chris seemed to be waiting for her to say something so he could voice his feelings. "You treat me different."

"*Jah*, you're right about that. It's a mamm's right to protect her children."

"Do I have to stay with the women?" Chris seemed to be in pain at the thought.

"The water in that river could swallow you up. But if you want to be with the men, you go find your daed and see what he has for you to do."

That lightened the mood, which was needed with what was ahead of them.

Abby stepped out and immediately went back in. The water was a few inches high, gaining in strength and volume right in front of her as she sat and watched.

"Doesn't look like we're going anywhere." Esther stayed in the driver's seat of the buggy. There was nowhere for them to go where the water wasn't deeper. It was higher as they got closer to the house. Henry's home was the closest to the river. It was a good spot for a farmer, with a water supply for the roaming live-stock or to take a swim in the hot summer months, but today it was the farthest from where a farmer would want to be.

"We'll have to drop off the supplies and go." Becca scanned the area. "Unless someone knows of some place we can park and still get out."

Abby looked over at Chris and reached for some supplies. "This basket is really heavy." Chris was by her side taking the huge load. "*Danke*." Then she smiled at him, and he grinned.

"You said an Amish word."

"*Jah*." She teased. "I know a little." She handed him a basket. When he started to complain, she tilted her head with a warning not to fuss. "I know you want to get out and help, but I need you here to give out the supplies." Distracting him helped Abby keep from wallowing over what obstacles may come to them. She wanted to keep her spirits up and help others to do the same.

She couldn't help but look for Mose. Her eyes went straight to him. Even though everyone dressed pretty much the same, she was learning to pick him out of a group. When she looked over at Becca, she was smiling, shaking her head as she'd done in the kitchen earlier. She seemed to be amused by Abby's lack of will-power to keep her eyes off Mose. When he made his way over to her, a rush of both excitement and foreboding went through her mind.

Mose waded through the water wearing thigh-high rubber boots. His face was gaunt and pale, maybe from being physically tired, but more likely from not accomplishing what they were there to do.

"How's it going?" She stared into his tired eyes and saw hollowness there.

"Slow. There's nothing to go on. It's as if he just vanished." He looked at the rushing river that had overflowed onto the nearby crop. "You ladies should go to the Bylers' store or the school haus. If the water keeps rising at this rate, that'll be the only safe place to go."

"How's your daed?" Esther asked from where she sat in the front.

"He's *gut*, but frustrated like the rest of us." Mose looked at the overflowing river with such a sad expression, Abby had to turn away. He seemed to be giving up, and by the looks of the other men, the mood was contagious.

She touched his hand with her fingers. "I'm sorry, Mose."

"*Jah*...me, too."

"I'd like to see Rachel. Any chance of that?" Becca leaned forward to look around at the mass of men around the water walking, pacing, and searching over the same ground they'd been over many times before.

"*Nee*; she refused to leave the haus, waiting for news. We've got to evacuate soon, and she'll have to go to higher ground like the rest of us." Mose poked his head into the buggy and looked at each one of them. "If you hear the bell, you head to the front of the community. Try to get as many as possible to go to the school haus." He reached down and squeezed Abby's hand.

Most of the women had gone after dropping off supplies, and when a wheel slid under the heavy water, Esther was ready to go. "You men have some sense about ya and get yourselves to the school haus too." She shook a finger at Mose. "The sooner, the better."

"*Jah*, I know." He spoke softly to Abby. "It's hard to know when to stop looking."

Abby's heart tightened with sadness at Mose's words. "I'll pray for your safety, and you pray for discernment." She didn't know where the thoughts came from, but it felt good and right to know something more powerful was watching over them.

Mose almost smiled with agreement. "*Danke* for the encouraging words." He looked down at the ever-rising water and squeezed her hand so hard it hurt. Then he turned slowly and walked away.

～ Chapter Twenty-Four ～

THE WATER LEVEL continued to rise overnight. The men worked to protect their farms until they were exhausted, and then they slept for a short period. The women didn't rest either, gathering their families together and working to keep everyone safe and fed. The dark clouds didn't let up, setting the mood that was thick as the mud they trudged through. The worst of it was there was no sign of Henry.

Nearly everyone spent the night in the schoolhouse or at the Bylers' store. When they ran out of room, the men slept in chairs and the children in their mothers' arms. Abby hardly slept. Every time one of the men came in, she hoped it was Mose, but he never came. When she woke up the next morning and asked around, no one could tell her where he was.

Abby sat down on the floor next to Esther. "I haven't heard anything about Mose. I'm starting to worry."

Esther began to stir at the sound of Abby's voice. "Every woman here is worried for their own. He'll show up."

"You don't know that for sure." Abby caught the pessimism in her words and changed her way of thinking. "I hope you're right."

Esther sat up against a wall. The schoolhouse wasn't completely finished, but the windows were in and the wood floors were down, and it was empty, so it had turned out to be a good place for shelter for those who needed it. "Any word yet on Henry?"

Abby shook her head. "I asked when I was looking for Mose." Although she didn't know Henry well, she felt a pain in her heart for him and his family. "Do you think they'll find him?"

Esther shook her head. "I think it's his family that needs to be tended to about now."

Coming from Esther, Abby took it as truth. She was one of the most positive people Abby had met, and if she felt it was time to let go, then it was probably true. "Are they here?" Abby glanced around the large room. Most had been up before the sun, and everyone except sleepy children were preparing for the day.

"They wouldn't leave their haus unless it was flooded. The fact that they're here is a *gut* sign, considering they were one of the farms closest to the river." Esther and Abby both stood.

Abby adjusted her dress and then looked to see a string of Amish walk in. She didn't know everyone in the community, but there wasn't a familiar face in this group of women.

"They're the Amish group from the other side of Beeville. They've come to help." Esther looked out the window with Abby to see the men shaking hands and talking.

"They weren't affected by the flood?" Abby questioned as she looked outside to see the men join together in a wagon and head in the direction of Henry's place.

"*Jah*, but they're not as close to the river, so they weren't hit as hard." Esther's voice wavered as the women came over to introduce themselves.

"*Gut* morning. We've brought hot coffee and doughnuts if you're hungry," an older woman offered, and she motioned toward a large folding table that was filling up fast with homemade doughnuts.

"*Danke.* Coffee and doughnuts have never smelled so good." They walked together, following the luscious aromas as they learned each other's names. Abby's mouth watered when she picked up a soft chocolate doughnut and relished the warm cup full of coffee. She took a bite, but her stomach suddenly lurched when she saw Henry's daughter walk in with a younger boy. Abby excused herself from the women and walked toward her. Others were approaching her, but that didn't discourage Abby from talking to her. An older woman clasped Rachel's hand, causing a tear to escape down her cheek. When the woman walked away, Abby stepped forward.

"Rachel." Abby's words left her as she stood there with an open mouth. "I don't know what to say."

Rachel's bloodshot eyes met hers. Abby had never seen such sorrow in a young person's eyes. She was used to anger, frustration, and indifference, but not the raw sadness Rachel's eyes expressed.

Rachel shook her head, and Abby instinctively reached out and hugged her. She reciprocated with a tight squeeze and then dropped her arms from what seemed to be exhaustion. "*Danke.*" Rachel took her brother's hand and accepted comfort from another Amish woman.

Becca came over and talked with Rachel for some time, and then packed up to leave.

"So, it's over?" Abby knew they were beginning to let go, but she couldn't believe Henry was really gone.

"The search continues, but the troopers told them after twenty-four hours, there's little chance of finding him."

"I'm so sorry for Rachel." Abby glanced over at her but didn't want to stare.

"She had a lot of support from people who cared about her and her daed." Becca watched the room full of women and grabbed her basket. "I'm going home to see my family and find out what needs to be done."

"Will you take me to Mose's house? I haven't seen him since yesterday morning." Hearing the words she had just said renewed her worry. She knew he was probably fine, but until she saw him, she wouldn't stop thinking about him.

"I'm sure he's fine, Abby. He's a stubborn one and is probably one of them who are still looking."

"You're probably right, but I have to know for sure." Becca knew Mose well. She was probably right about him staying until he found something or physically couldn't push on, but Abby would feel better if he was with his family.

As they walked out of the building, Abby thought about the irony of it all. The timing of the school being built, and that it was not only their children's future but also a refuge for them as they endured this storm. She couldn't help but wonder what was in store for this community, but she prayed all that had happened would make them stronger. Abby knew the events had already changed her. Until the crisis she hadn't asked God for anything since before her mother's death.

When they got outside, the heavy rains had stopped. Puddles of water inches deep covered the area, but only small drops of rain continued to fall.

"It's letting up." Becca closed her eyes and held out her hands while taking in a breath.

"Thank God," Abby whispered. The words were heartfelt with new awareness of the Lord's power to give and take away.

When she got to the Fishers' house, she hoped to see Mose opening the screen door and walking out onto the porch. He always seemed to have a sense about her whereabouts, even when she didn't tell him. She wished for that right at that moment. "*Danke*, Becca."

"I'll see you soon." Becca seemed hurried. The separation from loved ones had them both rattled.

She waded through the water up to the house. The ground was so saturated, the water stood stagnant a few inches deep. The sound of her boots on the porch was loud but drew out her senses, as did the voices coming from inside the house. But none of them were Mose's.

Abby plopped down on the porch swing, worry and disappointment gathering in her heart and mind. She gently rocked in the swing, not knowing what else to do. She wrapped her arms around her, wishing they were Mose's strong hands.

Chapter Twenty-Five

MOSE THOUGHT HE'D taken his last step. There wasn't an ounce of strength in him, but he willed himself to move forward. He couldn't feel his feet, and the numbness was spreading upward around his ankles. The water was colder than usual, even cooler during the night. But it wasn't clear enough to see much underneath with the storm stirring up mud into the water. They'd gone up and down the river even after it had been barricaded, with no sign of Henry, so they'd decided to drag the river. They were supposed to work in teams, but he and Joe got separated. The silence over the past twenty hours pounded in his ears, waiting for the sound of the life-giving bell that was never heard.

The water surged up around him, at some points up to his stomach. When that happened, he had to move up toward the bank. The water poured over the sides of the river's edge, sucking him in. He stuck his sharpened walking stick into the ground, but the undercurrent surrounded it, and the dirt mixed with sand washed it out of the ground. He stumbled, falling facedown, pushed by the force of the murky water. He stood, gripping the rod, and vigorously shook his head, throwing water into the air around him.

Frustration set in. His muscles ached with each step he tried to take. He wouldn't be any good to anyone until he got some rest and food in his belly. He looked at the turbulent river and let himself go into the water that was rushing forever forward, floating to save energy. Although the sun was rising, he shivered. If Henry was alive, he'd have been found by then.

When he reached the closest farm, he pulled himself up and

out of the river, flopping onto his stomach on the soggy ground. As he pulled himself up, he saw Rachel's oldest brother coming from the barn. Mose looked at the sun and figured he had just finished milking.

The young man stopped and stared for a moment. "Mose?" He raced toward him and put a helping hand around his shoulder. "Did you come out of the river?"

"*Jah*, spent the night looking for your daed."

He was quiet for a long while. "Troopers are saying time's run out."

Mose used what strength he had left and turned to look at him. "We won't quit until we have to." Mose clasped his shoulder

"How do we know when that is?" He averted his eyes to keep from getting emotional.

"You'll know." Mose leaned on him as they made their way to the haus. "Can you take me to the school?"

"Don't ya want something to eat first?"

"*Nee*, but *danke*." Mose's stomach rumbled at the thought of food, but he had to check on his family and see Abby before he could enjoy a meal.

Rachel pulled in as they were almost to the house and jumped down from the buggy to see Mose. "You look awful, Mose."

Mose forced a smile. "It's *gut* to see you too." He teased, then he instantly became solemn again. "I'm sorry, Rachel."

"Mose, you did what you could." She wiped her nose as she walked along beside them. "Everyone has."

"It's a difficult thing that's happened. But it may still end well." Mose felt weak and tripped over a clod of dirt in the muddy ground. "I'd like to know if everyone in my family is safe and sound."

"I just came from the school to see if there was any news. I saw your mamm with the boys and Abby."

Mose paused and moved his head just enough to look at Rachel. "That much is *gut*. Did you hear any news?"

"*Nee*, nothing." She took in a deep breath as if to push it all

153

away. "Take care of yourself." Rachel tried to smile and walked back to her house.

Mose couldn't imagine what the mood was in there with her family. No mamm, and now a missing daed, with four boys and Rachel to run things. Mose knew things in life weren't fair, but this was one of those times he just couldn't make sense of. He was thankful to hear his family and Abby were together and in good health. Now it was only his daed he had to worry about.

They got settled in the buggy and went straight to the schoolhouse. Mose was too tired to talk and concentrated on not falling over when his eyes shut. When they pulled up, some Amish women he didn't know brought him coffee and doughnuts before he even got out of the buggy. He accepted as politely as he could, but the only face he wanted to see was Abby's.

Mose asked around, but no one knew anything more than Rachel did. There were still a number of men away, so his daed must be with them. "They must have left already."

Rachel's brother grabbed Mose's arm. "I'll get you out of here and take you home."

Mose didn't complain—he dozed off once but caught himself before he crashed onto the buggy floor. When they got close to his farm, they ran into a deep puddle that sucked them in, threatening to trap them. "I'll walk from here."

"I can get up closer."

"Don't even try. I'm too tired to push you out." Mose jumped down from the buggy and started walking home. He waved to Rachel's brother in thanks. Everyone should be with their families, reuniting and appreciating that they were together, especially him.

The walk seemed to take forever, but the closer he got, the more adrenaline surged through him, and he picked up speed. The sweet smell of corn and clean country air flowing through his lungs made him grateful that exhaustion was his only repercussion from this whole ugly ordeal. His thoughts and prayers would continue for Henry. Mose did believe that miracles happened, so he wouldn't give up hope just yet.

As he got closer, he could see someone on the porch but couldn't make out who it was. His first thought was of Abby, and he wondered about his change in loyalties. This young woman who had come to him in the most peculiar circumstances was now first in his thoughts.

⌒ Chapter Twenty-Six ⌒

ABBY DIDN'T HAVE the will to get up and make her way to Becca's. Then a stirring through the cornfield caught her attention. Someone or something was moving through a tall row toward the house. She wondered whether the wild animals had lost their food source due to the flooding and were now looking for farm animals. But no, the rhythm was consistent, without stopping. An animal would pause, check the surroundings, and be more hesitant.

When Abby couldn't stand it any longer, she stood, ready to face whatever it was. The green leaves curled back and Mose walked out into the clearing, making his way to her. His clothes were filthy, his hair was askew, and his pale face was a fright. He marched forward, even though his reserves were surely depleted.

She ran down the porch steps and straight to him, letting the water splash over her. When she got closer to him, she slowed to catch her breath and then wrapped her arms around his neck. He held her tightly around her waist, but she didn't mind the slight discomfort to her ribs. Neither one of them moved for the longest time, each taking in the other and the assurance that they were both alive and well.

Abby finally moved back just far enough to see his face and moved her arms onto his shoulders. "Henry?"

Mose shook his head. "It doesn't look promising, but I'm not ready to give up hope."

"Good. Neither am I." She dropped her head, looking down at the muddy mess below her feet. "All of this makes me think about Jim."

"I've wondered about your dad too."

"As much as I don't want to, I should go see him. Just see how he is. I know he's sick and too stubborn to go to the doctor. But there's no one to take care of him." She was filled with the same sadness that she'd felt when she first arrived in the community— scared and hopeless—but not bitter like she had been. She'd been humbled by coming to the Amish, and that way of thinking had remained throughout her time there. "But right now there is a lot of work to do here."

"*Jah*, we need to find out what there is to be done." He turned to admire the endless land. "The cotton is gone, but most of our corn made it through."

"That's something to be thankful for." Abby had realized even more how important the crop was to the Amish. They could make a partial living from working a trade, but their crop brought in a great deal and was the heart of what they stood for. The closeness they were rumored to have when working the earth was sacred and couldn't be replaced by any other way of making a living. As she watched Mose looking over the cornfield, she understood for the first time how much it meant to him.

"Most of the corn looks good." Her comment brought a smile to him, but then she watched it disappear.

"Corn is more durable than cotton. I'm sure the cotton couldn't stand all that rain." He pursed his lips in disappointment. "But we'll count our blessings."

Eli rode in on one of their horses and came over to them. "Look what the storm dragged in." He shook his head proudly at his son. "Are you both all right?" Eli looked from Mose to Abby.

"Glad to be alive, praise *Gott*."

Eli hiked a leg over the horse and dropped both feet to the ground. "I feel like you look." He turned to Mose. "Wish we could find Henry."

"Did they call off the search?" Abby was disappointed. They couldn't give up, not yet. What would it do to Rachel, and then what it would do to her if Jim was injured, hurt, or even...

"There are still some looking, but his place was one close to

157

the river. Flooded the crop, a couple feet of water filled into their house, and muddy water up past your ankles still around the barnyard. Henry was trying to do what any of us would have done—save his farm. He probably just didn't know when to quit."

"How could you not know when to leave? Wasn't it obvious when the water was just too much?" Abby knew she still didn't fully appreciate the value they put on their farms, but when it came to life and death, she wished Henry would have been more cautious, and she wondered if Jim had been.

Eli held tight onto the reins as his horse fidgeted. "Rachel said Henry sent them all off the area and stayed trying to block the water from overflowing onto his property."

"Makes a person wonder what they'd do in the same situation." Mose asked himself the question, more than asking Abby and his daed.

"It's hard to know unless you're the one in it." Eli looked up as if thinking. "Rest up, you two. We have a lot of work to do around here and at Henry's place." He led the anxious horse to the barn, and Abby followed Mose to the house, her mind on Jim.

Mamm was in the kitchen. Chris sat at the table, half asleep with his head on his arms, as Esther looked up as they came in and walked over to wrap her arms around Mose and Abby. "Where's your daed?" She studied Mose with pensive eyes.

"Putting up the horse. If he doesn't come in, I'll go fetch him," Mose offered, but Abby couldn't see how he had the energy to do anything but eat and sleep.

A few minutes later Eli returned. They sat down to a silent dinner but didn't have as much as usual after giving to those who had none. They used canned food from the cellar, but no one ate their fill. There might still be a need to give away more food. Chris was restless, so he went out to milk while Abby, Mose, and his parents stayed seated.

"This storm has done a lot of damage. The railroad bridge is out, and Highway Fifty-Nine is closed, leaving us to stay put until they can clear the roads. Once the Chase River is under control, we're back in business." Eli was starting to show signs of fatigue, rubbing his tired eyes.

"Rain from the hill country's what got it coming down this way," Mose added. "It was more than they expected."

"There are a lot of buildings that will need repair." Esther gathered the dishes, and Abby got up to help, thinking about her comment and how they didn't have flood insurance or any insurance, for that matter. She knew they would rally together and help each other with the costs, but with so many homes hit by this disaster, she wondered how they would pull it off. That was a different way of thinking, one she wasn't used to.

"We should try runoff irrigation," Mose suggested, and Eli turned to him with interest.

"That would be a *gut* suggestion to tell the bishop. There is a gathering at the school haus later tonight. We should all go to see what the restoration plan is."

Abby was glad to hear Eli include everyone. This affected every single person in the community, so it was only right. When she looked over at Mose, he was watching her. Dark circles under his eyes made her wish he could sleep for a while, but she knew better than to even suggest it. The answer would be no, there was too much to be done.

They examined the water damage and found most to be in the barnyard. The barn had barely been affected, and the house wasn't too bad. The most damaged was the crop. All they could do was pray for a lot of sun and wind to dry up the moist ground.

There was a lot of work ahead of them, but the community meeting came first. Abby admired the way they worked on fixing the problems together instead of each family fending for themselves. If her own family would have had that kind of support, they may have had an easier time during the hardships they had endured.

Although Eli's buggy was big enough for all of them, Mose asked if he could ride in the two-seater with Abby. Eli half smiled and nodded. But once they got in the buggy together, they were too tired to talk.

Mose slowed the horse and looked over at Abby. "What are you thinking about?"

"Jim. I've thought him from the time I left, but after all that's happened, I'm worried." She looked down in thought. "I'm so conflicted as to what to do."

"What would your mamm have done? She seemed to know how to handle him, or is that too far gone for him to appreciate?"

Abby liked Mose's question, but she couldn't see Jim appreciating anything. He seemed to lose his love for anything, including Abby. "He is a bitter man, but he is still my father. I should find out if he's all right."

"If he needs anything, you know you can bring him here, although it doesn't sound like he would."

"No, he wouldn't. There's no doubt in my mind about that. He has ill feelings about the Amish." That was watered down as far as Abby could make it. Jim had a hatred for the Amish, one Abby couldn't understand. It was if they had done something awful to them, but what, Abby didn't know.

"That's hard to understand, but there must be some reason for it. He's not the only one who doesn't appreciate our ways. And then there are others who want to become Amish and appreciate our way of life. Like you." He smiled and glanced at her, as if needing confirmation.

"For the most part, but then I think the Amish are cordial people, usually welcoming." She remembered some people in town commenting on the Amish, how they weren't always friendly, but now she could see that it was more that they kept to themselves. It was not to be rude—it was just their way.

"If you decide to see your daed, tell me and I'll take you there." He didn't move his eyes away from her as he spoke, letting her know he meant what he said. But if Jim saw an Amish on his place, there would be trouble, so Abby didn't respond.

When they drove up to the schoolhouse, they had a hard time

finding a place to tether the horse. It seemed that the entire community was there. The bishop was talking about restoring the buildings and gathering the stranded animals. Mose offered his ideas about the runoff irrigation and building greenhouses to grow some crop. Once they delegated and found out what needs individual families had, they were sent their own way until the morning. It would be a long day, week, and maybe even months before they got back on their feet.

The bishop spoke to the minister, who stepped forward. "Before we depart, let's say a prayer for Henry and his family."

Abby watched every head bow as Rachel and her brothers went forward. The minister laid hands on them and prayed. His heartfelt words stirred Abby's heart. No matter how tragic it was to lose Henry, this community would make it as bearable as possible.

~ Chapter Twenty-Seven ~

MOSE RUBBED THE back of his neck as he tried to explain his idea about building a greenhouse to his daed. The stubborn old man was in a cross mood, so Mose didn't know whether to push the subject or come back to it later. Everyone was still on edge, but they needed to start making things right on their own farm as well as helping others. This was a bigger disaster than they'd gone through before, so the protocol wasn't clear.

"I don't know the first thing about building a greenhouse," Eli told Mose as Abby walked into the kitchen after a nice walk from Becca's.

Mose waited for her to look over at him, and they both smiled, distracting Mose momentarily.

"You two are starting early." She grinned and took a pan Esther had washed that needed drying.

"*Danke.*" Esther gave Abby a long look. "Mose thinks we should build a greenhouse to make up for some of the crop we lost."

"So I hear. Why doesn't Eli let Mose do it?" Abby continued to dry as Esther washed.

"That's what Mose is trying to talk him into." She shrugged. "I don't know why he's so stubborn. Anything new makes him jumpy." Esther smiled and drained the sink. "I'm going up to the school haus later, if you want to go. Everyone's bringing food for those who got hit hardest by the storm."

Abby grinned. "Sure."

Mose noticed Abby's eyes flicker in thought. "What are you thinking about?"

She lifted her head and stared at him. "Oh, nothing…" She

turned to Eli. "I hear you're building a greenhouse." She changed the subject, but that wouldn't stop Mose from finding out what was on her mind.

"I guess so. I just hope Mose knows what he's doing." Eli scrunched his forehead with skepticism.

"What I don't know, I'll find out from Joe. But for now there are a couple of hauses that need tending to." He turned to Abby. "Wanna go with me to the Lapps'?"

"What happened to their house?" Abby was already walking with him to the back door.

"Water damage. Probably need to replace some boards and whatnot. It shouldn't take long, but there are plenty others that need repair."

"See you at dinner then," Esther told them more than asked. His mamm and daed still wanted them to be under watch, and Abby reluctantly relented, feeling she was too old to be told what to do.

"*Jah*, Mamm." Mose opened the screen door for Abby to walk out first, and then looked down the path that led to their haus to see someone walking toward them. Mose took the stairs two at a time, and Abby followed. The tall trees created a large overhead of shade that made it hard to see their face.

"Who is that?" He heard Abby's voice, but he was too intent on seeing who the person was to answer. Then it clicked. He knew who it was. He'd know that confident stride anywhere. As the person got closer, he walked slower, like he was trying to make out who Abby was.

"He looks like you."

Abby was right about that, but only in appearance; they were nothing alike in any other way.

"*Hallo*, little brother." Jake held out a hand that Mose reluctantly shook. "You look surprised." He chuckled and looked over Mose's shoulder at Abby.

She came around in front of Mose. "I'm Abby, a friend of Mose's."

Jake lifted his brows. "Just a friend?" Jake winked, and that was all it took.

Mose took the three steps between them at full force. He hit Jake in chest, knocking him to the ground. Mose stumbled, trying to keep his balance.

Abby moved her hand away from her mouth. "Mose!"

Mose regained his composure and bent over to catch his breath.

"That's some greeting." Jake stood and slapped Mose on the back, hard. "He's missed me." Jake told Abby. "A little protective of this one, are you?" He pointed to her.

"You never did know how to treat a lady. I'm sure it's just gotten worse since you've been out there." Mose nodded with his head to the lane Jake just walked down.

"I came to help, but you obviously don't want me here. I'll go to Henry's."

Mose shot off a prayer for patience so fast, he said it again just to give himself time before he said or did something he'd regret...again. "Fine." He walked past Abby but couldn't look at her. He knew he was being a jerk, but what Jake had done to his bride and unborn child was more than Mose could find in him to forgive.

He heard Abby talking to him and stopped.

"You can't stay at Henry's, Jake. No one's seen him since before the flood."

Mose heard Jake scoff and turned around to face him.

"I'm sorry to hear that. *Danke* for telling me, Abby," Jake said to her, but he was staring at Mose.

"You were gonna let me go over to their house without telling me?" Jake shook his head then looked around the farm. "Looks like most of the corn made it through the storm. How's the rest?"

"Cotton's gone, at least most of it." Mose couldn't help but talk crop, even with him. "There'll be enough to feed our family and make some on the corn."

"Mose is building a greenhouse to help make up for the loss."

Abby seemed proud, but Mose didn't appreciate her telling Jake. He'd figure out some way to make it negative.

Jake folded his arms over his chest and grinned. "A greenhouse. Really?" His sarcastic tone increased Mose's distrust of him.

When Abby stepped forward, Mose did too. She placed her hands on her hips and locked eyes with his brother. "I don't know you, Jake, but I don't like the way you're treating me or your brother, so I'm going to go get the horse and hitch up the buggy." She brushed past him, making Jake smile, and walked to the barn.

Jake watched her go. "She seems like a bit of a spitfire."

Mose shrugged, not sure what Jake meant, but sure he probably didn't want to.

"So, there's still no water running under that bridge between us." Jake's words stung. It was the Amish way to forgive, but how could he when someone was so incredibly wrong?

"I'm not going to lie to you, Jake. You should have done the right thing and stayed with Katie and Solomon."

Jake nodded. "She named him after her dad?" He stuck his hands in his pockets and turned away.

Mose wasn't sure what to say or do next. He'd let his anger get the best of him. Half of the problem was that Jake liked to pop up out of nowhere. A little warning would allow people to be prepared. When Jake was around, the pot was always stirring. Mose couldn't help but wonder if he was there to help after the storm, or if he was there to make one.

Jake's emotion over his son he'd never seen surprised Mose. It had been months since Jake left the community, leaving the mother of his child, and Mose figured he was gone for good. It wasn't often Jake lowered his defenses. But that was because he was usually doing something out of order. No way was Mose going to let his guard down.

"You think it was easy to walk away? I'm not gonna stay some place where I have to follow a code that I don't believe in. I am doing the right thing, for me."

"*Jah*, for *you*." Mose shook his head again. "You always did have a different way of thinking."

"Just because I don't follow silly rules that don't matter to me doesn't mean my faith is any less than yours."

Mose didn't like his words, but he understood. Jake was judging just like he felt judged. He hadn't been in the community long enough after their move from Virginia to honestly know the differences they'd made versus the Old Order ways up north.

But there was a part of Mose that understood what Jake was referring to. Sometimes there was a reprimand from an elder over something Mose thought unimportant. There were ongoing discussions over indoor toilets, lamps instead of gas or battery, and limits on technology. It was still questionable for an Englisher to drive an Amish in their community. The new group by Beeville was more progressive, which meant even more decisions to make. For once in a very long time, Mose felt akin to his brother, and even though he didn't completely agree with Jake, he understood his meaning. "Then why are you here?"

Jake lifted his head as the wind rustled the leaves on the tree above him. He studied the fields and house. "Just thought it was the right thing to do."

"Is that all you brought with you?" Mose pointed to the duffle bag lying on the ground in front of Jake.

"It's all I left with, and all I'm bringing back."

Mose grabbed it and started for the house. When Jake didn't follow, Mose turned around to see him staring, eyes squinted. "You coming?"

"*Jah*, I guess I am." He didn't try to make up the distance between them but kept a steady course to the house. It couldn't be easy for him, but Jake had to have known that before he came.

Mose still wasn't happy about him being there, no matter how good his intentions might be. And he really wasn't looking forward to seeing the family's reaction, especially Katie. "Is the flooding the only reason you came back?"

Jake was silent so long Mose wondered if he heard him. "No, I wanted to check in on the baby."

"Almost a year old."

"Yeah, I know."

As they walked in the back door, Mose had second thoughts. Maybe he should have had Jake lie low until he could prepare the family that he was there. But knowing Jake, he wouldn't want to wait. He'd be gone before they knew it, anyway.

"We have a visitor." Mose laid the duffle bag on the floor in the kitchen and waited for the fireworks.

Mamm had her hands full of hamburger for a dish she was making for lunch. "I haven't put up the blueberry pancakes from breakfast yet."

Daed downed the rest of his coffee, looked over to them, and then sat back in his chair. "Well, I'll be."

Mamm turned to see what caught Daed's attention. She dropped the meat in a pan and wiped her hands on her apron. "Jake, we weren't expecting you." She stumbled over her words, worried about what his daed would say more than why Jake was there.

"What are you doing here, son?" Daed's tone was difficult to read. His wide-eyed expression was almost as intense as Mamm's.

Jake took a step forward into the room. "I heard about the flooding around these parts and thought I'd come down to lend a hand." He was less confident around Daed, but he held his composure. "And I'd like to see Solomon."

"We call him Sol," Daed corrected him quickly. His pride for the youngster's name was evident.

Jake smiled slightly at Daed's reaction. "Sorry to hear about Henry."

"*Jah*, it's a sad time for the Kings, with no parent to guide them." Mamm shook her head slowly but still held tight to a rigid posture, uncomfortable, as were the rest of them.

"They're all grown by now. They'll get along."

Mose cringed inwardly. He'd known that as soon as Jake joined in the conversation, something would start.

"What would you know about that, with you being gone?" Daed didn't blink, waiting for Jake's response. "You don't know this place or your own son."

The conflict between them started later than Mose had expected, but he knew it would come. The disappointment Daed felt concerning his eldest son would not change, couldn't change. Daed had disowned Jake in his mind, and nothing could alter that. Jake had done the unspeakable by leaving his family after a baptism.

Jake reached for his bag. "I think it best that I be going."

"*Nee.*" Mamm moved forward and looked at Daed and then to Jake. "Jake, you'll stay here."

"*Jah,* I don't want you bothering the Yoders. It's up to Katie if she wants to see you." Daed stood to his full height, which was a couple inches taller than Jake, and walked out the back door. His boots sounded louder, and the screen door hit the frame with a sharp *slap* as he walked away.

Mose wrestled with his emotions. He'd felt the same way his parents had when he first saw Jake, but after seeing all he'd already been through, Mose wondered whether he was regretting coming back yet. If he wasn't, he probably would be. He caught Jake's eye and let out a sigh. "You sure you want to stay here?"

"I expected this, but it isn't the hardest part."

"What if Katie doesn't want to see you?" That could be a definite possibility. She was as stubborn as he was.

"Then at least I tried."

"Is that the real reason you came back?"

"When I heard how bad the storm had hit you all down here, I had a strong conviction to come back whether I wanted to or not."

"Sounds like seeing Sol came in second." Mose had never been able to discern Jake's true intentions, even with something of this magnitude, and he wanted to know the truth.

"It's been hard knowing I have a baby and not knowing

anything about him. I didn't even know if it was a boy or girl." He grabbed the duffle bag. "The storm was an excuse to come see my boy." And with that he marched up the stairs, leaving Mose standing in the kitchen alone.

Abby stood by the screen door and called his name. "Let's go."

He made his way to the door and followed her to the buggy. "I'm sorry about this mess."

"*You* are apologizing to *me* about a family matter?" She shook her head. "It'll be nice for me to be able to support you for a change."

He climbed up into the buggy and sat down in the seat as she spoke. He felt better already. "It does help to have someone who understands." He tapped the reins, thinking it would be a lot easier to mend hauses after a hurricane than see his daed and Jake making amends.

⮑ Chapter Twenty-Eight ⮕

THE SUN WAS intense but helped dry the soggy ground that was saturated with water. And an ominous mood hung over them with thoughts of Henry. The entire community silently mourned in remembrance of one of their own who was gone so suddenly. Once his family was ready, they planned a memorial that would take place that coming Sunday.

They went from one farm to another in order of how much damage had been done. It was almost like another barn raising when they went to each house and there was a crowd of people to mend the home. The men would do their part and the women theirs, all joining together as one, and Abby was learning how she fit in. She learned some recipes from the women. Abby hadn't known much about baking until she met the Amish. These women could have opened a bakery if they wanted to.

The restlessness Abby felt regarding Jim increased each day. It had been days since she'd left, and a lot could have happened in that amount of time. Abby hated that she didn't want to go see her own father, but the guilt of not seeing him bothered her even more. She would never forgive herself if something happened to him and she never saw him again.

"What are you thinking about?" Mose looked up at her quickly and then piled more food on his plate.

Abby startled, deep in thought. "Jim. My dad." She clarified quickly, knowing it confused Mose when she used his first name.

"You haven't mentioned him, so I let it alone, but I've wondered about him too." He waved away a fly and then studied Abby for a moment. "Now that the roads are safe for the buggies to travel on, we could go see him."

Abby's head snapped up. "You don't have to go, Mose."

He drew back, hurt or angry—she couldn't tell which. "I want to, not only to support you but also for your safety." His furrowed brows warned her to tread lightly. Mose's feelings were at stake as well as his fierce need to always protect her.

Abby looked up at the bright sun and held up a hand to shade her eyes. "Jim will be defensive if you're there." That was true, but she really wanted to do this alone. It was between her and Jim, and there was too much history behind them that someone new to the situation wouldn't understand. They were as dysfunctional a family as any she'd seen, and Abby's job provided her with a fairly accurate way to gauge it. She didn't know the particulars about the oldest brother who had returned, but even that situation surely couldn't top hers.

"I have to go to the furniture shop to pick up a payment, anyway. It would be silly for us to go separately." He stared at her until she answered.

"All right, you can drop me off at Jim's and pick me up when you're done in town."

Mose shook his head with frustration. "I can't promise you I'll leave when you get there."

Abby crossed her arms over her chest. There was no way Jim would cooperate if Mose was there. It would be hard enough to have a conversation with him without Mose. "You can't come in the house, Mose. If he sees you, I won't get anywhere with him."

Mose's wrinkles unfolded across his forehead. "*Jah*, I'll settle for staying in the buggy." He didn't seem totally convinced, but this wasn't about him; it was about Jim.

"What are you two so serious about?" Becca walked up and set a bowl of egg salad on the table. The aroma of whipped eggs and mustard tickled Abby's nose and made her hungry.

"It's time I go to see Jim, my dad." Abby realized she'd made it seem like a prison sentence and changed her tone. "It's been too long. I need to see how he is."

"I've wondered about that but didn't want to pry."

"Oh, Becca, you know more about me than anyone. You can ask me anything and I'd tell you."

Becca took her hand. "You know I feel the same." She glanced at Mose. "Mose is taking you, *jah?*"

"We were just talking about that." Mose smiled at her.

She knew he meant well. He also had to know by then how independent she was, but overall he was fair with Abby and her opinionated ways. "And yes, he's taking me."

"It will be *gut* for you to go, *jah?*" She seemed concerned like Mose was. Abby understood, with the way she first came into the community that horrible night that seemed so long ago. "You know, I have an errand to run in town. Maybe I can go with you?"

Abby turned to Mose. "Sure. Right, Mose?"

"*Gut* by me." Mose seemed happy with the growing number and rolled back on his heels.

"Go where?" Joe bit the tip of his leather glove and pulled it off.

"Into town. Can Joe come with us?" Becca asked Mose.

Mose grinned at Abby, who gave him a playful look of irritation. She figured he was betting the bigger the crowd, the more likely Jim would behave. But what Mose didn't understand was that her dad would act up no matter how many people were around. That was just how he'd become after her mother died. As if he was determined not to be happy without her.

They sat together as they ate and talked about other less-stressful topics. There was always the talk of food—who made what—and going for seconds until everyone had their fill. With the Lapps' farm finished, they decided to go to Henry's place.

In light of the family tragedy the community had done a minimal cleanup and then given the family some time before invading their privacy with saws and hammers. But if they wanted to save any of their crops, they needed more help.

The women packed up everything and went home in some of the buggies, and the men went over to Henry's. They didn't want the bustle of the entire community at their place, and the ground still had standing water round the barnyard and most of the fields. Becca and Abby offered to go so they could see Rachel because they were close in age. It was so like Becca to offer to make the visit.

Becca and Abby took Becca's buggy to their place so they could catch up. Everyone had been so busy after the storm there hadn't been time to socialize much.

Becca glanced at Abby. "Do you feel up to talking about your daed?"

Becca looked so interested Abby didn't feel she could say no. Not that she would, anyway. She trusted Becca more than anyone, maybe even Mose.

"I don't like to talk about him, but I can't stay in denial."

"He's the one who hurt you."

For a brief moment Abby didn't know whether she meant emotional or physical. Even though they were intertwined, the emotional part was what lingered. Her bruise was gone. No one would ever know it had been there but the people here in this community, and they seemed to be colorblind. "Yes, he was."

"Then you shouldn't see him alone."

Abby scoffed. "There's a buggy full going, thanks to you."

"Going into town, but you need to have someone with you at the haus."

"You sound like Mose."

"I'd like to meet him." Becca was so serious, Abby knew she couldn't deny her request. Becca wasn't intimidating and was good with people. But then she'd never met Jim.

"Okay, but you may regret it." Abby already was, and it was a day away. She made a conscious effort to think of the present like the people there did so well. It seemed to work for them, and it was contagious. They didn't seem to worry about anything, although that was impossible. But then they'd say nothing's impossible with Christ, and she had no recourse but to agree.

Becca slowed the horse and watched Mose hop down and walk

to the front of his buggy. "Who is Mose talking to?" Joe walked over to Abby's side and motioned toward Mose.

"He's talking to Jake. When did he get here?" Joe was usually a fairly laid-back guy, but he wasn't at the moment. There was something about this Jake character that had everyone upset, and Abby wasn't sure she wanted to find out what it was.

"Early this morning. He wants to help rebuild."

"Give him a chance, Joe," Becca cautioned, but Joe ignored her request and stared as the two brothers talked. His brown eyes were darker than usual, intense, studying them. Abby wondered whether he was more concerned about Mose or upset with Jake.

Joe finally walked away when Mose and Jake headed for the house. "I'll come by later." Joe waved and caught up with them.

"Well, I hope those boys play nice together." Becca tapped the reins and followed them. She sighed. "During a marriage and baptism ceremony Jake made some decisions that the community didn't agree with."

"Did you agree with him?" Abby asked, puzzled.

Becca took a moment before she answered. "I didn't like the personal decision he made about his own family, but I respect him for not saying he believed one way of thinking when in his heart he felt another way. Most probably wouldn't agree with me on that, though."

Abby wondered whether she could ever follow the many Amish rules. She didn't even know them all, so she couldn't answer the question. "When is the next ceremony that you're talking about?"

"In the fall, when the couples get married." Becca smiled at her question. "They go through marriage classes and then are baptized."

"Who's getting married?" Abby suddenly wondered about Elsie, who Mose had been interested in at one time, and also whether Joe and Becca would be going through the ceremony. With the plans Becca had, she doubted it, but she wondered how Joe felt about waiting.

"No one tells until it's announced at church, and that's before harvest."

"What about you and Joe? Or can I ask you?"

Becca blushed and pulled on the reins when they got close to the house. "Joe has hinted at it." Then she became serious. "But you know why I can't commit right now. He had his time with *rumspringa*."

"You haven't told Joe?"

"*Nee*, I told you. You are the only one." She looked so deeply into Abby's eyes she knew this must remain a secret, one she couldn't break.

"This is really important to you, isn't it, Becca?" Abby didn't know where she got the courage, but she admired Becca even more for reaching out and doing what her heart told her to do.

"I've been planning this since I was a young girl. I've seen many Amish go out into the world and do things they regret. The images I formed in my mind from their experiences are engraved on my soul. I've never heard *Gott* call me more clearly than He did that day." She blinked and looked away. "I've never told anyone. But you being separate from everyone else gave me the chance to finally share it with someone." She took Abby's hand. "You're here for a reason, Abby. You need to find out what it is, just like I did."

Abby was moved by Becca's confession and her belief that Abby had a purpose there among the Amish. She couldn't imagine what that might be. They had served her. She had done little in return.

"You're pretty amazing, Rebecca Troyer." Abby beamed at her with admiration.

Becca's eyes welled up. "So are you. You just don't know it yet."

Her words gave Abby new strength and made her begin to wonder what God had in store for her. She smiled. "I've never had a friend like you."

"It's been quite a surprise for me too, you being an Englisher and all."

Abby laughed. "You say it like it's a dirty word."

"Heavens, no. If that were true, I'd be the worst of hypocrites." They both chuckled even though it wasn't that funny. It just felt good to laugh.

"What are you two giggling about?" Jake pulled on his gloves and walked over to Becca.

"*Hallo.*" She bent down and embraced him, and then he stepped back.

"That's the first hug I've gotten. Probably the last too." He grinned.

"If you'd ever give a little notice, it may help for people to get used to the idea that you're coming." He helped her down from the buggy, and Abby slid off her seat to the ground. "This is Abby." Becca pointed to her.

"We've met." He nodded toward Abby.

"How are you today, Jake?" Abby felt a little differently about him after hearing some of the story. She admired him for being honest, but she could imagine from his disposition that he may not express himself in a manner agreeable to others.

He looked back at her, seemingly surprised. "Better than yesterday, but the day's not over yet." He gave her half a smile, and for a moment she saw Mose. They looked so similar with their blond hair and blue eyes she took a moment before looking away.

"How long do you plan to stay?" Becca handed him as much as he could carry before she and Abby got the rest.

"As long as I'm needed. Not a day longer." His response was unreadable. He seemed to feel the need to be there more than a desire to be. Maybe not only to help with the flood damage, but also to be around people who used to be his own. Changing a lifelong decision had to be hard—even if you knew you'd made the right one.

"Who did you end up staying with?" Becca asked casually as they walked into the kitchen. It was too hot to have the food outside.

"The Yoders'."

They searched for a place sturdy enough to lay the spread of victuals on. Unloading all of the leftover food from lunch at the Lapps', they set up enough for people to snack on until supper.

Becca stopped arranging the food and stared at him. "How did that work out?" She had the nicest way of saying things, and Abby decided she needed to take notes.

"Well, I'm in the barn. I guess it's the only way I can be with Solomon."

"Don't let Eli hear you using his full name. He's sort of possessive of the little one."

Jake's expression changed from irritation to defensiveness. "I'm sleeping in the hog pen just to see him. I think I should be able to call him what I want." He shook his head and walked away.

Becca started working with the food again when some of the men came in. "I can't figure him out."

"It's all right. Neither can I." Abby got fidgety and took a plate. She picked at the food more than ate it. "I almost thought he was a different guy from the one I met earlier."

"I've known him all my life, but he's a stranger to me." Becca glanced at him.

"That's odd."

"*Jah*, that's just Jake."

As Abby watched others ignore him or give him cold glances, so unlike the Amish she had grown to admire for their friendliness, she became curious. "Why is everyone acting that way?"

"Jake's shunned. No one is supposed to talk to him."

"You and Mose did."

"I shouldn't have. But I can understand Mose wanting to have a word with him. He caused a lot of pain when he left."

She'd seen the way Jake dealt with her and Mose when he first arrived and the complete opposite with Becca until he turned on her so abruptly. Then Mose walked into the room, and Abby wondered how two brothers could be so completely different.

∽ Chapter Twenty-Nine ∾

ABBY FELT LIKE crying when she set eyes on her family's farm. It was as if no one tried to do anything to protect it from the storm, and afterward nothing had been repaired. There was no sign of the animals. She was glad Ginger and Blackie were safely in a nice bed of straw at Mose's place. The day after the storm had kept her occupied with life-and-death issues, but now that she was here, she wished she could have been in two places at one time. Jim didn't or couldn't do anything to save this ranch.

The runoff from the storm had stripped the fertile topsoil, creating thin lines of water through the dirt. The wheels on the buggy sank into the muck before they got to the house. "We're gonna have to walk the rest of the way." Mose walked over to Abby and helped her down.

She'd borrowed Becca's boots and was glad to have her help, but she only wanted Mose there with her. If things went well, Becca would meet Jim later. It was hard enough for Abby to have Mose there, but looking around the place, she was glad he was.

Mose was by her side as they walked up the road to the farmhouse. "It looks abandoned."

"I don't know where he'd go, except to the hospital."

The barn and other buildings were already in bad shape, but the storm had taken its toll, leaving them in scattered heaps of broken boards and beams, finishing some of them off completely. The ones still standing were missing boards, doors, and windowpanes, all needing to be replaced. But what worried her most was the animals. There wasn't a single one in sight.

"Where's the livestock?" she whispered.

"Most of the fence lines are down. They could have easily run off to the other farms when the storm hit." Mose's creased brow showed his concern, which made Abby worry even more.

With each step Abby took up to the house, she changed her mind. One step she wanted Jim to be there, the next step she hoped he wasn't.

The stairs creaked behind her as Mose followed. "Do you want me to go in first?" he asked, but he moved ahead of her without waiting for a reply. He turned the knob, but the door was stuck, so he slammed his shoulder against it. It scraped against the wooden floor as it opened.

Dust mites swirled in the sunlight, and the musty air was pungent. "It must have been empty for the last couple of days." Abby held her nose and went into the kitchen. Crusty food was dried on plates that were left out on the counters and in the sink. The tang of rotten milk was so strong that she gagged. She took the glasses to the sink to rinse them out.

Mose's hand suddenly clasped hers and pulled her away. "He's not here, Abby."

She stared at him, not wanting to give up yet. "We haven't checked the bunkhouse or the barn."

"There's no life here. Everything's gone." He didn't let go until she understood and was ready to leave this place to find Jim.

She nodded and took his hand as he guided her out. They walked over to the only two structures left standing, but nothing stirred in the eerie quiet as they walked the grounds. The sounds of her childhood were mute. No cows lowing their complaints to walk to the barn to be milked, no rooster crowing to wake them. Only silence, but it wasn't the peaceful quiet that she'd found at Meadowlark Valley with Mose. The ghosts that haunted her remained here, and that was all she felt from this place.

Mose seemed to understand and was quiet until they got to the buggy. "I'm sorry, Abby. I didn't think it would be this bad."

"This place was hit hard." She scanned the entire farm, slowly taking one last look before they left. She had to remember what

179

she was leaving, that it wasn't what she remembered growing up there. It had become as broken as the people who lived there.

"I'm ready." Abby closed her eyes as Mose encouraged Frank to pull them out of the mud pit where the wheels had stuck. Abby prayed they could get through. She didn't want to be there for another second. When she felt the wagon move, she opened her eyes and focused on the road.

Mose put a hand on hers. "Is there anywhere else you want to look or go to see someone he might be with?"

"No, there's no one else. Maybe we should go ahead and check the hospital." And that's what scared her. Since Jim had no friends or family to watch over him, he could have wandered off somewhere, and no one would know to look for him. She blamed herself for being gone so long. She knew how he was and that he was getting sick.

"Stop." Mose's voice jolted her out of her thoughts.

She looked over at him, wondering what was wrong.

"It's not your fault. If you wouldn't have left, you would have been a fool. And I wouldn't have let you come back any sooner than you did." He kept his eyes forward when he spoke, as if he didn't want to lose his confidence in telling her what was on his mind.

"Thank you, Mose. I needed to hear that." She squeezed his hand and admired the profile of his strong jawline and the slight bend in his nose that she was curious about. They were silent as they drove, but when they got on to the highway, she wanted to hear his voice, but not about any of the reasons they were there until curiosity got the best of her.

"What did you do to your nose?" She grinned slightly, glad to have something to smile about.

He scoffed. "My bruder hit me when we were messing around one day. I made him mad, and he popped me one. He caught it from my daed. But my mamm was even sorer at him than Daed." He grinned at the thought. "It was always fun watching Jake get it because he usually got out of punishments."

"Why do you think he didn't get caught?"

"Didn't have the conscience to 'fess up is my guess."

"But you would have told the truth even if you knew you'd be disciplined?"

"*Jah*, I never wanted to carry the burden of a lie."

"So, you did the right thing even if you got punished?"

He turned to Abby and studied her for a moment. "How does this relate to Jim?"

She smiled at his insight. "It relates to me, doing the right thing. I'm going to need someone by my side who will keep me on the right path. Because I can tell you now, there will be times that I don't want to."

"You got all that from my busted nose?"

"Your brother and Jim think alike in a lot of ways."

Mose looked over at her again. "You hadn't mentioned that before."

"You didn't tell me you had an older brother until he just showed up one day."

"*Jah*, I guess we both have someone who keeps us on our knees."

Abby smiled at the comment and said a little prayer right then, before she faced Jim, if they found him. If nothing else came of her seeing him again, she at least wanted him to know she'd tried. And all the things before this, like taking her mother's role cooking and cleaning after she died, and that she tried to be a good daughter to Jim, even though he was mentally as well as physically abusive, and she worked to help provide for them when he lost his reputation as a horse trader. He'd never appreciated anything she'd done, and she doubted she could expect it now.

When they got to the hospital, they were fortunate to be in a buggy, as the parking lots were full and they could squeeze into a space by a curb. Mose tethered the horse to a parking meter occupied by a small car and fed the meter a few coins. The closer they got to the front doors, the more anxious Abby became. It was even worse than the farm. This was unknown to her, and so was her father's fate. If he wasn't here, where else could they look?

They stood in line at the registration desk and watched the bustle of people going every which way. The waiting room was filled with people, and the employees looked harried and overworked.

When they finally got up to the desk, a clerk with puffy brown hair and bright-colored lips began asking one question after another. The barrage of information requested overwhelmed Abby, and she held up a hand for her to stop. "Jim Barker. He's my father. I just need to know if he's here."

"There's a certain protocol we ask each person, ma'am." The woman punched in some numbers in a computer and shook her head. "No one by that name is registered here."

"Where else would someone be who is hurt or needs help?" Mose leaned over and stuck his head over the desk to get her attention.

"You can check the churches. They're taking in the needy." Her heavy stare told them that was all the information they were going to get.

Mose took Abby's hand and led them to a quiet area where they could talk. "Is there any certain church he might go to?"

She shook her head. "He didn't go to church. But there's another hospital I want to check first—the St. Phillips Episcopal Hospital."

"The same name as the school where you teach. I should have thought of that. I hope your daed did."

She wondered how it would feel going back to work at the school after spending time with the Amish. She loved her job, but it was difficult to think about leaving Meadowlark Valley. And as she looked over at Mose, she especially couldn't imagine not being with him.

He kept her close as they passed by the line of people waiting for assistance and made their way to the buggy. The traffic was heavier than usual, but not as bad as Abby had thought it might be. A lot of people were on foot, going to grocery stores, fixing the mudslides that had caused damages, and repairing their shops.

"There's still a lot that needs to be done around here." Mose maneuvered through the people and traffic with more ease than the cars, and they were soon at the hospital. "It doesn't seem well organized."

"This is what you call quiet chaos." The organized ways of the Amish would be helpful in a situation like this. No one seemed to be helping each other, but she hadn't noticed any escalations or problems.

A nurse with blue scrubs caught them at the door. "Can I help you?"

"*Jah*, ma'am. We're looking for Jim Barker," Mose replied, peering over at the small computer she held as she tapped in some information.

"This way." She guided them into the crowded waiting area and pointed to the hall. "The elevators are down to the end. Go to the second floor, and you'll be directed to him."

Although helpful, everyone was abrupt. Abby knew she shouldn't expect more; there were a lot of other patients that needed to be taken care of. She was just anxious about the possibility of being so close to seeing Jim.

What will I say? What if he doesn't want me here? Will he be as nasty as ever, or will he be humbled?

If he was the latter of the two, Abby wondered whether she'd even know what to do with him. But she prayed for a gentle spirit all the same.

The *ding* of the elevator was sharp in her ears as she stepped out and then looked down the long hall filled with busy nurses and doctors. Mose walked away to ask a nurse where Jim was, and Abby slowly walked down the hall, looking for a familiar face.

Then she saw him. He lay perfectly still, with a breathing mask over his nose and mouth. His gray hair had turned white, and his skin had lost the touch of sun that was usually on his arms. His eyes were closed, and his mouth was open, as if to let in as much oxygen as possible.

She felt Mose's hand rest on her shoulder as he silently stood behind her for a moment. "Are you okay?"

She nodded, not ready to speak yet. Mose started to move his hand, but she reached up and held it tight against her shoulder.

What would I do without him here with me?

She used to be alone all of the time, but now she couldn't imagine being without him, especially now.

The nurse came in and put two fingers on Jim's wrist. "Are you relatives?"

"I am, yes. How is he?" Abby didn't recognize her own voice. It was so filled with emotion.

"I'll have the doctor come in and talk with you." She wrote on Jim's chart, smiled, and left.

Abby felt Mose's hand slip away and heard his footsteps. Soon he walked in with a doctor, who was explaining something to him. "You must be Mr. Barker's daughter. I'm Dr. Warren, the attending physician." He checked the chart and turned back to Abby.

"What's wrong with him?" Abby examined the machines. One was giving him oxygen, but she wasn't sure what the other was for.

"Your father has a tumor." Dr. Warren paused to let it sink in, but Abby only responded with a blink.

Numb as she felt, Abby made herself speak. She needed to know what was happening to him, whether she wanted to or not. "What does that mean?"

"If he would have come in earlier, we might have been able to help him. But at this stage, his chances of recovery are not favorable." The doctor's words were hard, but his demeanor was kind. "Did he show any symptoms of chest pains, fever, or weight loss?"

She shook her head. "No, the first time I noticed anything was when I saw him cough up blood." The remorse she felt grew.

If I had made him go to the doctor earlier, they may have been able to do more for him.

"Where is the tumor?"

"In his small intestine. That explains expelling the mucus and blood." He paused and studied her. "I can explain in more detail."

She shook her head. "What can you do for him?"

"We can do an endoscopy to find out the size and exact location of the tumor to see if chemo or radiation would help, or surgery, but I don't think he's strong enough to undergo a procedure."

Abby watched Jim's mask fill with condensation and his chest heave with each breath. "How long would he have without doing anything?"

"Medically speaking, not long." He moved forward and stepped closer to Abby. "But I've seen miracles happen." He patted her on the arm and walked to the door. "Let me know what you decide." He turned and walked out of the room.

"He makes it sound easy." Mose let out a breath. "It isn't fair for you to have to decide. I'm sorry it's left to you."

"He pretty much gave me the answer." She looked up at Mose. "Jim would be happier with my mother than with me."

"It's a quality of life question at this point." Mose looked over at Jim. "When he wakes up, maybe he'll help you with what to do."

"It would be good for him to decide, not me." She didn't want this burden. It wasn't fair to have gone through so much misery with him all of those years and have to decide what to do about his medical issues.

Why did I get the worst of Jim and my mother the best?

She stopped her thoughts. But he hadn't treated her mother well when Abby grew older. Looking back, she wondered whether Jim was envious of the attention her mother had given her. It would explain him abusing her. Nothing else made sense. And it explained his unreasoning disdain for Abby. She'd always felt it was something she'd done, but now she was realizing it wasn't her fault at all—or her mother's.

Mose's voice brought her back. "What about the miracles?"

Abby couldn't imagine anything even remotely close to something that pure or holy involving Jim. She swallowed hard as the reality of her family transgressions were revealed to her. The

185

worst part was she couldn't explain it to Mose. He wouldn't understand her not caring if her own father lived or died.

"If it's meant to be." She shrugged, not sure of anything at the moment—especially miracles.

"What is it, Abby?" Mose bent down to look at her, but she didn't meet his eyes, ashamed of what she was thinking. The more she thought about it, the more Abby knew she'd realized much more than she was willing to admit. It had taken Jim being near death to bring it up to the surface.

~~ Chapter Thirty ~~

MOSE WAS ANXIOUS to pick up Abby for Henry's memorial, knowing she would be going back to the hospital after the service. These were the times he wished she stayed at his home and they could leave together and communicate better. He decided to leave early to have some extra time with her.

Mose enjoyed the morning cool, before the heat stirred up the thick humidity. Most of the crops were beat up, half or completely gone. The autumn harvest wouldn't be plentiful, by any means. It would mean everyone gathering their crops together and sharing what they had equally. They would eat their regular fill, but they wouldn't have enough to sell and make a profit. The only good way of thinking about it was that they could put food on the table. Only one had perished, but one was more heartache than any of them could stand. It was a comforting peace of mind to think of Henry going on up to heaven with an angel by his side.

When Mose drove up to the Troyers' house, Abby was sitting on the top step waiting for him. He was pleased they could talk a little before getting to the service. As soon as she stood, Becca walked out with two of her sisters. He didn't want to appear rude, but he was a mite resentful that he and Abby wouldn't be alone. But he'd pushed that too far too many times. This was for the best.

Joe pulled up in front of Mose's buggy and grinned at him. "Morning, Bruder Mose."

Joe must have seen the irritation in Mose's face to grin like he was, but he wasn't going to pull out of it quickly.

"Mornin'." He switched gears and started focusing on the

meaning of the day. He shouldn't be thinking about himself first, second, or third. This was Henry's day.

"I hope it's okay to have the Troyer girls ride with us. Becca's folks sure appreciate it."

Mose must have given some clue that he was annoyed, because Abby and Joe were giving him subtle warnings. "No problem. *Gut* morning, ladies," he said in a most cordial voice.

"Thanks for driving us, Mose."

"*Jah*, it's nice to be together on a day like today."

The young women continued to chatter, and Mose politely responded when he should, and when he got the opportunity, he looked over at Abby to make contact. She tapped his knee and smiled at his reserved demeanor. The sensation of her touch distracted him from anything else he had been thinking about. She couldn't have realized the effect it had on him, and he was surprised that it did in such a powerful way. He hoped her attraction to him was the same as what he felt for her. A moment like that gave him hope that she did.

Mose dropped the Troyer girls off, and then he and Abby found a spot along a long thick rope that had been tied up to tether their horse. As they walked together to the Zooks' home, Mose instinctively wanted to hold her hand but didn't. Even though they knew they lived in two different worlds, Mose found himself forgetting she wasn't meant to be there.

The longer she stayed, the less foreign it felt to have her there. He could see that others were starting to feel the same. She could have been one of the Troyer girls to a stranger, and they wouldn't know the difference. Mose was becoming blind to it as well, and that was a dangerous place to be.

Abby's back stiffened, she stood straight, and her face was taut. Her eyes darted from one person to another in question. When she turned to him, he touched her hand. "It's just like most funerals. Don't worry."

Abby let out a breath she'd been holding. "Okay, good."

Many from the group near Beeville came to give their respects, overcrowding the room out past the front door. The setup at the Zooks' home was the same as any other Sunday. The plain pine casket was set up in the center of the room as Minister Miller gave a sermon. "Henry's earthly journey is over and his new life has begun."

Another sermon was given, and they sang a song. At the end of the service mourners walked past the family as the preacher recited Henry's name and said a prayer. There had been visitors at Henry's home, but the service wasn't over until the soil was placed on the ground around the headstone.

One of the elders led them in a song, and then Minister Miller read passages out of the Bible. There was never a eulogy, only the deceased's name said. The minister then gave a sermon and the congregation sang another song. With the service over, they got in their buggies and took the coffin to the cemetery in a hearse wagon.

When everyone got there, the minister led the mourners to the gravesite. The cemetery was not large, as they were a small community and not much time had passed since their arrival. So they hadn't had a reason to lay a soul to rest.

"Join with me in song." One of the elders led them in all four verses. The a cappella voices mixed together to make a varied, beautiful harmony. A white tombstone next to Henry's wife had only his name, date of birth, and date of death engraved.

"It seems there should be something more on the headstone," Abby mentioned as they walked past it.

Mose glanced at the tombstone. "Somehow, I find peace in that—a simple man with a simple tombstone, just enough to tell you he was born, lived, and died."

"Simple. I don't know how many times I've heard that word since I've come here. It has a whole new meaning here than it does out there." She pointed toward the highway that led to Beeville.

"And does it suit you?" Mose thought he knew what her answer would be, but he still found himself hoping she preferred this way of life that many Englishers thought was slow and boring.

"Simple? Hmm, I'm not sure…" She lifted her face to the morning sun and took in the air, and then looked over to him. "Peaceful. That's the word you used. Yes. Peace is what I've found here. That's what I like."

As they walked back to their buggies, no one spoke. A respectful silence reigned as each person got into his or her buggy and went back to the Zooks' for brunch. Mose and Abby stayed together as they ate, talked, and helped with the meal. Although they were not a couple, it felt as if they were, and others treated them that way also. When a question was asked, it was directed to both of them. His furniture business was implied as taking up a lot of *their* time, and her horse training had come to a temporary halt but was mentioned as something they both had the talent for. Mose wondered whether Abby picked up on it. He didn't know how she could have missed it.

"What did the minister mean about the beginning of a new life?"

Mose was glad she asked. He'd wondered what she was thinking about the ceremony. "It's a reference to what lies beyond, with a strong conviction he is taken by *Gott*."

Abby glanced around the room "Everyone seems surprisingly festive."

Mose watched people smiling and laughing. "We view death as a time of reflection when we celebrate the deceased's life. The opportunity to commune and eat together is always a joyous occasion. Usually the meal is at the deceased's home, but since there are no adults, Bishop Omar offered."

"Rachel and her brothers don't have relatives around?"

"*Nee*, they stayed in Virginia. Some of the older generation found it too hard an adjustment with the heat, and all. They're living with friends and getting along."

Abby looked to the ground and then back to Mose. "I feel like I should be doing that with Jim."

"It's harder in your case. It's part of our culture." Mose didn't want her to feel worse than she already did, but he also couldn't understand leaving your own flesh and blood to fend for themselves once they were too old to be self-sufficient. He took her hands and looked her in the eyes. "We'll go see your daed."

Her smile was all he needed to finish a full days' work in half a day so he could keep his promise and take her to her daed. A very selfish part of him wanted to keep Abby where it was safe and bring her daed to him so he couldn't hurt her. But he had no control over the situation, except for one thing. He would do whatever he needed to keep her out of harm's way.

The afternoon stretched on, and they spent time talking with Henry's boys. They had a farm to run, and a couple were school age. Rachel was used to doing most of the indoor chores, but the boys would need to discipline themselves to take the initiative. They took the information well, and Mose encouraged them to keep busy.

"I'm around too if you need me, as with everyone here."

Mose paused at hearing Abby's voice, appreciating her talking with the boys who ranged from his first day in school to the oldest in his eighth grade.

"But it comes down to you." Mose peeked around the corner at them, referring to the older boys.

The youngest one looked up at Abby. "Are we strays?"

She tried not to furrow her brows, but the reaction came anyway. The boy couldn't be more than five, but he was obviously a big thinker. "No, why do you ask?"

"When we find kittens in the barn, we call 'em that 'cause they don't have a mamm or daed." He scrunched up his nose as he waited for an explanation.

Abby bent down to look at him in the eyes. "It's different with animals. You're a special young man about to be running a farm. You're no stray." She looked around. "Every one of these people here is your family." She seemed to want to say more, but he was a little guy, and she probably didn't want to overwhelm him with more words. Mose noticed she'd said enough to make the boy's eyes soften a little.

Right on cue, Esther held out her hand to them. "Come with me and have a bite of my berry cobbler."

The boy smiled, but not as brightly as he probably could have. He silently took her hand. Abby winked at Mose, and then his daed walked up. He could already hear what his daed was going to say to them, so Mose shook the other three boys' hands and then caught up to meet Abby at the barn.

On their way he noticed Jake standing in the rear of the barn. He leaned back, watching as people ate and talked around him. For the first time in a long time Mose felt something other than disdain for his older brother. He'd always been a drifter at heart. Mose didn't understand why. Maybe he didn't have to.

"Jake!"

Jake looked for the voice and then spotted Mose. He gave him a half-smile, probably unsure of Mose's intentions. Mose realized he'd been hard on him—it was difficult not to, with the choices he'd made—but they were just that—his. "It's a fine day."

"I guess so. There are a lot of fine things to remember about old Henry. He was always good to me. Didn't find the need to form an opinion or make me feel low."

Mose didn't know whether he was trying to tell him something or was just being thoughtful. He saw the duffle bag at Jake's feet. "You leaving?"

Jake pushed away from the wall and reached down for his bag. Mose grabbed it a second before Jake did and handed it to him. "It was *gut* of you to come back."

Jake's hesitation was understandable. He was usually scorned for whatever action he took. Knowing praise was unfamiliar to him here made Mose's throat tighten.

"Thank you, brother." Jake grinned, then grunted, his way of pushing back the emotions. "It wasn't a prodigal son reception, but I got to see my boy." He slugged Mose's arm. "Didn't see much of you, though."

Mose was surprised that he'd care. Two very different people wanting to live a different way of life, they hadn't spent much time together since they were boys. Much like Abby, stuck in a place she wasn't meant to be in any longer. "Some people aren't in the right place and have to figure out where home is for them."

"Didn't expect to hear that from you." Jake grinned. "It's Abby."

"Maybe." Mose chuckled, wishing it wasn't so obvious. "Come back again."

He clasped Mose's shoulder and then turned and walked away. His cocky swagger gave off the appearance he was independent of them, but Mose knew he'd needed this visit as much as they'd needed to see him.

Mose went back into the house and then back outside, but not many gathered outside due to the muddy grounds. As he walked by the side of the house, he heard a slapping noise and what sounded like singing. When he turned the corner, he could see Abby's head above the banister. A group of girls were sitting in chairs or on the porch watching Abby and Esta play a clapping game. They were sitting across from one another, slapping each other's palms and thighs in planned-out moves to the rhythm of songs. The other girls were singing songs such as "Pop Goes the Weasel." Mose remembered some of the games his mamm used to play with them when they were young, but it was much different with boys.

He sat at the top of the stairs and leaned against the white wooden railing. When one girl missed a slap, she was replaced with another player. When the singing stopped, the girls spotted him and began to persuade him to play.

"*Nee*, I'd never slap someone." He teased, which only made them want him to play the game even more. They tugged on his arms, but they couldn't budge him, until one little bright-eyed girl looked him straight in the eyes and said, "Abby is awful *gut*."

Although competitiveness was frowned upon, Mose had a bit in him, especially in this situation. Abby grinned when he stopped resisting and let the girls drag him over to the empty chair. "Are you ready?" She held up her hands, eager to start.

"Hold on. I need a lesson." The minute he asked, three girls came over and started explaining the rhythms to him. He waved them away. "I'll pick the song."

"Fair enough." Abby agreed.

"You Are My Sunshine." He grinned back at her and watched her melt a little. They played two games that ended horribly for him, but he enjoyed every minute of it.

"Another game?" Abby was enticing, but he knew when he was beat.

"*Nee*, the loser asks for the winner to take a break." He rubbed his thigh in a bid for sympathy.

Abby chuckled and then stood. "All right, we'll let you heal a little before the next game."

The girls giggled, and soon two of them were playing the game with the others singing along.

Mose and Abby walked slowly in the afternoon sun, trying to avoid the puddles and muddy areas in the yard. "I hope it's okay to sing those songs. We do at school, and Esta never spoke against it."

"That would be up to the bishop. But on a day like today, it's *gut* to celebrate life after a death."

"I doubt you and your brothers played that one."

"*Nee*, can't say that we did, but I've heard the girls playing similar games at school. Sometimes I think the boys want to do it but wouldn't admit it."

"So you won't be playing it again anytime soon?" she asked playfully.

"Depends on who I'd be playing with."

She laughed. "You're a good sport."

"I guess that's worth my thighs stinging."

Her grin grew wider throughout the conversation, and he liked to see her smile. "It was nice to do something to lift the mood."

"That's the way Henry would have wanted it." Mose looked

up at the sky, thinking about his friend, Abby, and now her daed and the circle of life they were each in. "Should we give Ginger a visit?"

She looked over at him in surprise. With the prognosis slim that she would ever completely heal, the best thing for her was to rest the leg, leaving her with little to do but go out to pasture. But no horse would mind that. "What a good idea." They turned around and went to find Mose's buggy, telling where they were going.

Joe eyeballed Mose. "Is everything all right?" He looked from Abby to Mose. Joe was one of the few people who could see through him. Mose must have made a gesture or said something in a certain way to let his friend know he had something on his mind.

"*Jah*, just going to check on Ginger." He gave him a gentle handshake and then took Abby's hand. It just seemed natural, even if he heard about it later.

When they got to the Fishers' farm, they made their way to the barn with care not to step into too much mud. Old Blackie made himself known, not wanting to be left out as Mose let Ginger out into the corral. Blackie followed close behind, as they watched Ginger toss her head and buck. "She's got a lot of energy."

"I'll let them out in the pasture. They need the space." Mose went to open the gate and nodded to Abby that it would be best for the horse. She pampered Ginger like a sick child. Mose wanted to help her gain confidence that Ginger was healthy enough to do what any other horse on the property could do, but it just wasn't true.

As soon as the gate was opened, Ginger took off, but was partial to her bad leg. "I guess you were right. She can do pretty well with three good legs." It was a beautiful thing to watch her go, and even better that Abby had seen it.

They sat on an old wooden bench that looked out over the

acres of crops and livestock. "Abby, what will you do with your daed in a bad way?"

Abby's face tightened, and she took a moment to answer. "I will do what I'm supposed to do."

"Which would be?" He knew what was coming, but he needed to hear it so he could prepare himself. No matter how much animosity was between her daed and her, he knew Abby would do whatever he needed her to.

"It's terrible to say, but I keep praying there's a way I don't have to be his caretaker. Not just because of the physical and emotional abuse. It's just so hard to be with him." She paused and took in a ragged breath. "The only thing holding us together was my mother." She cleared her throat. "I'd be taking care of him for her."

Mose quietly watched her go through a flood of emotions. "That's just as *gut* a reason as any." He put his arm around her and pulled her close. "But if that's the case, you can't take care of him alone."

She moved away to see his face. "How would that work?"

"I don't have it all figured out, but you just can't. Not after what you've been through." He did have plans—big ones—but it wasn't the right time or place to tell her. At that moment, all that mattered was that he got her to agree she couldn't be alone with her daed. He didn't think it would be difficult to get her to cooperate, but he had a plan for that too if it happened. He'd never thought so much through or felt so ready to make sacrifices for someone. But for the here and now he would support her with doing whatever they could for her daed, no matter how difficult it might be.

Abby had been staring at him while his wheels had been churning. He didn't want to give her any answers, so a change in conversation was necessary. "Are you ready for me to take you back to the hospital?

Abby nodded, watching as the pink clouds were shaded with darkness as twilight drew near. "This is the best time of the day."

"It is peaceful."

She turned away from him and looked up. "But it's not just the sky. It's whenever I'm with you."

⌐ Chapter Thirty-One ⌐

ALTHOUGH MOSE HADN'T wanted to leave Abby at the hospital, at her insistence he rode into town to pick up Becca and Joe at the furniture shop. Mose knew better than to think Becca would leave without seeing Abby, but he'd pass on the message, all the same.

He tethered the horse and buggy, and then walked toward the shop. He didn't miss working there. Having a shop right out his back door was convenient and flexible. When he walked in, Joe was showing Becca the furniture he'd made.

Becca tapped Joe on the arm and walked over. "Did she see him?"

"*Jah*, he's in a bad way, so she hasn't talked to him yet. But for right now, she's just glad to know where he is."

Joe held out an envelope with Mose's last paycheck. "They said they'd take ya back in a heartbeat." Joe smiled.

"*Danke*. I'll be needing this for my own shop."

Mose didn't quite know what to do. He wanted to give Abby time with her daed, but he didn't like leaving her alone with him. Not because of her safety. Her daed obviously wasn't in any condition to hurt her physically, but the verbal abuse could be worse. And there were decisions to be made that would be hard for her to make alone, though it may come down to that.

"What's wrong, Mose?" Becca was staring at him with concern in her eyes.

"Her daed might not pull through, and that leaves Abby with decisions to make."

Joe looked down at his boots in thought. "She doesn't have any other family?"

"*Nee*, she was an only child, and her mamm passed away awhile ago." Mose waited for Joe to look at him. Joe was a sensible man, and Mose needed some good common sense about now. He had seen the conflict in Abby's eyes and knew she'd need a lot of help in making the right choices. The procedures the doctor was talking about doing would cost a lot and may not help. But if there was a chance they would make a difference, was it worth putting her daed through it? They were questions Mose wouldn't want to answer, and it made him feel for Abby even more.

"That's tough that it was just the two of them." Joe shook his head.

"What does Abby need?" Becca placed her hand on Mose's arm. "I'd like to see her, Mose."

"I'm sure she'd like that."

Mose led them to the buggy, but the drive was slow. It was around supper time, and people were probably driving home from work. By the time they got to the hospital, it was getting late. They didn't like to drive buggies on the highway after dark. It would have to be a short visit.

"Not much daylight." Joe climbed out of the buggy and helped Becca down.

"I won't stay long. But I have to see Abby." Becca didn't wait for a response. She was walking up the stairs before Mose or Joe had a chance to respond.

Anxious to see Abby, Mose led them to the room. He could tell her mood and how she would react just by reading her face. When she turned to see them at the door, he decided to caution Becca. "She's tired and stressed, worried about having to make decisions."

"*Jah*, I know. I won't talk long." Becca walked to her and pulled over a stool to sit next to Abby, who was seated in a chair. "How are you?"

"I don't know what I'm doing here, Becca." She slowly turned her head to see her dad.

Mose could feel the tension but didn't know how to help. At

this point, no one could, except the doctors, and the prognosis didn't sound good. They could only wait, the hardest thing to do.

"You're doing it." Becca gave Abby a warm smile. The sound of the oxygen machine push and flow was calming and maddening at the same time. "Just being here is enough right now."

"The doctor told me how much the procedures would cost." Abby's face contorted, and she let out a long breath. "We don't have insurance, Becca."

Mose's heart thumped. He couldn't let Abby have to make a decision like that alone. Not if it was a matter of money. "We can help with finances, Abby."

She turned around to see him. "I couldn't take money from you." He could see she was fighting back emotions that were right at the brink. Her nose flared and her chest moved quickly. "You've done too much for me already."

Joe stepped in and started to explain in a calm tone. "Don't get worked up about it, Abby. That's the way we do things. If someone needs money for something like this or anything else they can't tackle on their own, we all chip in."

Abby's face was a pink tint, and she let out a breath. "I couldn't pay you back."

"You don't. You just help out someone who needs help in return." Becca put a finger under Abby's chin, lifted her head, and looked her in the eyes. "Is that what the doctor said to do, surgery?"

"He said we could do the endoscopy to see where the tumor is."

"And then you'd decide from there?" Becca's soothing voice visibly calmed Abby.

As Abby was about to answer, Jim coughed and his eyes fluttered open. He turned his head to the side and saw Abby. One of the machines whined, causing a nurse to come in. Jim pulled at the mask with his right hand. The left arm went rigid against his leg. He stared at Abby with wild pale blue eyes. He opened his mouth to speak but couldn't.

"We should go." Joe took Becca's hand. "We'll wait outside."

Becca stubbornly stayed still until Joe pulled her up.

"I'll be back, Abby." Becca reluctantly walked out the door, leaving Mose and Abby with the nurse and then the doctor who came rushing in.

Mose stood behind Abby, far enough back to stay out of their way, but close enough for Abby to know he was there.

"What's happening?" Abby asked them, but they ignored her while they checked Jim's vitals. The beeping slowed and Jim's breathing became so shallow that his chest barely moved.

The doctor turned to them as the nurse continued to check the monitor. "I'll need to run some tests to know for sure, but it shows all the symptoms of a stroke." He bent over so he could make eye contact with Abby. "I know this is difficult. I'll do everything I can to get a definite answer and get right back to you."

"*Danke.*" After he left, Mose raked his fingers through his hair. Jim's health seemed to be going from bad to worse. He took the couple of steps between them. Abby and Mose stared at her daed. His eyes were barely open and his lips were moving.

"What is he saying?" Abby seemed as paralyzed as her father, unmoving and unblinking.

Mose walked closer to Jim and bent over to hear what he said. His pale eyes were uncomfortable to look at, almost translucent. Mose turned his head sideways to hear the two words Jim was repeating.

"Get—" Only a whisper of the graveled words eked out on a breath.

Mose slowly moved back and stared at the old man who seemed to be breathing his last few breaths.

"Out!" He rasped as his eyes focused on Abby.

Mose was stunned that this man could be so bitter and hateful even in this condition—and that he held such a heated grudge against his own daughter who had come here to see him. It may have been that he couldn't finish what he meant to say. That was the only way Mose could digest what he'd heard.

"Did he say something?" Abby's red-rimmed eyes stared deeply into his. Would he be doing her a favor by telling her, or was this one of those times when it was all right to change things just enough to spare a huge heartache?

"I think he wants some privacy, Abby."

She held up a hand. "Is that what he said?" Her pinched face and bloodshot eyes told him she couldn't take any more, and Mose decided to spare her with a lie rather than let her hear what Jim had said. Mose could pretend it was harmless and misunderstood. But the look in Jim's eyes told him differently.

"I'm not sure." He took Abby's arm and helped her stand and walk to the door.

She turned around once, but Mose quickly pulled her back. *This is what her daed wanted, so this is what he'll have.*

There would be no one to sit beside him waiting for test results or to talk with the doctors, someone who cared enough to be there. That person was turned away, and why? Because she'd left when he hit her? Took the horse that was hers? Came to the hospital to see if her daed was alive? What had Abby done that made him hate so much?

"Mose." Abby was watching him, hurt and confused. If Jim hadn't been a sick man, Mose would have been in that room telling him how much pain he'd caused his daughter. But Jim knew that, and he didn't care. Mose let out a breath. That was the hardest part to swallow. How could her own daed turn on her for something she hadn't done?

"I'm sorry, Abby. I guess he didn't want visitors." He tried not to look at her, to see her face that was confused and worn.

Becca and Joe saw them and came over. Mose glanced at each of them, plagued with worry. "Abby should eat something. And someone should take the buggy home."

Becca turned her gaze to Abby. "I'll stay with her."

"*Nee*, you two go back and rest," Mose insisted.

Becca and Abby embraced and then talked quietly as Mose talked to Joe. After a few minutes they returned to the room, which worried Mose. It seemed that something kept drawing Abby back.

Joe's eyes locked on to Mose's. "Is everything all right?"

"*Nee*. That's why I'm staying. There's more than just health issues at stake. That old man is a mean one."

Joe drew his brows together. "Even now?"

"I'd like to think I misunderstood him, but I'm afraid I didn't." Mose pursed his lips and looked away, then back to Joe. "Pray for me, bruder. I'll need strength to know what to do." He thought back to Abby's request that he keep her on the straight and narrow when it came to her daed, and now he understood why.

"Isn't there anything I can do to help?" Joe's concern made Mose back off a bit. This was nothing new with Jim, but it was more than he could take, considering the circumstances. Jim was dying but too stubborn to turn over a new leaf and accept the gift of his daughter's presence at his bedside. A part of Mose wanted to draw the hatred out of Jim before he was gone. That's what he should try to do, but the main thing on his mind was Abby and to protect her from Jim's miserable ways. She'd tortured herself enough without Jim making it worse.

Mose knew his reaction to Jim wasn't realistic. The man wasn't of sound mind to have healthy relationships before his health failed. Mose couldn't expect that to change now. It wasn't uncommon for people to square things up while on their death-beds, but he didn't think Jim would be one of those.

Becca finally came out of Jim's room and was ready to leave. "I feel a little better after talking with Abby. She has hope this might give her the opportunity to mend things between them, even if the worst happens."

Joe's eyes flickered over to Mose, waiting to take his lead.

Mose let out a breath and stared at Becca for a moment. "That's *gut* of Abby to hope for the best, but I'm not sure Jim will reciprocate."

Becca frowned. "I don't understand this man." She turned

and glanced back at Jim's room. Abby sat in a chair beside him looking out a window. "It's as if he doesn't know her."

"He has a lot of anger in him. I'm not sure why, but it's there all the same." Mose shifted his stare to Jim. His chest lifted slightly, taking in small amounts of air then sank slowly.

"Maybe it doesn't matter at this point. Just being here for him is enough for now." Becca raised a hand to Abby when she looked their way. Becca grabbed Mose's hand. "Take care of her, Mose."

"You know I will." As Mose watched Becca walk down the white tile floor over to Joe, he wondered whether what she said was true. Maybe no one needed to know just how hateful Jim was. But the knowledge of his harsh words was a hard secret to keep, especially if he became coherent and spoke them to Abby.

Mose woke and sat up in the chair, peeling his eyes open to see his daed sitting in a chair across from him. Turning, he saw Abby lying on a cot in the corner of the room. "When did you get here?"

His daed's tight face conveyed his discomfort at being in these surroundings. He was one of the Old Order who didn't appreciate hospitals. He'd have to be in dire straits to set foot in one. Mose was more than surprised he was there.

"Came into town to get some supplies and heard you were here, so I thought I'd stop in."

They both looked over at Jim, the reason they were all there. Mose knew this was his chance to talk with his daed about the financial end of things, but this wasn't the best place to bring it up.

"They might need some help with bills." That's all Mose had the energy for, and all that was needed. His daed would say yes or no, and that would be it.

His daed looked from Jim to Abby. "I've become fond of Abby. If I was told she was raised Amish, I'd have no trouble believing

it." He crossed his arms over his chest. "But this man here..."
He stuck out his bottom lip. "It's hard for me to forgive this man
for all we've seen and heard he's done." He sighed. "But the *gut*
Lord forgives me, so I'm called to do the same."

Mose wasn't sure where he was going with this, but one thing
about his daed, he was a God-fearing man, and that would work
to Mose's advantage in this case, although it brought up the bile
in his throat to be asking for help for Jim. "It's hard to figure
sometimes."

His daed tapped on the brim of his hat, where it lay in his lap.
"What's that, son?"

"Right from wrong."

"In this situation, it's best to err on the right. No use dwelling
on the wrong, even if it is. *Gott* takes care of the rest."

The longer he thought about Jim, the harder it was to see his
daed so easily help him unconditionally. Jim surely wouldn't do
the same for his daed if the tables were turned. "You mean ven-
geance is the Lord's?"

"*Jah*, son." He turned and stared at Mose straight in the eyes.
"Let it go." He stood and patted Mose on the shoulder. "You're a
gut man, Mose."

Mose tried to respond with the same thought about him, but
he was too choked up to speak.

⌐◦ Chapter Thirty-Two ◦⌐

ABBY SAT STARING at Jim. He had opened his eyes and stared at the ceiling for a second or two before closing them. This had just happened again, and Abby didn't want to miss the opportunity to say something to him if she had the chance. She was also waiting for Mose. After spending the night alone this time, she found herself missing him even when she was sleeping. She drew comfort from knowing he was there with her. But he had chores to help with, and customers were beginning to come to him to make furniture.

She looked out the hospital window. The parking lot was full, and people were walking in and out at a steady pace. Abby could see some of their faces filled with sadness, others with a smile. Abby wondered where she would be when this was all over. Jim seemed closer to death than life, but a part of her wondered if that was what he wanted. He led a bitter life, and he'd come to hate, not love those around him. And then there was the farm that was close to demolished. There was no life for her there. But did that still give her reason to stay with the Amish?

The hospital Bible on the bedside table caught her eye. She took it in her hands and looked up at Jim. If there was any way to forgive him, now was the time to try. Abby realized she hadn't been good about lifting up her transgressions toward Jim. She had made herself the martyr, overlooking the need to look inward.

She glanced over at Jim and then opened her Bible and spoke the words from 2 Corinthians out loud. "And in their prayers for you their hearts will go out to you, because of the surpassing grace God has given you. Thanks be to God for his indescribable gift!"

Jim stirred, then stopped, dead still as before. She wondered what state of consciousness he was in. Could he hear her? Did he even know she was there? She kept reading through the morning hours, speaking with a thread of hope that Jim could hear her. Even if he did, he would most likely be bothered by her reading to him, and not to mention from the Bible. For once she had the upper hand and he couldn't stop her, so she continued until her mouth went dry and her stomach growled.

"Your mother...stop..."

The sound was but a whisper, but Abby clearly heard the words. Her head snapped up and she turned to Jim. He was staring straight at her. Their eyes locked. If she even blinked, he would be gone again, so she sat stock-still. He didn't say another word, challenging her with his unblinking stare. But why? To stop reading? Stop the machine that was keeping him alive? Tears drifted down his cheeks. She didn't know if it was because he didn't blink or if it was an emotional response.

"Mom, *my* mom?" Abby moved closer and watched his eyes drift to the Bible she clutched in her hand. "Do you want me to stop reading?"

His head moved. Abby didn't know if it was a gesture telling her yes, no, or nothing at all. "Amish...she stopped..."

"She stopped what, Dad?"

When she said his paternal name, tears flowed down his cheeks. Then his eyes closed again. His face relaxed, and his breathing slowed. She stood over him, waiting to see if he would open them again. One thing she knew for sure was that he wanted to be with her mother. Abby's only hope was that he would be, that he had a quiet faith with God in some way, somehow. All she could think of to help with that thought was the Good Book.

"Morning. Or should I say afternoon?" The doctor twisted his wrist to look at his watch. The dark bags under his eyes showed his exhaustion, but he smiled despite the fatigue. "Have you thought any more about what to do?" He moved forward and checked Jim's chart.

Still shaken, Abby forced out the words the doctor needed to know. "He opened his eyes just now, and he spoke."

The doctor studied his chart and then the monitor. "I don't see any change."

He looked up at her with concern. "Could you understand what he said?"

"He said stop, I think. And something about my mother." She didn't know how much she wanted to tell him. He obviously thought her dad was too far gone to even believe he had responded.

"I understand. It's hard to let go." He looked at the monitor again. "But it would be helpful for us to have a plan of action in place."

"I've been hoping I wouldn't have to decide." This had thrown her off, but only for a moment. She looked over at Jim's worn-out body and knew what she would want if she was in his place.

He handled the chart and set it down. "You don't have any other family?" He frowned in question, confused over the fact she didn't.

Abby looked down at her hands in her lap and felt very alone. "No, I don't."

He grinned. "I'm used to the Amish saying *nee* instead of no."

She looked up at him, bewildered for a moment, and then realized he thought she was Amish. She was dressed in the appropriate attire and was with others who were. She opened her mouth to explain but then changed her mind. She not only didn't want to clarify, but she also felt comfortable with the faux identity. Even though she wasn't truly Amish, she liked the idea of it.

He crossed one foot over the other in thought. "When I said I've seen miracles, it didn't always mean the patient was healed. I meant the answer was given to the surviving family, clearly enough for them to feel they'd made the right decision." He looked up, waiting for her answer.

"He's not been the same since my mother died." She glanced at her dad again. "He's wanted to be with her for a long while." In thinking back, his anger had gotten worse when they knew her mother wasn't going to survive. It didn't make sense, it wasn't right, but that's the only logical way she could figure things out.

The doctor moved closer. "It sounds like you've made the decision."

"I just can't see putting him through this anymore." She searched the doctor's face for a trace of confirmation. Although he didn't say a word, she found solace in his presence.

He walked over to write on the chart again. "He has a Do Not Resuscitate, so that might make things a little easier."

Abby nodded her acknowledgment. Her emotions kept her from speaking, so she kept her head down, digesting what they'd just decided. She knew this doctor was going out of his way to help her, and he couldn't know how much she appreciated it.

She stood and offered her hand in thanks, but impulsively gave him a hug. She quickly moved away. "Thank you." It was all she could say without breaking down. But a part of her felt a sense of relief.

"I would have expected a '*danke*.'" He smiled and turned to walk out, but stopped short.

Mose stood in the doorway. His eyebrows drew together and his eyes flickered from the doctor to Abby.

"Excuse me." The doctor walked past them and Mose watched him go.

"What just happened?" Mose slowly turned his head to look at her. He walked into the room, closing the door partway.

"He woke up." She looked at her dad, watching his chest rise and fall.

Mose's stern eyes softened a little. "Were you able to talk to him?"

"I'd been reading him the Bible all morning, and I thought that maybe that was what he wanted to stop."

Mose shook his head. "He's still stubborn, until his last breath."

"He mentioned my mother stopping, something about her stopping the Amish."

"Is that possible?" They were quiet for a moment, and then Mose took her hand. "Maybe you broke his spirit enough for his stubborn heart to concede."

Her eyes moistened as she took in Mose's words. Abby blinked through the tears to see her dad's eyes blink then shut again. She took quick steps to him and bent over, lending an ear his way. "What? Tell me, Dad."

Mose sat with her, and within moments her dad's machine rang and the nurses and doctor came in. Abby didn't understand where the thoughts came from, but she found comfort in hoping that her heavenly Father took her earthly father, and he was with her mother again.

Mose sat waiting for Abby at the hospital. There was paperwork to fill out that he couldn't help with. They'd already agreed on selling her farm. That would hopefully pay for the medical bills, and if not, his community would pitch in. Now was a time of mourning and healing, and Mose planned to be with her every step of the way.

When she'd finished, they drove the buggy back to the community.

"What's all that?" He pointed to a folder filled with papers, brochures, and a Bible.

"Information for the funeral. He has a plot by my mother, but I'm not sure what to do with the rest. I haven't seen any of his family since I was young. The only friends he had were the ones he saw at the bar in town, and I never even knew their names. He didn't attend church, so he has no ties that I know of." She took in a ragged breath and put the folder aside.

He didn't know what to say but wanted to be supportive, so he offered the only suggestion he could think of at the moment. "We'll figure things out. Think on it a bit, and maybe something will come to you."

She nodded, and he watched her flip through the Bible with curiosity.

"What are you looking for?"

Abby stopped, as if she'd forgotten he was there. "I'm looking for a verse to give me some peace about my dad."

He understood. But he couldn't imagine how hard it would be to wonder about whether your own family believed. "'For the grace of *Gott* that brings salvation has appeared to all men.' Are you looking for something like that?"

She stared at him but looked away when her eyes watered. "Yes."

He held the reins with one hand and flipped toward the end of the Bible, stopping on Titus. "It's somewhere in there."

She found it and smiled at him. "Thank you. It's false hope, I know. He didn't have a belief in anything. Neither did I, except for the bits and pieces I got from working at the Christian school."

"But your mamm did, didn't she?"

She shrugged with exhaustion, and Mose wasn't sure she would answer. Her face darkened to a shady pink and she turned away. "She kept it to herself, more than I ever knew. Maybe she was scared to share it."

"What about you?"

"It wasn't worth it, knowing it would cause issues at home. The few times my mother did say anything, it just led to problems."

"What about now?" Mose didn't want to push too much, but he could almost see the desire in her eyes to learn more about the faith he and her mother lived by.

She fingered the pages of the Bible in her hand and glanced down at it. "I'd like to have what you have. What the community has, without doubt or fear."

He tried not to overdo, but he couldn't be happier to hear the words she'd just spoken. If there was any future for her to be in his life, making her faith a priority was the most important part. "I'm glad to hear that."

He had kept quiet about something that had been on his mind, but he couldn't hold back any longer. "What were you and the doctor talking about when I came in?" He turned to see her.

She smiled. "He thought I was Amish." She kept her eyes on the road and continued. "He didn't understand why I don't have any family members to help make decisions."

Mose was relieved to have somewhat of an explanation, but he still wasn't satisfied. "So you hugged him?"

Abby turned toward him. "Are you jealous, Mose Fisher?"

He couldn't read her face, but he felt foolish now for asking. "Just curious." He shrugged. "Why didn't you tell him you weren't?"

She was quiet for a moment, looking out over the ripe corn that would soon be harvested. "I sort of liked the idea." She glanced over at him. "Not that I would become Amish, but I have enjoyed the time that I've been with the community." She stuttered a bit and spoke quickly, obviously uncomfortable responding to the question.

Mose gave her a minute and then asked the question that had been rattling around in his brain for weeks. "If you like living in the community, why wouldn't you consider staying there?" He waited for the expected, reasonable answer that would close the conversation.

"I have considered living there, if there was a place for me."

He couldn't help but stare at her, and when he did, he could see the conviction she had for what she was saying, and he felt his chest warm.

"It's been more like a home to me than living with my dad."

Mose caught her eye and smiled, she used Jim's paternal name, a sign she might have forgiven him for the hard times during their last few years together. She was in a fragile state, so he tried to hold back from saying too much, but more than anything he'd ever wanted before, he wanted her to stay.

He knew part of his desire was selfish. It was a big commitment, and it had to be for the right reasons. So he thought through his words carefully. "This would be a good time to start over."

She nodded. "There are many things I like about living among the Amish. But there is one part that concerns me. The separation from the rest of the world is the way my father lived after my mother died. So I did too." She stopped and took a deep breath. "I know it's different in that there are a large number of people who live in Meadowlark Valley." She paused again and waved her hands. "It's completely different, really. But even those words bother me. I don't want to live separated anymore."

"We're separate from the outside world so we don't stray, not because we don't want to experience other people and their lives. It's staying clear of temptations." He hoped she understood. Because he was around the English when he worked in town, he had learned to talk about these questions to them. But he still had a lot to learn when it came to explaining their ways.

"I've been secluded for so long, I don't know if I can let go of the outside world again."

"Do you feel that way when you're in the community?" With each question he asked, he hoped for the answer he wanted to hear. There would be no swaying her. He had to stay as neutral as possible, considering how much he wanted her to stay.

Abby was quiet for so long, Mose wondered whether she was going to answer, but when he saw her face, he knew it was because she was giving her answers a lot of thought. "No...the more I think about it, the more it feels right." Then she looked up at the blue sky, thinking again. "But this isn't a *gut* time to decide anything. Once everything is taken care of with my dad, maybe I'll know better what to do."

Mose's stomach dropped. It wasn't fair of him to expect her to know or to think she realistically would end up in the community. His assumption that she would be with him was even more far-fetched. But he couldn't keep his feelings from coming into play. He was *ferhoodled* with her. As he took in her Amish dress, apron, and kapp, he could see why the doctor took her for one of them, and he liked the thought.

"Is that why the doctor said *danke*?"

She grunted a laugh. "*Jah.*" She teased. "He expected to hear that, as well as a *nee* and *jah* now and then."

Mose did admit he felt a bit of jealousy even though it was foolish. Simply the fact that he felt that way told him how fast and hard he'd fallen for her. She seemed to feel the same about him some of the time, but not always, and it made him wonder whether he was setting himself up for heartache. Only time would tell…but he wasn't in a patient frame of mind.

Chapter Thirty-Three

THE SOUND OF hammers and saws fast at work rang in Abby's ears. A dozen men were tearing down what was left of her family's farmhouse. Bittersweet emotions surged through her as she watched Mose throw down a handful of shingles from the roof. Her dad's funeral was the next day. All plans had been made, but somehow being at the farm made his passing surreal. She expected him to walk out the door and climb down the stairs, but the steps were gone, along with the rest of the structures. A few of the animals had wandered back, but there was nothing else worth trying to save.

When Mose looked over at her, she forced a smile. Abby was grateful for the men and women who had come out to help, and she knew this was what needed to be done, but it still stung. The house held both good and bad memories. The ones with her mother were tender. The time spent with her dad was a mix of confusion. In thinking back, she didn't really know what her relationship with her father truly was, and that's the way it had stayed until he died.

She watched Joe and Mose climb down the ladder and sit with Chris while they showed him how to pull out the nails from the shingles that could be saved and reused. Abby filled three glasses with sweet tea and walked up behind them. She slowed her walk when she saw their somber expressions.

"But you like her, right?" Chris looked at Mose with a furrowed brow.

"*Jah*, and so do you."

"So why don't you marry her?"

Mose paused as if pondering how to answer Chris. But he

215

didn't seem to know the answer, so Abby wondered how he could give Chris one. "She's English."

Mose handed him a handful of nails. "You're doing a *gut* job—"

"So why does that matter so much?" Chris interrupted without a blink.

Mose's usual placid face was pinched with discomfort. "Amish have different ways than the English." He grabbed a bag and handed it to him to put the nails in.

"If Abby learned them, could she stay?" Chris asked.

When she saw Mose's exasperated expression, Abby felt a lump form in her throat. She had thought long and hard about all of the questions Chris was asking. But from the way Mose was answering him, he hadn't. She let out a long sigh, preparing herself to give them their drinks without her emotions getting the best of her.

"It's been done." Mose finally answered, but he took a step back as if to end the conversation.

"She already lives with us." It was obvious by his questions Chris had no idea how uncomfortable the discussion was for Mose. Even Joe shuffled his feet as if he would prefer running away. "So is she gonna?"

Joe looked over at Mose. "It's hard to do, but if they all agree, the church will let them."

Mose nodded to Joe, as if silently thanking him for answering. His response made her wonder whether there was anything else Mose was agreeing with. She let her mind wander so far as to hope he was actually considering what was being discussed. If what Joe said was true, whether an Englisher could marry an Amish was up to each church.

Mose suddenly turned around to see her standing just a few feet behind him. Abby felt her face heat and broke eye contact. Joe turned to where Mose was staring with the same look of surprise.

"Come on, Chris. Grab your bag." Joe touched him on the shoulder to set him in motion.

Abby glanced down at the tray of glasses, almost forgetting why she was there. "I have tea."

"Just had some, but *danke*." Joe caught Chris by the arm.

"*Nee*, we didn't." He started to go to her, but Joe stopped him. Chris frowned at Joe but obediently followed his lead and walked away with him.

Abby threw back her shoulders and moved forward. "Thirsty?"

Mose took one of the glasses but didn't take a drink. "Did you hear us talking?"

She nodded, feeling guilty that she hadn't made herself known. Abby took a glass and then set down the tray on the ground. Mose sat on the trunk of a tree that had fallen in the storm. She moved over next to him, remembering the shade the old tree had given on hot days. "Some of it, yes."

"I would never talk about such things, but Chris is full of questions." He glanced over at her and then away as if ashamed.

"I understand."

He stood abruptly. "*Nee*, you don't. This should not be discussed by anyone but the couple."

She leaned back, shocked by his defensive words and stature. Then it clicked. He was telling her she didn't know their ways, and this was one of them. But she also knew he was probably embarrassed and took that into account. "Then why were you talking about it?"

He pursed his lips and sat down hard, causing the tree to creak. "Chris is fond of you. I wanted to set him straight." Then he looked straight into her eyes. "I didn't want him to be disappointed or misled."

Abby's heart thumped. He wasn't just talking about Chris. Abby thought she knew what he was saying, but with the intensity of his gaze she wanted to know for sure that she understood what he was referring to. Abby only became more confused. She couldn't stand the way he stared at her, so she looked down at the bark peeling off the tree, once so vibrant and alive. "I'm sorry I didn't leave when I heard you talking, but I have the same questions that Chris does. I wanted to hear the answers."

She made herself look at him. Abby needed to see his face to know what he was really thinking. If only he wanted to make the effort for her to stay the same way Chris did. But it was good for her to know Mose didn't have that same desire. "*Your* answers."

He slowly turned to her. "I was just teaching him our ways—"

She stood up next to him. "You don't need to explain." Abby didn't want to hear his reasons for not wanting to go through the demands of committing to an Englisher. He had a right to how he felt. She just didn't understand how she could have misunderstood their relationship to the degree she had.

Mose moved a step closer, but before he could speak, she walked away.

She faintly heard him say her name, but thoughts of her dad filled her mind, drowning out Mose's voice. She'd lost her father, and now this with Mose. She sucked in a breath. There was nowhere for her to go. The community had become her home. Regardless of what happened between her and Mose, she didn't want to leave. The biggest piece she hadn't let soak in was her dad's last words.

Something about the Amish? He had no patience for the Amish, but she had come to admire them. What an odd shift that would create in her life. To live among them.

When the sun had almost disappeared, they packed up and rode back to Meadowlark Valley. They had made good progress on leveling the buildings and cleaned up the place better than it had been for years. Abby rode with Mose and his family, but she didn't have much to say. Her mind was in a whirl, conflicted, between Mose and her dad and also her mother. Although one had nothing to do with the others, they tangled together in her mind. Mose gave her quick glances. Whether they were of remorse or concern, she wasn't sure.

Abby looked out over the open grass land scattered with cacti and shrubs. "Farming wasn't meant for Texas," her dad would say, believing that raising livestock was the only reasonable way to make a living. Sheep and cattle were the norm, making ranchers a good living. Then the Amish had come alongside the few farms that existed and found soil that they could work with. She looked at each member of the Fisher family and felt the same admiration for them she had when they'd taken her in on that horrible day that seemed so long ago.

Maybe she was more attached to the community than she realized. Maybe it wasn't so much about Mose as she thought. But when she watched him as he drove the buggy with his capable hands and strong arms, she knew it was more than just the people she had fallen in love with. As much as she didn't want to admit it, Abby was enamored with the entire package, but it started and ended with Mose.

As soon as they pulled up to the house, Becca was by her side. The bond between them was stronger than any friendship she'd ever known. Abby was vulnerable and needed to confide in someone. She hadn't been this out of sorts since her mother died, but this time it was so much different being older and living in an Amish community, of all places. As she watched the women there, Abby wondered whether she would honestly be accepted or whether she was still just a friend on a long visit to get her life together.

"What is it, Abby?" Becca hooked arms with her and was dragging her away before she was even off the buggy.

"I'm not dealing with anything very well."

"Why do you expect yourself to? There's been too much happening for much of anything to make sense right now." She stopped when they were away from listening ears. "Tomorrow will be difficult. At least this day is almost over for you."

Her simple but consoling words were as gentle as a healing balm, covering Abby's emotional bruises and cuts. All but those created by Mose...or had she misunderstood? "I shouldn't say or do anything until I feel right again."

Becca took a moment to study her, but Abby wasn't

uncomfortable. She had gotten used to Becca's gestures and behaviors. "What do you mean?"

Abby waved her hand as if to dismiss what was really tearing her apart. "It's nothing, just my emotions running away with me." She glanced at Becca, who was eyeing her suspiciously. "Really."

She smiled to cover up her hurt and gave herself permission not to think of her dad or Mose while she helped prepare supper. A chore she once did begrudgingly, it now provided satisfaction and growing relationships.

Abby tried to appear interested in trimming the excess dough off the cherry pie she made. When she noticed Esther watching her from the other end of the room, she knew they would be having a conversation Abby didn't want to have. Esther gathered the pieces of dough and rolled them into a ball.

"That's a beautiful pie, Abby." She handed the dough to her and leaned against the counter so Abby couldn't see Becca, obviously wanting her individual attention. "Mose's favorite."

Abby blushed. She knew that, but she hadn't intentionally made the pie for him. Or had she? She was flustered, uncertain what was bothering her and how much attention she should give to everything that was brewing inside of her. "It hasn't been a good day."

"And tomorrow will be worse." Esther's sympathetic eyes spoke of her true concern, and Abby knew it was as strong as what she felt for Esther. This woman had taken her in without question and never said an unkind word to her or judged her situation.

"Thank you for everything you've done for me." The well kept springing up, more like a tidal wave that couldn't be stopped. She had no more energy, and she hoped nothing else would take her over the top.

"*Nee*, Abby, thank you for making my son happy. We're blessed to have you."

Abby choked on a sigh. She was the one who was grateful, yet every person she came into contact with brought out what she cherished about them, making her wish even more for a place there. Even those who didn't know Abby as well showed a quiet sense of mourning with her and understanding for her ridiculous sentimental outbursts.

Esther's touch on Abby's arm started a rush of tears that rolled down her cheeks. Abby fumbled with the pie and lost her balance, and it went *splat* onto the wood floor. She bent down, grabbed the tin, and tried to wipe up the gooey mess.

"It's all right." Esther's hands touched Abby's. "Let me."

Abby stood, wiping her tears, and rushed to the door. She kept walking until she found a spot by the river and sat down on the ground. As she watched the rushing water, the tension of the day began to float away with it. She hugged her knees and rested her head on them, listening to the rhythmic sounds of the never ceasing river.

She heard something behind her but kept her eyes closed, wishing for solitude. Someone sat down next to her but said nothing. It was then she knew it was Mose. She didn't move, feeling at peace with his presence in the comfortable silence. Fearful for what his answers might be, she didn't ask him about what they'd discussed earlier that day. She wasn't Amish, and he would never leave his community. There was nothing left to say.

⌐ Chapter Thirty-Four ⌐

HE DISTANCE BETWEEN them was both physical and emotional. Mose watched Abby climb into a buggy with Becca without so much of a glance his way. What had he done for her to distance herself so? His explanation to Chris was just that—the particulars of how the Amish dealt with outsiders wanting to join their community. He didn't make the rules; he just lived by them.

Mose followed behind her. He knew from the sloping of her shoulders and her lack of conversation with Becca that she was fully mourning Jim's death. Mose could only imagine the torture she was putting herself through, wondering what would have happened if she'd found him earlier. If he could talk with her, he'd tell her that and a lot of other things to help ease her pain.

"Pay attention." His daed called out beside him as a car went flying past them. "Watch the road, not the buggy in front of us." His daed glanced over at him. "Everything all right?"

"Is the railroad bridge still closed?" Mose asked to keep from answering the question, though he honestly didn't know how much had been repaired since the storm.

"*Jah*, but Highway Fifty-Nine is open." His father looked out at the feedlots where cattle had been stranded during the flooding. There were about half the number of cows as usual, but the aroma was as strong as ever.

As the buggies pulled up to the funeral home, bystanders stopped and watched, mainly tourists who were finding out the Amish had moved to the area. Those who lived in Beeville were used to them.

Mose tethered the horse next to the others, all in a row. As they continued to file in, Mose was touched by how many from the community came to the ceremony, and those who couldn't had already paid their respects to Abby. Some were too frail, others under the weather, and many of them stayed back to prepare the meal after the funeral. Each had a way of helping according to his or her talent. Mose expected this of the Amish, but they were treating Abby like one of their own.

He and Abby joined together as they walked up to the funeral home, but neither spoke. No one did as they entered the large foyer. Mose watched her face tighten as she looked around the room. The flowers and coffin were just a few feet away. He saw her chest rise and release, and then she took slow steps to view her daed. Mose followed behind her.

"His gray hair seems lighter." Tears welled in Abby's eyes as she spoke her thoughts out loud. "His cheeks are so hollow."

The cancer had taken its toll and consumed his body. He looked as if he'd passed away a long time ago, and in a metaphorical way, he had. "I'm sorry you have to see him like this."

She clasped Mose's hand and squeezed once tightly, then let go and walked away. He didn't follow, wanting to give her some space, but he kept a close eye on her as she spoke to those gathered. He knew her well. With every facial expression or word she said, he knew what she was thinking, and sometimes he could tell how she felt. Although people meant well, they didn't know her dad. Some knew he was the reason why she'd come to their community, but that was all they needed or wanted to know.

When everyone had taken a seat, Mose and Becca walked with Abby to the front row of the small chapel. Many stood in the back, but the service was short because there was no one there who knew him, except Abby and Mose. Not a single English soul had attended, but an Amish community whose only connection was his daughter was there. Mose turned slightly and studied her. She looked and acted much like any of the rest of them and seemed comfortable living with the Amish.

He turned away. But she wasn't. And as much as Abby meant

to him, it wasn't possible for Mose to ever leave this group of people or their way of life. It wasn't even a consideration.

The ceremony was short. "Amazing Grace" was sung, which Mose thought appropriate considering Jim's doubt. The pastor gave a generic sermon, and did as well as one could, not knowing the deceased. Then they were released to the next room for refreshments, but few stayed. They went back to Meadowlark Valley to prepare the midday meal. Mose's family was the last to leave, sitting in the foyer quiet as church mice.

"You don't have to stay with me, Mose." Her voice was raw from crying, and when she looked up at him with bloodshot eyes, he knew he couldn't leave her.

"I'll wait." He wouldn't be swayed. Becca and Joe waited outside. Mose's family left, leaving Mose and Abby alone in the funeral parlor. When he came back in, she was praying, head bent and fingers intertwined. He knew how conflicted she was about her faith, but there was a peace about her that gave him hope she was growing spiritually. If so, she might be able to deal with the loss as *Gott* intended. He sat down beside her and did some praying too.

When he opened his eyes, she was smiling at him. Her features had transformed from dark to light. *"Danke."*

He chuckled at her choice of word. "There's nothing to thank me for."

"I have everything to thank you for. If it weren't for you, I'd be doing this alone. And I wouldn't have a friend like Becca or a community of people who support me." She put her hand on his. "Thank you, Mose."

His eyes misted, partly because of Abby's gratitude, but also because he wanted to share the life he had with her but didn't see how that could happen. Even after all she'd said, there was no mention of her wanting to stay. She knew the conditions, but she had made no commitment to make it happen. He had hoped he meant enough to Abby for her to consider it, and it hurt that he was wrong.

Mose waited out front while Abby firmed things up with the funeral home. Once she had a buyer for the farm, Abby would have some money to help her out. With all of the beaten-up buildings, tearing the place down was the best way to sell it, even before the storm. It was one less thing for Abby to deal with that took an emotional toll. Mose had wanted to talk with the funeral director with her, but she was set on taking care of the business, as well as everything else concerning her daed. "Were you able to work things out with them?"

"The funeral costs weren't too bad. Now I need a serious buyer for the farm to pay the medical." She looked at the sun overhead, then back to Mose. "Do you think Joe and Becca would mind stopping at the farm one last time?"

"I bet they'd be happy to take you, as long as I can hitch a ride. Mine left, already."

She grinned. "Always..." was all she said. She seemed to want to say more but forced her lips together.

The warm sun beat down on the ten acres of land that was Abby's home. Most of the fields had finally dried out, but the topsoil had been stripped away, creating a tough planting season. Autumn harvest was around the corner, along with "wedding season," as Mose put it with sarcasm, despite his mamm's disapproval. He admitted he was envious of those who joined together each year, and another year had rolled around without a significant other for him. As he looked at Abby now, he wondered how he'd mixed the signals up about the two of them.

"It's so bare," Joe commented as he scanned the area. "Did it grow pretty *gut* crop?"

Abby took a minute to answer, as if she was lost in her thoughts. "I remember it did when I was a girl, but not over the past few years. My dad pretty much gave up on everything. Looking back, I don't know how we got along."

"How did you?" The question slipped out before Mose could think. If she wanted to answer the question, she would have.

"He was a horse trader but lost his reputation after making

some shady deals. But as I got older, he was gone for longer periods of time. I think he went to nearby towns where people didn't know him and did some trading." She kicked a clump of dirt. "Things changed after my mom died."

Joe and Mose looked at one another. They hadn't had to face the same obstacles Abby had. They had a set of their own, but family wasn't usually a great problem. The difference between them was that Amish didn't give themselves the option of second-guessing or backing out. They stuck things out despite their differences, through whatever hardships came their way. It didn't make them better, just made life a little easier.

"The next family who lives here will make a *gut* home for themselves." Becca smiled at Abby. "All of the *gut* memories you have here will live on for them."

Abby gave her a sad smile. "You always find the good in everything."

Joe scoffed. "You're right about that." He grinned playfully at her. "Take your time, Abby. I'm gonna take a load off and sit in the buggy."

"I won't be long." Abby was turning away as she spoke, heading for the foundation that had once been her home.

As Mose made his way over to her, he tried to put himself in her place but couldn't. There was nothing he could say that would make any difference in the way she must be feeling. "I'll give you a minute."

"No," she said on top of his last word. She turned backward but didn't meet his eyes. "Stay, please."

He didn't answer. Abby knew he would; all she had to do was ask. He watched her take careful steps so as not to dirty her shoes, staying clear of the puddles of mud. She walked the perimeter of the cinderblocks that were still visible and stopped where the front door used to be. Abby looked around the grounds and rested her scrutiny on Mose. Her stare was so intense, it became unnerving. It was if she was reaching down into his soul, searching for every last bit of him.

He had to break the tension. "Are you ready?"

She nodded, walked up next to him, and thanked him before sitting in the backseat with Becca. They were quieter than usual on the drive home, but when they were almost there, Abby and Becca started up a conversation about tomorrow being wash day.

"Becca, you know how much I've appreciated staying with you and your family."

"You're like a sister to me, Abby. You don't need to thank any of us. I'd miss you if you ever left."

Abby paused. "When school starts, I'll need to decide if I should find a place in town."

Mose couldn't see her and didn't want to be obvious and turn around. He peered into the mirror in the side door, but he couldn't get a good look at her. He'd known this day would come, but not this quickly.

"You could take a little more time to heal." He wished he could say something more profound, but his mind was whirling. This was too soon. She might think she was ready, but he would convince her she wasn't. "And you could still help out here."

"*Jah*, I don't want you to be alone—not yet. Not ever, if it was up to me to decide." Becca's voice wavered, unusual for her. Her soul was gentle as much as it was strong.

"I can't stay at Meadowlark Valley forever." Abby's mechanical voice, unemotional and dry, was much the same as when Mose had first met her, not the vibrant young woman she had become over the last weeks.

Mose tried to contain the rage that was building in his gut. He didn't have much of a temper, but when he did, his emotions went beyond reach. He raked his fingers through his hair once, and then again, trying to shake the reality of what Abby had just said. He forced his straw hat on his head as he stewed.

"It will be hard to leave, though." Her words were spotty through the anger in his head. At least she'd said that something made it a harder decision than when she'd first made her announcement. He would have liked to be the first to know.

227

The minute the wheels stopped, Mose was out of the buggy. He tried to stay put but couldn't. There was nothing she could say that would calm him down at this point, so he marched home. Thoughts flew through his head. One minute he was so angry, he tried to trick himself into thinking he didn't care. The next second he was trying to figure out ways to talk her into staying.

His boots hit the ground in rhythm with his breathing, in and out, until the repeating sound calmed him. He glanced behind him to make sure no one had followed him. He was in no mood to be around anyone, but that was difficult, so he made a dash for his bedroom. He was almost to the landing when his mamm stepped from her room with a basket of dirty clothes.

"What happened to you?" She moved the basket under her arm. The crunchy sound of the wicker pierced his ears.

He didn't want to talk, especially with his mamm, and thought of a number of excuses not to talk, but he knew his mamm wouldn't let him go without an answer. He took the easiest way out. "Tired. It's been a long day."

"The sun's not down, so the day's not over." She motioned to the basket of clothes she'd gathered to wash the next day. She read him too well, and he was not in the right mind to deflect her.

"Let Chris do the milking. I'll make it up to him in the morning." He took the last step up the stairs and rounded the banister toward his room.

"Aren't you going to eat supper?"

He felt like a child, going to pout in his room and ditch his chores. He let out a long breath and looked at his mamm. She set down the basket and waited.

"Abby is leaving." He looked down at his dirty boots. Knowing his mother's pet peeve, he stopped his thoughts long enough to know he should have taken them off.

"Why? Did you two have a disagreement?"

He shook his head, wishing he wouldn't have told her, but he knew she could see right through him, so he had no choice, and that made him angrier.

"Then why would she leave?"

"Wants to go back to teaching in town." He said it quickly as if it was poison on his tongue.

"Humph, I thought you two might get together."

Mose's anger simmered as his curiosity grew. "You did?"

"Why does it surprise you? You did everything two young people do when they're courting."

When he thought back, she was right. He just hadn't considered being with an Englisher would hold the same merit as if he were with an Amish girl. "She's made no gesture or talk of being with me. I was dense to think she might. Abby needed help, and I gave it to her. I've served my purpose." He could hear the bitterness in his voice. None of what he said came from the heart, but he kept sputtering it out all the same.

"I've never seen you so passionate about anything in your life, Mose Fisher." She half smiled, and her eyes misted. She made him want to dig deep down and let it all out, but his defenses wouldn't drop to a level that would allow him to. The thought of being rejected was too daunting.

"What am I supposed to do about it?"

"Tell her how you feel. If you don't, you're being prideful."

He frowned at the accusation. "She's English." He threw up his hands in frustration. "And she hasn't said anything about staying here, so that ends it."

"Have you made the offer?" She lifted one eyebrow in question.

"You want me to marry an English woman?" He scoffed, confused to the point of wanting to run away like a child.

"If I wait for you to marry an Amish girl, I may never have the pleasure of seeing more grandchildren."

Mose's head snapped up to see his mamm smile and realized she might be right.

~ Chapter Thirty-Five ~

ABBY HARDLY SLEPT. Not wanting to talk to anyone, she had turned in early. Becca, being Becca, seemed to understand and didn't prompt her to discuss her decision. Abby knew she owed everyone more of an explanation. The first person she needed to talk with was Mose. It had tugged on her heartstrings to watch him storm off. She regretted not telling him alone, but she'd finally gathered the courage to tell them and wanted to get it over with. She hadn't intended to hurt Mose so much.

She turned over in bed and watched the sunrise, feeling the familiar calmness that she'd noticed when she first came to the community, so unlike the tense environment she had lived in for years after her mother died. When she thought about leaving, the stress came back, but she couldn't stay and live this close to Mose and not be with him. She cared about him in a way she had never felt toward anyone before, but if he didn't feel the same, she couldn't bear to stay. She wondered whether it was because she was English or whether the feelings just weren't there.

If they were, he would have made an effort for me to stay.

"Becca, are you awake?"

"*Jah.*" She sat up and rubbed her eyes. "Abby, I'm worried about you."

"Don't be. It will all work out."

"Don't try to be strong with me, Abby. What do you really want?"

"The people of this community, your faith, and Mose." Abby feared she would get emotional, so she avoided Becca's eyes. It was that simple. No matter how complicated she made it in her

230

mind, it came down to him. Suddenly she said, "I'm going to see him."

"*Gut*, very *gut*." Becca threw off her quilt and jumped out of bed. "Abby, don't let pride separate you." Becca was so kind in the way she rebuked others. It was gently spoken, not to hurt but to help.

"I don't know what to think, Becca. That's why I'm going to see him." She jumped out of bed and hugged her friend, more eager than ever to go to him.

Abby dressed and walked out the front door to avoid going through the kitchen where the girls were making breakfast. The smell of bacon wafted through the air, but she had no appetite. She passed by the two farms between Becca's and the Fishers' and soon ran into a group of children walking together in groups. Esta came up behind her carrying a bundle of books. The sight of her made Abby's heart twist. She missed teaching. That was one thing she knew for sure. Someday she wanted to take more classes to get certified and have a class of her own.

"Morning, Esta. Where are you going with all of those books?"

"We're going to the new schoolhouse and dropping off our supplies. The parents are there having a meeting. Are you going?" She tucked a blonde wisp under her kapp and happily marched down the dirt road.

"No. I'd like to, though." Abby was curious, but it made no sense for her to attend.

"So you're going to see Mose, then?" Esta crinkled her nose and squinted against the bright sun. Surprised the child would notice, Abby took a moment to respond, then nodded. "But I may stop by, if that's all right."

"See you later, then." She gave her a quick wave and ran up to some girls, chatting away. Abby felt the excitement and wished she was part of it. As Esta talked to her friends, they turned around and waved while they giggled.

Esta probably told them about Mose, which made Abby wonder what people in the community felt about them. She was never one to care what others thought of her. She'd never been truly accepted or cared enough to want to be, until now.

When she reached the Fishers' farm, Abby went straight to the milk barn. Mose should just be finishing up, and Abby knew she would be alone with him and he couldn't leave. She didn't know what to expect, but she owed him a private conversation. The closer she got, the more nervous she became. What if he was still as upset as he had been yesterday? She didn't know how to deal with *that* Mose. But she'd come this far, and it needed to be done.

"Morning." When he didn't respond, Abby wasn't sure if it was because he didn't hear her or that he was ignoring her. He turned and startled when he saw her. His face tightened, and he looked away.

"Mose, do you have a minute?"

He pointed to one of the milking stools they used when they milked by hand, before the gas-powered units were approved by the elders. The stools had one middle leg to balance on so the person milking could lean in under the cow. Mose sat down on his with no effort. Abby sat on her stool but wobbled around, trying to gain her balance.

"I'm sorry I didn't talk to you first about my plans. It just came out. And honestly, I wanted to get it over with." She paused to see if she could gauge him, but his face was void of any expression, so she continued. "I appreciate everything you've done for me. You know that I do, Mose, but I can't stay here indefinitely—"

"Why?" His lips didn't seem to move, but he said the word so loud she knew he had spoken.

"I'm not a member of the community." She stated what she thought was obvious, but when he didn't respond, she added more. "It's not like I can just stay here forever without some sort of recourse." She waited for him to say the words she wanted to hear, hoping he would tell her he felt the same way about her that she did for him and wanted her to stay.

"You know you can. You heard me telling Chris." His blank face was worse than if it had been red with rage.

"Exactly—you told him, not me."

His eyebrows drew together, and his mood was condescending. "And through that conversation you learned there was a way for you to stay here if you wanted to."

She shook her head, causing the stool to wobble, and reached down with both hands to steady herself. When Abby looked up at him, she noticed him ready to reach out and catch her. She lifted her eyebrows to caution him. The conversation wasn't going as she'd hoped, and even though the stool was irritating her, she didn't want his assistance.

"But it wasn't directed to me." She placed her hands on her chest to express what she was saying and caught herself before the stool fell over. When she looked up, he was hunched over with his fingers intertwined, grinning up at her. She stood to save face before she went tumbling down off the stupid, little stool.

"Everything I said to Chris was what I've been wanting to say to you. But I've gotten so many different signals from you, I didn't." He crossed his arms across his broad chest.

"You don't exactly wear your emotions on your sleeve either, Mose."

Mose frowned with confusion at her turn of phrase, exemplifying their different cultures. "As much as you like it here, I had hoped you might stay. But I guess I was wrong." His voice continued to rise with each word, the fire in him heightening. He stood abruptly and hung up the stool.

"If I stayed here, it wouldn't just be because of the community or the way of life. It would be because of you." As soon as she said it, Abby felt so exposed, she had to turn away. He stared at her, his jaw dropped, but he didn't speak. She turned, kicked the stool, and walked away. She heard him say her name, so she walked faster and didn't stop until she got to the dirt road. Abby wanted to look back but didn't. If he wasn't there, she'd be hurt, and if he was there, she'd be angry, so she kept walking.

"Abby." Esther sat in her flower garden, waving to her.

Abby hoped she hadn't overheard her conversation with Mose.

233

She was disappointed at the way it had turned out and embarrassed about the way she'd left him. She let out a breath, and then walked over and climbed up to the porch. She stopped, noticing a blue patch of flowers. "Those blue flowers are beautiful."

Esther stuck the spade into the dirt and smiled at her. "How are you, Abby?" Her face showed small lines from age, but she was still a pretty lady with a lot of wisdom and energy. Abby wondered whether she could be the woman and mother Esther was. She was so far from knowing what she wanted for her life at the moment. She couldn't even imagine being anything like Esther.

"I honestly don't know how to answer that question." Abby sat down and hugged her knees, and they sat quietly together looking over Esther's garden. Pink-lace cactus flowers and yellow daises among a plethora of other plants filled the white picket fencing that surrounded them.

"What's next for you, Abby?"

Abby sat to the side, propped up with one hand, trying to figure out the answer to Esther's question. "I know what I want, but I'm not sure it will all work together."

"So what are you going to do?"

Abby hadn't seen Esther so serious, yet she was gentle with her questions and patient with Abby's time in answering.

"You're worried about Mose."

"I'm worried about both of you, that you'll miss this opportunity for all the wrong reasons."

Abby sat up. Esther's words were what she was struggling with, and she was open to hear Esther's advice. "What opportunity?"

"To be together despite your differences."

"The obstacles are pretty big."

"It's all relative—depending on how much you want the relationship to work and what each of you will sacrifice."

"I don't have as much to give up as Mose."

Esther smiled. "I was just thinking the opposite."

"Mose doesn't want to leave this place, and I don't have anything to go back to, except teaching."

"You could do that here too. The timing couldn't be better."

Abby frowned. "They wouldn't choose me. And it wouldn't be fair if they did."

"It's only right to hire the person best suited for the job."

Abby took a minute to consider the possibility. It was more than she could hope for, but not realistic in her mind. "I just can't imagine that happening."

"You have the experience. The other criteria is a religious foundation." Esther shrugged. "And I've seen your students who live here interact with you. That says a lot when it comes from the children."

Sudden emotions caught Abby off guard, as thoughts of her mother flashed through her mind. She had encouraged Abby much the same way Esther was doing. "Can I share something with you, that's just between us?"

"Of course. What's on your mind?"

"When my father died, he said something about being Amish." She paused to let it soak in again. "Do you think that's possible?"

"*Ach*, anything is possible, but does it really matter? Most are born into the community, but there are those who come to us who aren't and live a *gut* life. After a while there is no difference." She stared at Abby and then smiled. "If you're doing it for the right reasons, no matter who your blood is, it's meant to be."

There seemed to be nothing she could say that Esther didn't have an answer for. Abby took a moment to reach into the heart and truly see where God wanted her to be. It might not become apparent today or in the coming days, but she knew a path would be made for her.

"I appreciate what you're saying concerning teaching the students here, but I still couldn't rightfully be considered to teach when I'm not a member of the community."

"That's your choice, but I beg to differ." Esther stood and took the small rake to clear away the weeds that were tangled around some sunflowers. The suffocating vines made Abby think of how tainted she'd felt when she first met Mose, and how the feeling had slowly slipped away once she started living a more God-centered life. But she could do that anywhere. It didn't have to be among the Amish.

"How do I decide?"

"Learn about our ways and what is involved in converting. Then pray for *Gott's* wisdom as to if it's right for you."

There was a long but comfortable silence between them. "Will you help me, Esther?"

Esther looked her in the eyes. "I would love to, Abby." She took a moment and then added, "Let's start with this. *Gott* is twenty-four hours a day, seven days a week, not just when you need Him. Here, prayer is every day, at any time, for any reason."

Abby nodded. "I can attest to that after living here. It's about time I do what I've observed."

"Set your mind to things above, and you'll soon find it a habit." Esther continued on with her gardening as their conversation came to a close. "Abby, let's keep this between us, at least for a while, until we have a better idea about what you'll decide."

Abby nodded reluctantly, knowing how hard it would be not to tell Mose right away. As she made her way to the road, she was encouraged after their talk and felt she had the direction she'd been looking for.

Abby was deep in thought about what Esther had told her as she walked. She was almost surprised when she looked up and found herself by the little red school with the charming bell on top. She started to walk by and then stopped, feeling drawn to it. Maybe it was just curiosity. Maybe something else drew her.

The children were outside playing together, and the older ones were in a huddle talking. Abby stopped at the door and heard the bishop speaking and listened awhile. "At this point I believe it's up to the school board of parents to decide, and we'll go from there."

She felt like she was eavesdropping, so she backed away and

enjoyed watching the children playing a game of ball. She was about to leave when Esta ran over and took her by the hand. "You're *gut* at this, and we're losing."

Abby's first reaction was to decline, but as Esta pulled her along, she felt her frustrations fall away. There were two teams, girls against the boys, and the boys were winning. When they saw her, they chuckled. Esta grinned at Abby and called for the ball. She kicked it to Abby, and she tapped the red rubber ball halfway down the field before handing it off to one of the other girls, who then scored. The boys saw they needed to step it up, and the game was on.

By the time they'd finished, Abby was tired and panting from exertion. But she hadn't felt this good for a long while. There was something about being out in the country air, exerting herself in a friendly with a group of kids, that could bring out that feeling. The boys shook hands even though they'd lost. The girls knew they'd given the boys a challenge, so Abby gave them high-fives. They all talked at once, the way girls do, and Abby decided she should get back to Becca's.

"*Danke*, Abby!" They all yelled in unison.

Abby waved and walked around the corner of the schoolhouse. She passed by a window to see a dozen parents talking with Becca's sister Arianna. The bishop shook her hand and opened his arms wide, as if showing her the school for the first time. As Abby passed by the next window, Bishop Omar watched her go by. She smiled at him and kept walking. Reality hit once again, and she pulled out of her Amish-school fantasy and switched to the school in Beeville. That was her place, not Meadowlark Valley.

∽ Chapter Thirty-Six ∽

WHAT'S ALL THE noise?" Mose's daed peeked around the corner of the milk barn.

Mose instantly felt ridiculous throwing the steel milk buckets into the bin. He didn't lose his tongue when he was angry, but he did tend to get physical when he reached this level of frustration. He thought about how Abby's daed dealt with his anger and let out a slow breath. He didn't ever want to take his frustration out on anyone. He needed to learn to talk instead of lose his top. "Sorry, got carried away."

His daed turned over one of the pails and sat down on it. He waited for Mose to do the same. "What's on your mind, son?"

Although couples didn't usually let anyone know of their intentions, Mose got the feeling his daed knew about his and Abby's conversation the day before, so he skipped the general and got down to the specifics. "I don't know what to do with Abby."

His daed frowned at him, so Mose started again. "What do you think about Abby staying here?"

His daed shrugged. "Wouldn't surprise me."

Mose turned and stared at him.

"Don't look so shocked. I told you at the hospital that I thought she fit in here." He stuck a piece of straw in his mouth from the bale of straw behind them. "The real question is what do *you* think of Abby staying here?"

Mose hated it when his daed turned it back around on him. If he knew for sure, he wouldn't have asked what his daed thought. "You mean it's not obvious?"

His daed chuckled. "Well, it is to me, but it might not be to her."

Now he had Mose's attention. "Can you expand on that?" Mose realized where he got his lack of words in serious conversations. Horseplay was one thing, but serious talks shut them both down.

"What have you done to let her know how you feel?"

"I hadn't really thought about it. There's been so much going on, I haven't had much of a chance."

His daed nodded. "*Jah*, her daed mistreating her is what got her here. Then the flood kept her here."

"And before that, her horse came up lame after the accident." Mose thought about how it had all come about and wondered if *Gott* had brought them together, but he was just too slow to figure that out. "Then her daed got sick."

"She was awful *gut* with the kids." His daed looked over at him. "That comes from her being a teacher, I suppose. Interesting that we need one right about now."

"Have we talked ourselves into an answer?"

"Maybe you needed to. I've known all along." His daed grinned and waited for his reply.

Mose took his time and gave it some thought. "I guess I have too."

"There's always obstacles, son. There's no getting around that. But Abby's solid, so you'll be all right."

Mose laughed inwardly at his daed's choice of words. He didn't know whether Abby would appreciate her finest attribute being "solid." But he knew what his daed meant. She had struggled with her faith, but since she had arrived, he'd noticed a quiet, spiritual growth about her that he admired. "Since I'm not supposed to tell you anything else about courting, you won't be hearing from me for a while."

"I'm glad to hear that." His daed's face softened to where Mose knew he meant what he said and that his daed must truly accept Abby into their fold.

He slapped Mose on the leg and stood. As he walked away, Mose heard him mumble, "It took long enough."

Mose grunted a laugh. He had taken longer than most, but it was worth it. Many Amish don't get to experience marrying for love, only convenience, because most marry in their prime. Mose might be past that, but he didn't have any regrets.

He finished feeding the livestock and then went to find Chris. He was on a wood swing tied to the biggest branch in a cottonwood tree by the house. There were chores to be done, and swinging wasn't one of them. Mose stopped behind him and cleared his throat.

"Mose!" Chris drug his feet into the dirt a couple times until the swing stopped so he could jump off. "I'm almost finished with the cracked corn."

Chris dragged his feet all the way to the side of the barn and pulled out the grinder. Mose was close behind with a bucket and a large bag of dried corn. Chris placed the bowl underneath the discharge shoot that caught the cracked corn as it was processed. Chris continued to fill the grinder with the whole, shelled corn until the bag was empty. Mose was restless going through the process, but he wanted to keep Chris on task.

When they were done, Mose went to Ginger's stall. She whinnied and walked over to him. She favored her bad leg only slightly, but the injury wasn't going away. It was something she would have to learn to live with. That was true of Abby, as well. But the hardships seemed to make them both stronger.

Mose got his horse and set off to Becca's. Frank seemed slower and the distance to Becca's longer than ever. Mose did not make his usual stops to say hello to anyone on his way. When he got to Becca's, he watched as Abby stood on a flatbed driving the horses in the cornfield. Becca grabbed the corn stalks as one of her sisters cut them down. Another sister took the stalks from Becca and secured them on the flatbed.

When Mose saw the efficiency of the four young women, he was impressed, especially with Abby. He couldn't help being partial. His daed was right in saying she worked as well as any of the women in this community, and even some of the men.

Unsure what kind of reception he'd get after their last conversation, Mose tethered the buggy and sat on the porch waiting for her. When she walked up to the house and saw him, the four of them stopped talking.

"Morning, Mose." Becca and her sisters walked past him. He nodded, sinking into the awkwardness that had suddenly come upon him.

Abby forced a quick grin. "This is sort of a bad time."

He held up a hand to block the sun. "Should I have called first?"

His joke made her smile. "Why are you here?" She wrapped her arms around her waist and gave him a blank stare.

"To see you and tell you I'm sorry for taking so long."

She frowned. "About what?"

"Telling you how I feel." The last word came out slowly. It wasn't a comfortable one for him to say. When he saw the beginning of a grin on her face, he knew he'd picked the right one.

"You're hard to be mad at."

"Yeah, I know." He grinned.

"Why are you in such good spirits?"

He looked around the green fields with yellow corn busting through the leaves, grateful for the crop. "It will still be a decent harvest, even after that flood."

She turned her head to look at him. "That's why?"

"*Jah.* Don't you think the crops will do good?"

She furrowed her brow. "Yes, but what does that mean?"

"You can't say no about the crop, so I thought I'd at least get one yes this way." He continued to study the swaying green leaves, unable to meet her eyes. "I'm going to propose to you, and I want to know you're going to say yes before I ask."

She shifted away. "That's the most ridiculous thing I've ever heard."

He looked at her to see whether she was getting angry or understanding his cowardliness. Her forehead creased with confusion and question. He hoped it wasn't just curiosity that was keeping her from slapping him across the face and walking away.

"But I'm glad you told me, because the answer would be no."

Mose felt the blood rush through him. All he could do was stare as his heart began to ache.

She looked down at the dirt under her feet. "I'm not ready yet."

He shook his head. Now he was the one who was confused. He finally got his lips to move but wasn't sure what would come out. "I don't understand."

"You will. Just give me some time." Her eyes shone brightly, like Mose had never seen. Whatever her secret was, it made her glow.

He shrugged with disappointment. "Do I have a choice?" Irritation began to overtake his interest in what she was talking about. He looked away to keep her from seeing the change.

"No, but I do, and I want to make sure I make the right one." She looked at him with those hopeful eyes, and he couldn't say anything against what she was saying even though it made no sense to him.

"I'll leave you alone, then, until you figure things out." He couldn't help but hope she'd throw him a bone. Any more information would be good about now.

"*Danke*, I appreciate your patience."

There seemed to be no end to her flustering him. But her last comment gave him a small bit of hope all would work out in the end.

She pointed to the house. "I'm making apple dumplings."

He was tempted, but it didn't feel right, like he was left out of something really important. "Maybe another time."

Mose turned to walk away, torn as to whether or not he should have stayed. As much as he wanted to be with her, she seemed to have something more significant than him at hand. He wanted to turn around and see if she was still there, but he didn't let himself until he got to the end of the gravel drive and onto the dirt road. When he did finally look back, no one was in sight.

He passed by his place and stopped by Joe's. He needed another opinion as to what was going on. He replayed the recent events in his head but found no reason as to how things had taken such a bad turn. He figured he was at fault for something, but he wasn't sure of what exactly.

When Mose got to Joe's, he started helping his friend with a chore; he always felt better working. He had time to figure things out and gather his thoughts. There was something about making or repairing that cleared his mind and helped him think more clearly.

Joe took one glance at him and then went back to sorting nails. "Look what the cat drug in."

"How do you know so much?" Mose took a handful and put the nails in containers by size.

"You and Abby are both acting strange."

"What do you mean?"

"I went over to see Becca, and Abby seemed like she was floating on air."

Mose was more than irritated that she wasn't more that way with him. She acted as if she couldn't wait for him to leave when he was there. "I didn't get that reaction."

"What did you say to her?" Joe snapped the lids on the nail boxes and put them in his toolbox.

"It wasn't so much what I said as how I said it."

"Which was?"

"Told her I was thinking of getting married."

"That's how you asked her?" Joe shook his head. "No wonder it's taken so long for you to settle down."

Mose remembered similar words coming from his daed and decided they must be right. It wasn't that an Amish girl would expect anything elaborate, but he could have done better. And she was English. He'd heard of some of the ways they proposed and was glad he didn't have those expectations put on him.

"You're not too far behind me." Mose tried to redeem himself.

Joe was two years younger but knew he and Becca would marry soon.

"*Jah*, that's true. We're going to the schoolhouse. Grab another hammer. It'll distract you." He took his supplies to the buggy with Mose carrying a few more tools close behind him.

"Glad I stopped by," Mose said sarcastically as he pulled himself up into the buggy.

"I know you wanted to sit around and mope, but we have better things to do." Joe clicked to his horse and they passed by the Zooks' and Yoders' farms. The schoolhouse's red exterior contrasted with the white interior and made both stand out. As they walked in, the women were scrubbing the floors with soapy water. The men worked outside to make sure every nail was flush with the wood siding. Some were finishing a second coat of paint, and others were painting the rim of the bell tower, the doors, and the window trims white.

"The kids should be proud of this school." Mose smiled at the children swinging in the back.

"This is nicer than the schoolhouse we had in Virginia." Joe admired the structure with Mose, and then they got to work.

Mose caught up to his daed to see whether he needed any help with setting the legs of the playground equipment. He stood over his daed, who was on all fours checking the stability of a teeter-totter. "How's it look?"

His daed sat back. "*Gut.* The bigger question is, how are you?"

"It didn't go as well as I'd planned." Mose hitched a thumb in his work belt, wondering what he could have done differently. "She's got something going on that's not clear, and she obviously wants to be alone."

His daed scratched his head. "You might want to talk to your mamm about all of this. I'm running short on words."

Mose groaned inwardly. He needed answers. "I know where I inherited it."

His daed smiled to ease the pain. "I say we work on that greenhouse you talked about building."

Mose was shocked. His daed hadn't liked the idea from the beginning. But it was a good idea. The crop wouldn't be as bountiful due to the storm, and Mose wanted to create something with his own two hands, completely different from anything else he'd ever made. "I'd like that. Just a little surprised that you want to."

Eli grunted. "To be honest, your mamm's been pestering me about it."

"Fair enough." Mose smiled, understanding a little better what was happening and looking forward to another distraction.

Everyone worked into the evening, stopping only for supper. The women cleaned the desks the men brought in and scrubbed the walls. The only tasks left to do were building the outhouses and organizing the supplies. That would be up to the teacher. As Mose packed up his tools in the one-room schoolhouse, he pictured seeing Abby sitting at the teacher's desk. And for the first time he could honestly consider it a reality.

Chapter Thirty-Seven

YOU'VE BEEN DILIGENT in learning the ordinances." Esther sat in a rocking chair, swaying slowly. The clacking of her knitting needles made a slow rhythm that synchronized with the motion of her rocker. The smell of beef roast lingered in the air, making Abby's mouth water. She hoped she could learn to cook as well as Esther. The women here loved to have their own secret spice or ingredient that made a dish their own.

"Yes, there are a lot of rules to remember." Abby found comfort in the movement and noise. She relaxed back into the sofa, waiting for Esther's direction.

"Hmm...speak as much Pennsylvania Dutch as you can. You probably know more than you realize."

Abby cleared her throat. "*Jah*, I understand it better than I speak it."

"The German helps. Where did you learn it?"

"Most in my high school took Spanish as their second language. For some reason I took German. It's harder to learn the Amish German language mixed with English." Abby knew the reason now, and it made her wonder whether God had planned for her to be here all along.

"You're ahead of most, so you'll be fine."

"Have many converted here?"

"Not here, but back in Virginia there were some."

"And did they adjust well?" Abby didn't want to seem doubtful—she already felt at home in the community—but she still wanted to know what would make them change their mind. She already knew the ways of the church, and Esther was coaching her in their ordinances. All she needed was for the church to vote her in.

"Most do, but others realize it's not for them."

"Esther." The sound of the knitting needles stopped, and their eyes met. "I don't have any doubts that I want to be here. I just hope that everyone wants me to be."

Esther set down the knitting needles and reached out for Abby's hands. "You're already one among us. I just don't want there to be any surprises. I'm here to answer your questions and guide you, but the decision is yours."

Abby reached out and hugged her, sinking into her arms. She rested there for a moment, enjoying the closeness and knowing there was no doubt where her home was. She pulled away. "When I think back to when I first came here and why, it seemed so dark and sad because of what I was going through." She sat back and plopped her hands onto her apron, thinking about how it was second nature to wear the Amish clothes. "I never would have dreamed things would end up this way."

Esther put a hand to Abby's cheek. "And I would never have expected Mose to bring home an English girl." They both grinned. The sound of Mose's name made Abby miss him. Abby was still frustrated that she was the one who had to finally mention something about their relationship. Although she was disappointed, she knew it wouldn't do her any good to dwell on it. This was a good way for her to be sure that he wasn't the only reason she wanted to live here.

The door opened, and she heard the sound of Mose's and Eli's voices. Esther turned to Abby with a gentle smile. "Before you see Mose, here's a thought. Give thanksgiving for what you have received and encouragement for living the way the Lord wants you to. If someone insults you, don't do the same to them. Our way is to turn the other cheek and forgive."

Abby knew the last part was concerning her and Mose. She wanted to see him and everything to be good again, but she felt he needed to put forth some effort if she truly meant anything to him. She understood his loss of words when it came to serious matters, but this meant too much to just assume she knew how he felt. She needed to hear it with her own ears to feel it in her heart. She paused and thought about how perhaps she hadn't been very forgiving or honest when she sold horses. She had observed a lot from watching her dad and learned to use his tactics well. Abby wondered whether she should ask for forgiveness for her dishonesty.

Mose walked into the living room and stopped when he saw Abby. "I didn't know you were here."

Abby smiled at his surprise. "Eli didn't tell you?"

Esther picked up her knitting and appeared to concentrate on her work, but they both knew she was enjoying being in the room with them.

"*Nee.*" He turned around as if to spot his daed, maybe to tell him off for not preparing him that Abby was there. "What are you doing here?"

Esther frowned at his lack of tact, but Abby was coming to expect it. His choice of words got worse when there was tension. The anxiety would continue until he could figure out what to say and how to say it. She wouldn't accept anything less at this point. Abby felt she was doing her part by learning their ways and taking classes to be baptized—something she had never done and wanted to do now. It was a good time for her to make the commitment, no matter what happened between her and Mose.

Mose scratched his chin. "I didn't know you were coming over."

"I came to see Esther."

He flinched and looked from Esther to Abby. "*Ach,* I see."

In the awkward moment Abby wanted to look into his eyes, to see what he might be thinking, but she couldn't find the courage. His short responses made her think he was upset with her. If that was true, there would be a standoff. The advice Ester had just given her went to the back of her mind. Abby noticed the striking blue color of his eyes as he brushed some blond wisps from his forehead. Maybe because they hadn't spent time together for a while or because she felt more accepted and assured of herself, she was looking at him in a new light. Abby felt as comfortable there as she had when her mother was alive.

"I'm going to the milk barn." Mose didn't so much as wave good-bye before he left. His guarded demeanor was upsetting, but then she must be coming off the same. For the moment it didn't matter. She was making big changes in her life, and Mose could support her through this or she could do it on her own. She was beginning to think this was the way God wanted it to be—just her and the Lord working together to find her niche in the world.

"Would you like to help me make dinner, Abby?" Esther didn't stop knitting as she waited for an answer.

"*Jah*, sure." She watched Mose walk out the door and second-guessed her answer. It was so automatic, she didn't think much of it, but she would wait and see whether or not it was comfortable for her to stay.

Esther set her knitting on a little brown stool by her rocking chair. "Let's get started."

Abby had learned a lot from Esther about cooking and was always ready to make something new, but Abby was more than ready to finish this task and go to Becca's. She hadn't had a heart-to-heart with Becca for a while, because she had been trying to figure out things on her own, but now she felt the need to talk to her friend.

Abby knew Esther wanted to talk about the mood she was in, but she had nothing nice to say about Mose, or herself, for that matter. "What's for dinner?"

"Hamburger subs. They're made with cheese, onions, peppers and ground beef, and my special sauce. We used to sell them to the English during tourist season. They've become a favorite."

"They sound good," Abby agreed, although she had no appetite. The thought of sitting with Mose and having a meal together made her stomach turn. She watched the shadows grow over the fields as the day ended. Come fall they would harvest the crop, a time she always enjoyed. Seeing how they'd prospered from the land with bountiful produce reminded her of why she enjoyed being there.

"Are you staying for supper, Abby?" Eli sat in the family room with *The Budget* newspaper in hand.

"*Jah*. It's almost ready."

"No rush. Patience is a virtue." He winked at her and began reading again.

It seemed everyone had words of wisdom for her. And it was beginning to bother her. She had come a long way since arriving there and had gotten along just fine. So unless there was something she was missing, she wished everyone would give her more credit. Her shoulders slumped, and she let out a dry breath.

Unless they are referring to my faith... but haven't I shown growth there too?

With dinner on the table, Abby waited to see what Mose's disposition was before speaking. Although she had a lot to say to him, what she had to say was not fit for the dinner table.

Chris came in pushing and shoving his friend, some sort of game they always played. Never having had siblings, she envied them. She was learning firsthand the saying that Amish children have never-ending playmates. The boys sat in their seats and became somber when Eli eyed them. Mose hadn't joined them, but she didn't want to ask about him. That might open up a discussion that she didn't want to have.

"Let us have a silent prayer," Eli directed, and he intertwined his fingers together.

Abby still didn't feel like she knew what to say to God. He seemed so big and ominous, would she ever feel worthy of His attendance?

The meal was congenial, as usual. She always enjoyed Mose's family—one she wished she'd had growing up—but she had stopped feeling deprived, instead appreciating having this family now to fill that void.

When the meal was over, Abby was overwhelmed with

curiosity as to where Mose was and why no one had mentioned him. She pursed her lips, trying not to ask about him.

"Let's fill the lamps with kerosene before it gets dark." Esther led the way to the barn, stopping in the mudroom to tidy some shoes that were in the way.

Staying busy on the farm had helped when her mother passed, and a task such as this helped in the same way. As she walked behind Esther gathering the lamps, Abby felt a certain kinship with this Titus woman who was leading her in so many ways.

The sound of Mose's footfalls as he approached made Abby realize she even knew the way his boots sounded.

Esther grinned. "Don't let the sun go down on your wrath."

Abby watched her turn and walk out of the barn, wondering how she'd become so transparent. She followed her into the kitchen and began cleaning up the dishes. She was too stubborn to greet him, but somehow she didn't think he was there for her.

"How'd it go?" Eli asked him.

"Still have one missing." His chair screeched against the floor as he sat down next to Eli.

Eli peered out the window. "No more daylight to keep searching."

Abby placed the last glass in the dish rack and walked over to the table to wipe it down. "What's missing?"

"A lamb. There always seems to be one that loses its way." Esther placed a plate of food in front of Mose.

Abby's heart fluttered, imagining wild animals catching and feasting on the little lamb. "Can't you take a flashlight... or something?" She looked outside, but only a tease of light remained in the darkness covering the land.

She wrung her hands with worry. No one spoke. Mose watched her with the rest of the family and then finally broke the ice. "I'll take one last look."

Abby let out the air she held in her lungs and felt silly for her overzealous behavior. All she could think about was the animals that had been lost after the storm at her farm the last time they went. For whatever reason, she felt she needed to find this lost lamb to fill that loss. "I'll go with you."

"I figured." Mose pushed away from the table.

"I'll keep your dinner warm." Esther smiled, and Abby knew it wasn't because of the lamb. She was pleased to see them together, even if it was chasing after lost livestock.

"You have to keep up with me." He was already walking ahead of her, making her wonder how she could.

"Where haven't you searched yet?" She looked at the flat plains and wished they had already harvested the corn. They could search forever in there.

"Nowhere." He scanned past the fields.

"I thought lambs followed their mothers." Abby wished she could scold the little one for going off on its own. Maybe because their farm was so much smaller and had fewer predators they'd never lost one.

"They do, but they're also curious. And straying is sometimes a sign of illness, so that might be the problem."

"They count on their sense of smell to find their mother, and the mother does the same. So why don't we find a bleating sheep and let her lead us?"

Mose's brows drew together. "I don't know about that."

She put her hands on her hips and frowned at him.

He blew out a breath in surrender. "What have we got to lose?"

"A baby lamb." She marched over to the herd and listened. She didn't know whether Mose was taking her seriously, but she kept making her way through the herd until she heard him call her name.

She walked over to see an ewe draped around his neck and one under his arm. Both sheep were bleating at him at the top of their lungs. Abby wanted to be smug but thought better of it—at least until they found the little one. She picked up Mose's shotgun and followed him. They walked until they were away from the herd, and he set down the two sheep.

"We have to keep them away from the herd." He pointed to a

small crescent, close to the river. "Let's head that way. The lamb may have gone for some water where they usually drink."

After a long trek to get there, Abby was losing her stamina. The baking and a full stomach were taking their toll. Even Mose slowed his walk, which made her feel a little better. She watched him a few steps in front of her. His faint swagger exuded confidence, and his silhouette framed his strong physique. A far-off sound broke into her thoughts.

Mose increased his stride, and she was soon by his side. The sound grew louder—the bleating of a lamb.

Mose took off into a jog and rounded the small hill. Abby followed and watched him pause as a grin spread across his face. When she peeked around the bend, one of the ewes was circling a small lamb, nuzzling him, guiding him home.

⌒ Chapter Thirty-Eight ⌒

MOSE PLOPPED DOWN in the grass and watched the heifers meander down a hill until they became so small, they were out of sight. To get Abby off his mind, he spent every spare moment he had working on the greenhouse. When he started moping around, his mamm gave him more to do. The only time he perked up was when Abby came to visit his mamm, but Esther would usually go to see Abby at Becca's.

He stuck a blade of grass between his teeth and lay back, letting the afternoon autumn sun warm his face.

"*Guder mariye.*"

Mose put a hand up to shade his eyes. His daed stood towering above him.

"*Gut* morning." He jumped up, feeling lazy for loafing around.

"Looks nice and relaxing." His daed looked down to the flattened area of grass where Mose was lying. "I'd like to join you, but we're needed at the schoolhouse. The local fire department is doing an inspection."

Mose rubbed his chin, trying to remember whether they'd ever been inspected when they were in Virginia. "Is there something wrong?"

"The fire captain said he didn't know the school was in his district. That's all I know. The elders are going to meet with the bishop to talk to them about it."

"It's a new building. What can be wrong?" Mose asked as they walked to the barn to hitch up the buggy.

"The captain said our schools can create special challenges."

"Humph. I wonder what that means."

"That's what we're going to find out."

254

On the way Mose limited the conversation to the school to avoid talking about Abby. He didn't know the answers, so he didn't want any questions.

The school was surrounded with buggies and two fire department vehicles. Children stayed on the playground while two fire captains met with the Amish elders.

Bishop Omar and the elders were talking amongst themselves when Mose and Eli walked in. Mose scanned the room for Abby but didn't see her at first. Then he looked out the window and saw her on the playground with the children. His daed noticed his wandering gaze and elbowed him.

"I'll be right back." Mose walked to the side door and went straight to Abby. She lifted her eyes and smiled when she saw him. "Are you coming in for the meeting?"

"*Jah.* What's this all about?" She helped a little boy off of the swing and turned to Mose, not realizing they would be face-to-face. He studied her, never having been that close, and noticed the deep color of her blue eyes and her supple skin. His impulse was to touch the softness of it, but he knew he couldn't. Feeling her warm breath on his face heated his cheeks and down his neck. If they had been alone, he would have done something he shouldn't.

"Mose." Her gentle voice brought him back, and not without embarrassment.

He took her hand, desperately wanting the contact, and walked into the school.

"Everyone gather 'round." The bishop's commanding voice caught the attention of the roomful of people. "This is Captain Barney Willis and Captain Chris Nelson. They are open to questions, so I'll start. Why are you here today?"

Captain Nelson was a dark-haired, tall, skinny man wearing a uniform. He stepped forward. "To start with, I'd like to thank you folks for meeting with us. There's nothing that can't be taken care of fairly easily. There are a number of hazards that need to be addressed. Nothing serious, but it could be if not dealt with."

"Why do you have to be involved in our school?" Bishop Omar asked, but it seemed to be more for the mass than him personally.

Captain Willis, who was equally as tall, answered, "Every school with twenty students or more needs to go on one of our lists according to district. You're in between the two."

Eli stood next to Mose, quietly listening, but Mose knew it wouldn't last long. His daed always had an opinion.

"Can you give us an idea of what you're referring to? Sounds awful broad for a little school like this to be saying there are 'a number' of hazards."

Some grunts of agreement were heard. There were probably all kinds of thoughts among the Amish. Most likely some were open to the codes that needed to be followed, and others thought it was an intrusion. Mose felt a little of both, depending on who was talking.

Captain Willis pointed to the wood-burning stove. "An example is how close this stove is to the wall." A mark that could have been from moving it in place, not a fire, served as evidence of the danger. "Other possible dangers are flammable liquids." He pointed to the kerosene used to fill the lanterns and power the lights. "If there are no phones, no one can reach us if there is an emergency."

Mose didn't appreciate his tone. He was condescending, telling them what changes to make and had no regard for their privacy, whereas the other captain was less demanding.

"We have a community phone. And the kerosene will be locked in a shed." He looked directly at Captain Willis, wanting to make the point they weren't ignorant when it came to protecting their children.

"Good. But until today we didn't even know your building was here, and because you have no address, it would have been difficult to find you. And there are other issues that are unique that we haven't explored yet."

It seemed as though this man was on a hunt to find deficiencies. And Mose was growing tired of him.

The bishop stood with his hands behind him. "We haven't opened our school yet, Captain Willis. We still have more to do before the children are in this building every day."

"See to it, as we'll be doing annual inspections to make sure fire alarms and smoke detectors are in working order." He looked around the room to see that there were none.

Bishop Omar stepped forward. "We are a private people, Captain Willis. How can we abide by your rules and keep our privacy intact?"

"A school is a school. There are no exceptions just because you're Amish. I'll notify a representative from the school district that you're here as well."

The bishop took a moment to make eye contact with the persistent fire captain. "Our operating standards are up to par as well as the curriculum, Captain. We've already taken care of that."

Captain Nelson eyed Captain Willis. "I can assure you that everything we do is done for the safety of the children and teachers," said Captain Nelson.

"Those are our priorities as well. We should be able to work together with that as the precedence." The bishop gave Captain Nelson a one-pump handshake, but Captain Willis was heading toward the door.

"Did we do something to offend the captain?" Bishop Omar inquired.

Captain Nelson shook his head. "Only that you're Amish. Some people think you all get away with some things. You know what I mean."

"*Jah*, from taxes to fire codes. It would be *gut* if people knew the truth, but it is a burden we have to bear." The bishop shook his head in disappointment.

Captain Nelson tipped his hat. "Thank you for making the time to talk with us. We'll be in touch."

The bishop showed him out, and everyone slowly filed out of the room. Mose looked at the newly made wood desks, the sparkling floor, and the books on the shelves. Everything had been thought out and made by someone in the community. And the children would be taught well, no matter who the teacher was. They would be well taken care of, no matter what any government official thought.

"Overall it went well. We can't let any of it put a damper on the opening of the school." Bishop Omar set his gaze on Abby. "Would you come with me?"

Mose watched as the two of them talked. His daed cleared his throat to distract Mose from staring, but that just made it worse. All sorts of scenarios went through his mind. Had the elders voted on her staying? Was she being scolded for not having a chaperone? *Nee*, that would be his chastising.

He drew nearer to hear the last of the bishop's words. "You know how to work with children and help them succeed, *jah?*"

Then he saw them both smile, so he walked over.

"Bishop Omar." They shook hands and Mose waited for an explanation, but none came.

"We need extra hands to make some wood boxes for the students to put their essentials in, if you're willing."

It was the perfect fit for him, and he readily agreed.

The deacon winked at Abby, and she smiled in return. They had only taken two steps away when Mose asked, "What was that about?"

Abby was beaming when she turned to tell him. "Bishop Omar has asked me to consider a teaching position."

"Here, at this school?" He pointed at the floor.

"*Jah*, here, silly. Where else would he be referring to?" She practically jumped into his arms, forcing him to embrace her. Not that he minded, just not around curious eyes. It was so unusual for her, he couldn't refuse the affection.

"What about Arianna? I thought she was going to be teaching."

She pulled away, her cheeks a bright pink. "The deacon said they would consider splitting the children into older and younger groups since it's such a large number of students."

He was silent, trying to figure things out in his head.

"Everything that I've wanted is starting to happen, at least in part."

"I'm happy for you, Abby." Mose meant what he said, in more ways than she could know. If she was considering teaching here, she would be committing to stay. And if that was true, all that remained was discovering what her commitment was to him.

Chapter Thirty-Nine

ABBY WALKED DOWN the road to Mose's place. She needed a ride, and she missed him—two good reasons to show up at his door. But she would have to find more patience. It seemed she was the one making the effort to make a life for her here, and she had told him how she felt about him. He was important to her. He knew that. She'd told him so that day in the barn. But she didn't have that same assurance from him.

As she walked up onto the porch, admiring the beautifully potted plants in large ceramic vases, she wondered whether she would ever have a home like this one. Esther was beyond the ordinary in whatever she did, and sometimes Abby wondered whether she could ever measure up.

She rapped on the door, calmly waiting for someone to answer. A few minutes later, after knocking twice, she decided to go to the back door, closer to the kitchen. But when she rounded the corner of the house, she saw the milk barn was full and cows were mooing. When she walked in, Mose was finishing up, with Chris by his side.

"Good morning."

Her voice caught all of them by surprise, and they stopped momentarily to greet her. She wasted no time telling him why she was there. "Mose, can you give me a ride?"

"Of course."

"I'll help you ready the buggy." She couldn't hide the anxiety stirring in her. A task would be helpful. Abby hadn't said a word until he finally asked her where they were going. "The cemetery."

Mose jerked his head over to see her. "To your daed's grave?"

"*Jah.* I keep remembering his last words." She rested her head against the horse's side, feeling the warmth radiating from his body.

"What do you think he meant?" Mose stopped, tightening the cinch and turned to her.

"That he wanted me to leave the room, his life...I don't know." She shrugged the hurt away and waited for him to help her get through the pain. "And then he mentioned the Amish."

"It could mean a lot of things." He squatted next to her, and she lifted her head up to face him. "He was very ill. What little I knew of him leads me to believe he wanted to go in peace, alone."

"I wish he'd had more strength so I could know for sure."

"I've been wondering why he told you to stop. Do you think it was because you were reading the Bible?"

"At first I thought he meant to stop treating him, but the more I've thought about it, I think he didn't want to hear me reading." A stirring in her heart gave her hope he may have heard something that bothered him enough to think on it before he died. But that was far-reaching.

"You did more than most would have after the way you were treated. But I wouldn't have expected anything less." His thoughtful smile lingered, giving her some assurance she'd done what she could, although she felt she'd never be completely released from the chains that dragged her into heavy guilt for being away so long, knowing he was ill.

She and Mose finished hitching up the horse and were on the highway in no time. Once they got to Jim's headstone, Abby asked for privacy. "Just for a moment, Mose."

"Are you all right, Abby?"

She understood why he asked. She was upset, but it was probably her intensity that worried him.

"I need to do some forgiving so I can start healing." Her smile was to reassure him, but she doubted it helped.

Mose stepped away, but she knew he stole glances as she

silently knelt and bent her head. She still questioned how to pray. Her lack of commitment to declare her faith for so long made her feel unworthy to come to God. Everything about her way of life now had integrated into her soul—her references to God, prayers, church, and singing hymns—but until she made a profession to Christ, she knew it was all for naught. The path to salvation was hard, and her choice had eternal consequences.

Mose was leaning against a tree, looking at the different grave sites. He noticed how simple her daed's headstone was compared to most of the others. It was more like Henry's than the English headstones.

"Did you finish what you needed to?"

"*Nee*, I haven't." Abby started walking to stay calm, and Mose followed close behind her. She wanted to know the extent of their relationship, and until then, she would not allow herself to grow any more attached to him. Not that she wasn't already, but it helped her feel that she was not hoping for something that wasn't there. It was too important to think it would work out on its own. She needed to hear him say the words.

Mose stuffed his hands in his pockets. "What have you and my mamm been talking about?"

This wasn't the conversation she wanted to have, but then she thought better of it. Maybe he would see the direction she had chosen and would share his plans.

"She's teaching me what's involved in converting." Abby looked straight ahead, not wanting to see his face. If his expression gave her any idea of what he thought about what she'd just said, she might be swayed, so she kept her eyes focused on the bright yellow sun climbing over the horizon.

His walk slowed to a crawl, his boots crunching against the ground. "When did you decide to do this?"

"It's been a slow process ever since I came to the community. And then when the storm hit...and my daed's passing, and I lost my home—"

"You have one with us." His voice was clear and his words concise.

She finally looked at him, prepared for whatever she could read in his face. "That's what your mamm told me. And that's how I feel." She looked around from one headstone to another, taking in the cool air.

"So that's what this is all about? You're staying here with…us?" He hadn't blinked, obviously shocked at the discovery.

"I wasn't going to say anything until I knew for sure."

"But now you are?"

The hope in his voice made her catch her breath. "*Jah*, I'm sure." She smiled until it hurt and watched him return the smile.

"Well, that's *wunderbaar*." He put a hand to his chest and nodded his approval. "I know I've missed the mark somehow." He paused. "But I'm not sure how to hit it."

She grinned at the way he worded his question. "You just did." She took one step closer to him. "By *telling* me you care."

Confusion and satisfaction mixed together on his features. "If you tell me what I did, I'll be sure to do it again."

"I needed to hear you say that *you* want me to stay."

He looked up at the sky, as the light took over the darkness. "Why would you think any differently? I've been with you every step of the way."

"By your actions, maybe, but not in your words. I don't want to assume and expect something that won't happen."

Mose scoffed as a sharp wind whipped between them. He pulled off his hat and tapped it against his knee. "I understand that I haven't expressed myself enough, but can you honestly say that you don't know how I feel?" He rubbed his forehead with frustration. "I might not do well when it comes to courting, but for me, I thought I was doing pretty *gut*."

She tried to explain what she needed and why, but when she started to speak, he cut her off. "Maybe you're worried about not looking the fool. But I already know I am."

He turned away before she could respond. She didn't know what to say after hearing what Mose said. It had happened so quickly. One minute they were beginning to understand one another, and the next he was upset. "I also needed to know if I'd be accepted here by the community and that I can live an Amish life."

"What do you mean? Of course you could." His shoulders moved up and down nonchalantly.

She stared at him in disbelief. "You don't know how different it is here compared to what I come from."

"I know it's a big change."

"Mose, there are people around all of the time. And not just relatives. These people were strangers to me when I first came. I used to buy my clothes. Now I make them. I've worn a long dress all summer, instead of shorts and sleeveless tops. My day went from nine-to-five to a sixteen-hour day, six days a week. No television or radio, books." She took in a breath. "I used to make meals out of a box. You have no idea...but I wouldn't take any one of those things back if it meant not living amongst the Amish."

"The sacrifice becomes real when it's about you." His entire body melted into relaxation, and he swiftly rubbed his eyes. "What you've done is more than I could have hoped for or dared ask for, and that makes it mean even more. I don't know what to say." He stopped and started again. Looking her in the eyes. "*Danke.*" It was only one word, but it was the one she needed to hear.

She nodded. "I did it for a lot of reasons, Mose." "I know, and I'm glad. I selfishly wish it was all about me, but a foundation like that wouldn't be an honest reason for making such an important commitment. I suppose you need to like the community as much as you do me."

"I don't know if I'd go that far." Her insides fluttered as she took him all in. "There's still more to do." Her face tightened with worry.

He drew close to her and hugged her lightly around the waist, placing his hands on the same spot she always did to protect herself when she felt vulnerable. It was if he wanted to fill that void with his support. "I'd like to help you through the process if you want me to." He looked deeply into her eyes. "But you're already there."

ᢦ Chapter Forty ᢧ

MOSE WOKE IN the darkness, full of anxiety. This was an important day. If Abby was baptized, it gave Mose permission to ask for her hand. If not... he couldn't think of that possibility. It had happened with Jake, reminding Mose of how much pain his last-minute recanting had caused. As much as Abby talked around it, there was never a definite commitment as to her faith. He hoped he wasn't expecting too much, that what she'd said was enough, but deep down he worried. What if he'd finally found someone to spend his life with, but she didn't commit herself to the community? The Amish didn't take what they wanted and leave the rest. It was all or nothing.

As the first sliver of sunlight showed through the stalks of corn, he got out of bed. Within a few short hours Abby would be baptized and made a member of the church. It was surreal to think that she would be a part of the community that had nursed her back to health. Minister Miller had been gentle with her questions but firm on how the Amish stood on every issue. Mose appreciated both his patience and conviction in explaining both to her.

Mose felt she sensed his concern and didn't want him to know how deep her uncertainty ran. But the minister had comforted Mose, telling him her situation was different and encouraging him to be patient.

Mose ceased his thoughts. From this moment on throughout the day, he would pray every time he started to worry. His stomach would be tied in knots if he didn't turn it over to the Lord.

"This will be a glorious day," Esther sang as she passed by his room. "A day the Lord has made."

Mose blew out a breath and walked out to do the milking. The chore kept him busy and his mind from wandering. When a heifer named Blondie kicked him on the thigh, it brought him out of his worries. He asked *Gott* to give him a less painful reminder in the future.

When he walked through the kitchen, Esther looked at his feet. "Forget something?"

He looked down to see his work boots covered with mud, milk, and he didn't know what else. He shook his head. "Sorry, Mamm."

"Get something in your belly and clean yourself up." She was already wiping the floor where his boots had tracked in muck. She patted his shoulder. "Why don't you go pick her up?"

"*Jah*, I think I will."

After a bath and his mamm's blueberry pancakes, he felt much better, ready to face the day as his mamm had been trying to tell him all morning.

When he pulled up to Becca's, Abby was sitting on the stairs with Becca.

"Morning," he said to Becca, but his gaze was on Abby. She was prettier than he'd ever seen her. She wore a kapp and a new dress for the occasion.

Abby held her hand up to block the sun that was directly behind Mose. "Are you my ride?"

"Your chauffeur on a day like today." He grinned, feeling better already. With only one look at Abby, all things were new. His focus was on her and this special day.

"I can't wait to see you after service as my sister in *our* community." Abby knew Becca understood this was more than just a baptism for Abby. She had picked Becca's brain about the teachings of Christ and her commitment to *Gott*—even more than the studies she had with Minister Miller after weeks of classes.

"There's room for you, Becca," Abby suggested.

Mose nodded his agreement, but he selfishly hoped it would just be the two of them.

"Not this time. You two go on. I'll be there shortly." She waved them off and ran up the stairs. Her energy always made Mose tired.

"You look nice."

"*Danke.*" She sniffed. "And you smell good." She grinned.

He shook his head, a bit embarrassed. "Are you ready for this?"

"*Jah.* I'm looking forward to it, actually." She turned to him. "Are you?"

She had no idea how important this was. The first priority was the baptism, but there was also his proposal. Between the two, he was more worked up than she was. "This is a life-changing decision that will transform your life. I'm glad you've made this choice."

She stared out the window at the acres of crop and took in a long breath of fresh air. "I feel closer to the community when I'm close to the Lord."

Mose felt his heart tighten. "That's as it should be." He couldn't help but look over at her. That observation alone told him she understood what this all meant.

"When I heard Minister Miller's sermon when I first came here, he talked about how baptism didn't save you. It's a symbol, a sanctification of one's faith. And that we should do it because *Gott* commands it."

He had a dozen questions to ask her, but he bit his tongue. It was between her and God. And he was a bystander. "The bishop told me when I was baptized, it was an opportunity for *Gott* to live in me. He wasn't part of me but all of me. That stuck in my mind."

She was quiet for a moment. "I hadn't thought of it that way."

Again her comment tugged at his heart, and he shamed himself for being judgmental. He was silent the rest of the way to church.

When they drove up to the Lapps' house, Abby went up to

the front with the others who were to be baptized. The music director led them in song, and Minister Miller delivered his message. Then it was time. Mose impatiently waited, praying one last time these baptisms would be blessed.

Minister Miller asked them to leave with him, and they were asked one last time if they were ready for the commitment or felt they should wait. When all of them came back out, Mose sighed with relief. They kept their heads down as the minister began the ceremony.

"This promise to *Gott* will be witnessed by those of us here today. This is a promise for life that they have all agreed to. And the young men know the possibility of becoming a minister may fall upon them."

They knelt, and each was asked four questions in response to the commitment to join the church. The bishop removed Abby's prayer kapp and raised her head. An elder held a bucket for the bishop to cup some water in his hands and dripped it over her head three times. "In the name of the Father, the Son, and the Holy Spirit, I baptize you."

Mose couldn't see her face clearly, just a profile as a tear slipped down her cheek.

"In the name of the church and *Gott* our Father, we offer you the hand of fellowship. Rise up and be a faithful member of our church." The bishop raised his hands as if *Gott* Almighty was right there with them. Some clapped, and others were tearful. Mose was almost one of the latter, but he kept his feelings intact—until he saw Abby walking toward him.

He instantly wrapped his arms around her as his eyes misted. "I'm happy for you. This is a *gut* day." He pulled away before too many eyes were watching.

"*Jah*, it is. But it could be better. I thought I should tell you that I'll say yes to your proposal now." She smiled brightly, enjoying his surprise.

"I was planning on that." But he wasn't expecting her to be so quick to get them married, although it pleased him to know they would be included with the others who would be joined in marriage.

"I promise I'll let you take it from here. I just wanted to make sure that I was marrying material in the Amish world." She was beaming, but her eyes never wavered, as she waited for what was next to come.

Chapter Forty-One

ABBY WALKED HAND in hand with Mose to their buggy after church. It was so nice to be able to show their affections to one another now that they were published as a couple to be wed. They had been announced in front of the church, and now a whirlwind of planning would begin.

When they got to Mose's home, Esther was already in the kitchen starting the noon meal. They met Eli as they were walking in. "Well, if it isn't the happy couple." He grinned. "So what day and time do you want the wedding?"

"I'd like to go to one more singing before the wedding date is announced." Mose looked over at Abby. "If that's all right with you."

"Of course. Whatever you want." Abby wasn't completely familiar with all of the customs, so she'd agreed with everything Mose wanted, but she was beginning to wonder what she was getting into with each promise she made.

"What happens after that?"

"I help you make a dinner and plan the wedding." Esther's sing-song voice cut through the room. She appeared and took both of Abby's hands. "It's normally done with your mother, but I'm happy to have the honor."

"And you'll be busy passing out invitations." Eli tapped Mose's shoulder.

"Doesn't everyone come?" Abby didn't understand the purpose of the invitations. They never excluded anyone and were practical people when it came to spending.

"It's a verbal invitation, and it gets around by word of mouth more than my visits asking everyone to come," Mose told her.

"It's just another custom, not a necessity," Esther said patiently.

Abby's emotions must have been obvious, because they were all staring at her. "This is a lot different than what I'm used to."

"Does it bother you?" Mose's brows drew together.

"*Nee*, I just need to get used to it, is all." Abby didn't know for sure, but then she realized why she liked it better. It was Amish—simple in every sense, but that's what she was, simple, hard-working, and frugal, all ways both her parents had taught her, and now she was glad for it.

Mose led her upstairs to Jake's room and made her close her eyes. "Okay, open." In the corner of the room was a beautifully sculptured rocking chair.

Abby lifted her hand to her chest. "For me?" She didn't take her eyes off the chair as she walked over and sat down, rocking slowly.

"It's your wedding present." He beamed, enjoying her surprise. She suddenly stopped rocking. "I wasn't prepared for gifts."

He shook his head. "You don't need to be."

Her eyes widened, and she went over to the closet, pulling out the disappearing hat.

He grinned and plopped it on his head. "Just what I wanted." Mose took off the hat and stared at it in his hand. "Wait here." He dashed off and returned with an envelope. He handed it to her but didn't say a word. Abby opened it, read through it, and then read it again.

"Where did you get this?"

"I bent a few ears. John Yoder helped quite a lot, and there's an Amish database with genealogy records. I thought you'd want to know." He shrugged, unsure of himself.

"So it was my mother my dad was talking about who was Amish." Abby read it again, "Kathy Yoder."

He nodded, more confident now. "She must have left the community after she was baptized."

Abby let it soak in—all the while God was guiding her here. It wasn't because of a piece of paper. She'd known this life suited her soon after she came. But now there was no doubt in her mind, and Mose was kind enough to help her along. "My dad *knew* of my Amish heritage."

"He wanted you to know." Mose's gift of this information meant more to her than anything.

"Maybe that's where the hate Jim had of the Amish comes in, if my mom was shunned and he knew that it hurt her. In his mind, that was enough reason to hate the Amish."

Mose grabbed her hand and tugged on her until they were out the door.

"Where are we going?"

"To where it all began."

"That's mysterious." Abby tried to think of what he was referring to, but she couldn't come up with anything. They kept walking and talking for quite a while until they were at Ira's place. Then she understood why they were there. "Ginger."

Mose tugged her hand as they went to her stall. Ginger bobbed her head and came closer to them. "She never did quite heal. But she's a nice-looking horse."

Abby stroked the filly's coat. "I've always loved horses. I started riding when I was thirteen and rode every day. I'd ride any horse my dad would let me, whether it was broke or not." Abby was silent for a second, studying the strip of hair missing on Ginger's leg. "Sometimes we need a reminder of what we've been through to appreciate where we are."

"It's all in one's perspective." He hung his arms over the stall and let Ginger nuzzle his hand. "What do you miss the most about the life you've left?"

She shook her head. "Nothing really. A lot of what we had didn't make things better, just more complicated."

"So you really don't miss your old way of living?"

She realized he was making sure that she wouldn't have second thoughts and was touched by his worry.

She stood and placed her hand on his shoulder. "I told you. There isn't anything out there that I want more than what is here." She poked a finger at the left side of his chest, and then flattened her hand, feeling the beating of his heart. His handsome face glowed as he pulled her close. Abby had never felt so content and safe. It was at that moment she was absolutely sure of her choice to stay there and in him.

Her faith had guided her, and now, she was finally home.

Glossary

ach — oh
Ausbund — hymnal
bruder — brother
daed — father
danke — thank you
dawdi — grandfather
drei — three
ein — one
ferhoodled — enamored
Gott — God
guder mariye — good morning
gut — good
hallo — hello
haus — house
jah — yes
kapp — hat
mamm — mother
mammi — grandmother
narrisch — crazy
nee — no
rumspringa — teenagers running around
shunned — disregarded
wilkom — you're welcome
wunderbaar — wonderful
zwo — two

Coming from Beth Shriver,
Spring 2014,
Season of the Spirit

Chapter One

THE STORM IN Emma's haus foreshadowed the impending weather. The bleak, Pennsylvania sky hung overhead with a threat of snow. She sat up in bed and listened to the commotion downstairs. Roy's voice lifted, rising to a decibel that would surely bring her daed into the kitchen. Their neighbor was a good man, but he'd had enough of her brother. Mark had continued to become harder to deal with once he reached adolescence. Letting loose a herd of thirty milk cows, staying out all night, and getting caught with a beer didn't seem to be enough. His latest pursuit happened to be Roy's daughter.

Emma willed herself to get ready for the day, but she didn't move, just closed her eyes and waited for the shouting to end. She didn't want to have to see Roy—not again, not already. He'd been over just two days ago when he caught Mark throwing rocks at Naomi's window one night. It wouldn't have been so bad except that he broke the window in the process. Daed had sent him over to work off the damage, but that gave him too much time with Naomi, and for whatever reason she seemed to be enamored with him now. Mark was a handsome one, and charming in his own way, but a pain in Emma's side. She seemed to get stuck dealing with him. Her patience was worn as thin as Roy's.

When the back door slammed shut, she pushed off her warm quilt and climbed out of bed.

What did he do now?

She stood on the cold wood floor, gathering her clothes to get dressed. Her mamm had promised her they would make soap this morning, but only if Emma finished with her morning chores before the noon meal. She wasted no time gathering the eggs, helping her brother with the milking, and hanging the clothes up to dry.

Monday laundry always took a long piece of the day, but when her sisters helped, they finished quickly. As soon as the last bed-sheet was clipped onto the clothesline, Emma headed for the house to start the first batch of soap, but the sound of boots scuffling in the pebbled dirt made her pause.

Zeb walked down the lane toward her haus, buried in a warm, heavy coat. His tall, skinny frame couldn't be missed, like a scarecrow in a cornfield. He gave her a smile as he strolled up to her white clapboard house. She wondered if her mamm had something to do with his visit. Emma was past the age most women married, but much younger than Zeb. His wife had passed away not long after they married, and then he started courting Emma. She had been reluctant; it seemed too soon. But her mamm was set on finding her a suitor, even though Emma had no interest in anyone—except for one. And he was no longer part of the community.

"It's a beautiful morning." Zeb's customary greeting made her realize what a stressful day it had been. The sun hadn't reached the middle of the sky yet. And now she had to give him her attention.

"Morning, Zeb." She picked up a basket of clean laundry.

He took one large step into the house with Emma, standing within inches in front of her, looking down at her with his dark blue eyes. "How are you today?"

"Busy with chores." That's all she said or wanted to say. She didn't feel like engaging in small talk, and there was nothing new to tell.

"I can't stay long. Do you have a minute?" Only Zeb would ask it in a way that made it hard to say no. He was kind enough and soft on the eyes. She wondered what he saw in her. Others had vied for his attention when his wife died. It was more common to lose a husband than a wife, but most Amish women didn't remarry. The men most always did. For whatever reason, Zeb continued in his attempts to court her.

The large home had sparse furniture except in the kitchen, where eight seats filled the large room. The fire in the family room warmed the cozy area. Multicolored rag rugs warmed the wood floors in every room. Four bedrooms were just enough to accommodate her family, with a washroom to share and outhouse out back.

She slipped off her coat and took his. He sat on the couch close to the fire and rubbed his hands together.

"I hope you don't mind me folding laundry." Emma plopped the wicker basket down on the family room floor. It was wash day, and she couldn't get behind. She wondered why Zeb had idle time this early in the morning. He had a large and thriving dairy with over fifty Holstein cattle. He'd nearly doubled the number after his wife passed on. He said the extra work would keep his mind off things. He had a large, sprawling farm, but he used it more for grazing land than growing crops. She wondered whether that was one reason her mamm was so adamant that she spend time with him. He would provide a secure life for whomever he married.

They talked a bit, and she listened as he told stories. He always had one to tell, and she had to admit they were witty. She never knew whether they were fact or fiction, but they were entertaining, either way. But today she was restless.

She had plans with her mamm and didn't want the opportunity to pass her by. With six children, it wasn't often she had time with her mamm alone. Being the oldest gave her privileges, but also responsibilities the others didn't have. Mark and Maria were only a year apart from one another, and in their teenage years. The younger three were all under ten years of age. Her mamm said the Lord knew she needed a break in between having babies so close together.

Zeb jerked his head up when he heard Maria's voice rise from the kitchen. "Should we see what she needs?"

Her sisters—Mary, Martha, and Miriam—were getting a baking lesson. The problem with that was Maria was instructing instead of Mamm. Martha peeked out the kitchen door. "She burned something again."

Emma couldn't help but grin, although she was sure her mamm didn't find it humorous at all. "What is it this time?"

"Cheese bread." Mary appeared behind Martha. They both had strawberry blonde hair like their mamm. People thought they were twins due to their being so close together in age.

"*Ach*, my favorite." Emma squeezed Zeb's hand and genuinely smiled for the first time that day. "I should go."

He chuckled. "You can accept my help every now and then." One side of his lips lifted.

She nodded, having heard the words too many times. She knew he wanted to be around her family. The more they knew him, the more she felt obligated to consider him. And he knew that. "Thanks for stopping by."

He zipped up his jacket then tipped his hat, like he did every time they parted, and turned to leave. "You're welcome to come over for dinner, if you like."

She hesitated. Her haus was her refuge, and she took every opportunity to be there. She didn't always feel comfortable sharing a meal with Zeb's family. He had built his mamm and daed their own haus attached to his, which was common, but premature due to his wife passing. "I'll be there in time to help with dinner."

"All right, then." He took a moment to catch her eye and lifted a hand to say good-bye.

The smell of spices filled the air as Emma walked into the kitchen. Mamm's herbal tea was brewing on the stove. She heard Maria talking with her in the kitchen. The room was warm with humidity from pots boiling on the stove. Mamm stood over them sprinkling in some salt, and Maria cut up sausages. Emma walked to the large picture window over the sink that opened to the cornfield.

"This is the first time I've been asked to go to singing." Maria twisted a straggling lock of her reddish hair and sat down at the large wooden table. Maria's tight lips drawn together told Emma what she needed to know to catch up with the conversation. Emma and Maria had a tight sisterhood. They shared most everything, from their hearts to their hairpins. Each knew the other like she knew herself. There was only one other person in whom Emma had ever confided in the same way.

"I understand, but you need a chaperone." Stray, gray hair floated around her plump face as Mamm walked to the sink. She washed her hands and looked over at Emma. "You've been working harder than usual this morning."

Emma didn't want to talk about the soap in front of Maria but felt silly for her thoughts. She cherished this time with Mamm, and on top of that, doing something she liked, not a chore like mucking stalls.

"*Jah*, I'll help with the noon meal." Emma nodded and gathered the silverware, not wanting to draw attention to her work well done, partly so as not to appear prideful, but also because of the reason she was motivated. As her sister looked at her and started to speak, she knew Maria had other things on her mind.

"Emma, will you chaperone me to singing on Sunday?" Maria wrung her hands, waiting for Emma's answer.

Emma wasn't sure of what to say. There was obvious tension between Maria and Mamm that she didn't want to get in the middle of. She took extra time in answering, hoping one of them would intervene before she had to. "*Jah*, if Mamm approves."

Maria beamed at Emma for only a moment until Mamm lifted a hand to speak again.

"Your brother can chaperone." Mamm had her back to them, cleaning up the kitchen from the breakfast meal. Emma knew she was trying to get Mark involved so he could feel included, but Maria must not want him to.

"*Nee*, Mamm. He'd ruin it somehow."

Her sister was probably right, but what else could her parents do? They had tried everything they could think of, but nothing had improved his behavior. Mamm seemed to be weakening; it had been apparent for some time now that reasoning with him time and again was wearing her down.

"It would be nice for Mark to be with you, Maria." Mamm never met her gaze, avoiding conflict that might arise with her answer.

Maria's shoulders slumped, and Emma knew she had disappointed her. "I'll ask him to be on his best behavior." She wanted to do more than that, but it did no good to dwell on the issue. Emma wondered why her brother had changed so much when he became an adolescent. He'd always had a lot of energy, but this was more than that.

Maria huffed and went back to the counter where she was preparing the meat for stromboli. "Some are talking about *rumspringa*."

She didn't look up, just kept working as if she'd said nothing at all. Although it was considered a rite of passage, *rumspringa* was still frowned upon by most parents. Emma understood you couldn't condone such a custom unless it was something you'd grown up knowing about and was accepted by the most of the Amish communities.

"Why now? Spring planting isn't for a few more months," Mamm asked, but continued with her work, adding the ingredients together. She stirred the mix together with more force than usual. Talk of *rumspringa* clearly upset her.

"A lot say they're going." Maria sighed. "They're going to talk about it after singing." She twined her fingers together as if sorry she'd said the words out loud. It seemed strange coming from her, but Maria was just passing along information. She would never leave. She was one of the many uninterested or scared to explore any place outside their community, but Emma had never felt that fear, and her interest was piqued.

Emma had heard there was a good number who said they were interested in participating in the adventure, but few actually went. It would ebb and flow. Some years they stayed on the farms and had parties; other years they would go outside the community. Emma didn't know what this group would do, but she hoped they would go to the city. She had always wanted to see what was out there, not to live but to serve. The only obstacle was Zeb. She knew he was planning on her marrying him, but she couldn't think about that—not now. Thank goodness she had a beau who didn't have any interest in going. He could be a chaperone, but he would never do that, and those on the trip never appreciated anyone looking over them.

Emma went about slicing the ham and cheese while Mamm cut up the onion. As Mamm waited for the water to boil, she glanced over at Maria. "It's early to be thinking about something that's happening in the spring."

"*Jah*, but there's been a lot of talk lately for some reason." Maria's words told all. She was either fed up with her brother being in the way of things, or she really did want to go. But Emma couldn't imagine she truly did. Maria was a gentle soul who was very content on the farm. She wouldn't know what to do in the city, but then most Amish don't.

Mamm's face tightened. Her cheeks were taut and eyes dark. "I see." When Mamm was upset, she held her tongue, lest she say something that she couldn't take back. She didn't have the patience to talk through the issue.

Emma and Maria waited to see which she would do at that moment.

"Emma, let's go make the soap." Mamm threw in two cupfuls of flour into the bowl and then wiped her hands on her apron as she walked through the mudroom. They both watched her go.

"I should have expected that. I shouldn't even talk about it." Maria grunted, and then gestured toward the door. "Go ahead. I'll finish this."

"*Danke*, Maria. But you know she's only upset because she doesn't want to lose any of us. And you would never go. She knows that." Emma held up her hands in frustration, not sure what to do. And at that moment she felt for her mamm. She must be incredibly frustrated to hear talk about leaving, which she could see Mark doing. Mamm's denial and her father ignoring the problem would only made things worse.

She sighed. "*Jah*, I just wish she would do something about Mark. He's too hard to deal with anymore."

"I know how you feel, but I think there's more of a reason for his bad choices. I don't think he can control himself like we can."

"Like what?" Maria's eyebrows furrowed, and she crossed her arms across her chest, clearly ready to reject whatever reason Emma presented to forgive their brother.

"I don't know, for sure. But sometimes I see him struggling with whatever it is." Emma was going on a hunch. She didn't know how to explain it, and she admitted to herself that she'd lost patience with him as much as Maria had.

Maria frowned and then went back to the misty pot that was rumbling with a strong boiling hum.

Emma grabbed her coat and followed behind her mamm, who was walking too quickly to catch. Mamm's arms swung back and forth as her short legs kept stride. The thought of having time with her and making the soap had lost its appeal. Mamm would be tight-lipped until she could get this off her chest by talking with Daed.

As she stepped into the old red barn, Emma thought about better times, before the problems had begun. Thinking back, she couldn't figure out what had started Mark's outbursts that had created such tension. As she watched Mamm gather the necessary supplies, her heart ached for her, for all of them. Mark was not easy to live with these days.

The cold wind moaned through the slits in the wooden sides of the barn. Emma lit a couple of gas lanterns and placed the glass chimneys over the flames. They would give light and a little warmth.

Mamm grabbed a handful of lard from a metal bucket. "Take as much as you can carry."

Emma had wanted her mamm to show her how to make soap, but until today Maria had always gotten to it before she did. Being the oldest, Emma's duties were greater and more demanding. She took on the role well, but sometimes she wished for the small pleasure of something different to do—something an opportunity like this provided.

She pulled up her apron and loaded it full of the lard until it was too heavy to hold. Following her mamm, she dumped the lard in a large kettle. "How much do we need?"

Mamm's mood lightened, and they both started enjoying the project at hand.

"Six pounds of lard, two and a half pints of water, and one pound of lye will make plenty to last awhile. We'll have enough to sell at the Weaver's store too."

Zeb's parents owned a small store and had a produce stand by the road. Emma would offer to help when he took his turn selling the goods they grew and raised.

Emma heated the kettle, and when it started to boil, she stirred the mixture. Once it melted, they weighed it.

"Now we let it cool, put the lye in with the water, and then let it set."

While they waited for it to cool, Emma watched the fluffy clouds glide by and thought about Zeb. He was good to her—never raised his voice—and worked hard for his aging parents. There was no reason to discount him. She needed to stop thinking of wanting something—or someone—different.

Her mamm sat down next to her. "What's on your mind?"

"Nothing, really." She could hear what her mamm would say and her rebuttal, so what was the point of talking?

"Are you happy?"

"*Jah*, sure." Their marriage would tie Zeb's land and her daed's land together, making the largest farm in the community. It wasn't something she could protest even if she wanted to. She could be happy there.

"*Gut*. You will be glad you have it all behind and settle in." Mamm turned away and went to check the lard.

They went about cleaning up and put away the extra lard and lye while they waited. "Ready for the lye?" Emma took the lye over to the kettle with the lard.

"*Jah*, then just stir until it's thick and coats the paddle in sheets." Mamm prepared the table to put the soap on to cut into bars. She laid a frame of squares they would fill with the melted soap, and then stood back to admire their work. "You're good at this, Emma."

"Adding some color into them would be nice. Like sky blue, green as the corn stalks, or yellow like the sun." Emma pictured the various hues she could add into the white soap.

Mamm nodded enthusiastically and wrapped her arm around Emma's waist. "*Jah*, next time we'll add color."

They looked up as dark clouds rolled over them and as the thunder began to pound.

FREE NEWSLETTERS
TO HELP EMPOWER YOUR LIFE

Why subscribe today?

☐ **DELIVERED DIRECTLY TO YOU.** All you have to do is open your inbox and read.

☐ **EXCLUSIVE CONTENT.** We cover the news overlooked by the mainstream press.

☐ **STAY CURRENT.** Find the latest court rulings, revivals, and cultural trends.

☐ **UPDATE OTHERS.** Easy to forward to friends and family with the click of your mouse.

CHOOSE THE E-NEWSLETTER THAT INTERESTS YOU MOST:

- Christian news
- Daily devotionals
- Spiritual empowerment
- And much, much more

SIGN UP AT: **http://freenewsletters.charismamag.com**

8178